She was so determined to keep any hint of her femininity hidden

A lopsided smile quirked up his mouth. "That wasn't so bad, was it?"

"Compared to what, dancing a reel with a tumbleweed?" Hallie managed, trying not to give away the effect being this close to him had on her.

Despite her light quip, Jack felt her quickening breath, saw her eyes widen slightly. She might not look or act like any woman he'd known, but she couldn't help responding like one.

"Come on," he said, sliding his gaze down her. "Let's get you inside and out of those britches."

"You don't give up, do you, Dakota?" Pulling away from him, she swung around and started toward the house, ignoring his call after her.

"I didn't intend to take them off you, darlin'," he said to her back. "Though I'd be glad to help, if you'd like."

Praise for Nicole Foster's recent books

Cimarron Rose
"A must read."
—*Rendezvous*

"A spirit-lifting, heartwarming story."
—Romance Reviews Today

Jake's Angel
"Finely rendered...expressive...
Jake's Angel is a classic romance, and any reader
devoted to this genre will love this book."
—Romance Communications

"A charming tale from a promising new talent."
—*Affaire de Coeur*

HALLIE'S HERO

NICOLE FOSTER

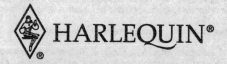

HARLEQUIN®

TORONTO • NEW YORK • LONDON
AMSTERDAM • PARIS • SYDNEY • HAMBURG
STOCKHOLM • ATHENS • TOKYO • MILAN • MADRID
PRAGUE • WARSAW • BUDAPEST • AUCKLAND

ISBN 0-373-29242-2

HALLIE'S HERO

Available from Harlequin Historicals and
NICOLE FOSTER

Jake's Angel #522
Cimarron Rose #560
Hallie's Hero #642

Please address questions and book requests to:
Harlequin Reader Service
U.S.: 3010 Walden Ave., P.O. Box 1325, Buffalo, NY 14269
Canadian: P.O. Box 609, Fort Erie, Ont. L2A 5X3

For our families near and far.

Best regards,
Annette and Danette

Chapter One

Paradise, Arizona Territory, 1876

It couldn't be gone. Hallie Ryan gripped the battered metal box in her hands, closed her eyes and took a deep breath to fight off the surge of panic. But when she looked again nothing had changed. More than half the money she'd so carefully hoarded all these months was missing.

She realized right then who had taken it. Only Ben would leave part of her money, thinking he'd sweeten her temper by not stealing it all. And Ben would do it even though he knew she'd been scraping together every penny, selling practically all she owned of value, to buy back Eden's Canyon before the bank sold their ranch to the first buyer who came along.

The only reason they were still living in the house was because she'd choked down her pride and begged Mr. Parsons to let them stay until the bank could find a buyer, giving her a last chance to beg, steal or borrow enough money before they lost everything.

Hallie welcomed the sudden anger flaring up inside her. For the moment, anyway, it pushed away the sick feeling twisting her stomach, and gave her the prod she needed to do something besides curse and cry. Shoving the box back into her wooden chest, she grabbed up her hat and headed for the barn.

She couldn't remember when she'd been madder at Ben, although her little brother had given her plenty of opportunities in the last year. He was always promising he'd finish one chore or another, always swearing he'd start taking on his share of the responsibilities. But then he'd sneak off to one of the saloons in town to gamble and guzzle a bottle of whiskey or two.

This time, though, he'd gone too far.

Yanking open the barn door, intent on getting to town and confronting Ben, Hallie nearly tripped over Tenfoot Jones on his way out.

"Whoa, there," Tenfoot said, holding up his hands and stepping back as Hallie stalked into the barn. He pulled a faded bandanna from around his neck and rubbed it over his weathered face and under his braid of iron-gray hair as he watched her drag out the rigging for the wagon. "You're lookin' as mad as a peeled rattler, Hal. What's young Ben done now?"

"Nothing a few years locked in the barn won't fix."

"Meanin' he's in town puttin' his money into someone else's pocket again."

"No, this time he's putting *my* money in someone else's pocket," Hallie said, as she led the piebald gelding out of his stall and started hitching him to the wagon. She didn't tell Tenfoot what money Ben had taken. Like everyone else who lived and worked on the ranch, the cowboy was already worried enough about where they'd be bedding down next month. "I aim to stop him if I have to hog-tie him and drag him home behind the wagon to do it."

Tenfoot snorted and shook his head. "That boy's wilder than a barn rat. Always has been. Be the best thing for everybody if you left him where he is, and let him learn about livin' the hard way."

"Maybe. Maybe I should've done that a long time ago. But I can't."

"So you keep tellin' me. But durned if I understand why."

Tugging one of the harness straps tight, Hallie's hands faltered. She swallowed hard, gritted her teeth and forced her fingers to finish the job without shaking. "Because I said I'd look after him."

"I don't think your pa meant until Ben was dried up and gray. The boy's old enough to look after himself. Hell, Hal, you were runnin' this whole spread when you were his age."

Hallie shook her head. "He doesn't have anybody else."

She'd made her pa two promises before he died less than seven months past: to keep Eden's Canyon thriving and to take care of Ben.

So far, she hadn't been able to do either.

Pa had always counted on her to help him with the ranch. He'd taught her to raise cattle and break horses, and to hold her head high even when people stared and whispered behind their hands when she walked down the street in her leather britches and beat-up hat.

But he hadn't told her about the debts he'd left behind, debts that had cost her Eden's Canyon. And he hadn't shown her how to corral a seventeen-year-old brother determined to get himself shot or thrown in jail before he saw twenty.

Climbing onto the wagon seat, Hallie tugged her hat down and took up the reins. "I'll be back with Ben and my money," she told Tenfoot as she slapped the leather against the gelding's back, "one way or the other."

Jack Dakota figured the kid had less than ten seconds to live.

From the way he swayed on his feet, and the unsteady fumbling of his hand at his holster, the fool boy wouldn't even get his gun drawn before a couple of bullets laid him facedown in the dirt.

Everyone in the Silver Snake had crowded onto the porch of the saloon to get an eyeful of the kid facing Redeye Bill Barlow. The noon sun beat down on the dusty street, rippling the air, and in a sudden moment of stillness when everyone in Paradise seemed to stop breathing, Jack swore he could hear the sweat trickling down the boy's face as he squinted toward Redeye.

Jack cursed under his breath. He'd come to Paradise to start new, to finally put down roots, not to get caught in the middle of the kind of trouble he'd been trying to sidestep ever since he was old enough to shuffle a deck of cards.

It had started out harmlessly enough, a quick game with his old rival Redeye to pass an hour or two. Then

Ben Ryan had insisted on joining them. Jack thought the kid looked too young to be emptying his pockets at a card table and had told him so a few days earlier, when Ben had tried to talk his way into a high-stakes poker game.

But today Redeye had had the boy's money on the table before Ben even sat down. An hour later, Barlow staggered to his feet, yanked out his gun and called the kid a cheater.

Now Jack didn't have time to consider how stupid he was about to be.

Taking two running steps off the porch, he slid his Colt out of the holster, aiming and firing in one swift motion.

The shot caught Redeye in the shoulder. Barlow staggered, lost his footing and fell on his backside, dropping his gun, an almost comical look of surprise twisting his face.

Glancing at Ben, Jack saw him drop to his knees and double over, clutching his stomach.

Jack shook his head and, holstering his gun, strode over to where Redeye still sat in the dirt, holding his bloody shoulder. Jack kicked Barlow's six-shooter several feet to the side, resisting the urge to kick Barlow along with it.

Redeye glared at him through bleary eyes. "Damn you, Dakota. The kid was cheatin'. He had this comin'."

"You had this coming. Although with two bottles of that rat poison they call whiskey in you, I don't know how you could tell one way or the other."

Before Barlow could argue, Jack reached down and

rifled through the other man's vest pocket, pulling out a crumpled wad of notes. Barlow made a grab for them, but Jack easily snatched the money out of his reach. "Part of this is mine. And you might remember next time that the game's played with only four aces."

He was just about to turn his back on Redeye, give Ben his share of the money and disappear before the sheriff arrived, when a wagon came clattering up the dirt street straight at him, the driver practically standing, urging the horse on in a headlong gallop.

At the last moment, the madman holding the reins reared back, jerking the horse to a stop and jumping down from the seat before the wheels stopped sliding.

"Ben!"

Jack first thought the wiry figure in the baggy duster was a boy—until he saw the lumpy braid underneath her sorry-looking hat slap her back as she ran toward Ben. Even then it was hard to believe anything that dusty and rumpled could be female.

"Are you all right? What happened?" the girl demanded, dropping to her knees beside Ben and running her hands over him. Ben, still bent over, answered her with a groan.

"He was trying to get himself killed," Jack said, walking up to them.

The girl looked up, ran her eyes over him and frowned. "What would you know about it?"

"More than you at this moment. Trust me, darlin', he was close enough to hell to smell smoke."

"It looks to me like he wasn't doing too badly," she said, flipping a hand to where Redeye still sat in the dust, chaperoned now by Joe Bellweather from the general store as Joe waited for his son to fetch the sheriff.

"C'mon, Hal, Ben couldn't hit a bull's rump with a banjo, even when he ain't been drinkin'," one of the cowboys still lounging on the porch of the Silver Snake called out.

A loud outburst of laughter greeted his remark, and Hallie flushed. But she kept her chin up and refused to look away. "And I'm supposed to believe one of you *gentlemen* helped him?"

"No, you should be thankin' your friend there for keepin' Ben out of a pine box. He drew so fast Redeye didn't have time to blink."

Hallie turned back to the stranger, who seemed to think very little of shooting a man on the main street in the middle of the day. He looked more like the fancy-dressed gamblers who came through town than a gunslinger, but you never could tell. "Is that true?"

"Oh, I think Bill probably blinked a couple of times. Here," he said, reaching down to take Ben's arm before Hallie could refuse his help, "let's get him in the wagon before he decides to sleep it off in the street."

More than ready to end being the afternoon's entertainment, Hallie helped get her brother to his feet and half carried him to the wagon. She started to guide Ben to the seat, but Ben's rescuer shook his head and hefted him onto the back floorboards instead. Ben, his eyes screwed shut, curled up on his side, moaning softly.

Jack pulled off his hat, wiping his brow with the

side of his hand. He wondered how many times the girl did this in a week. From the way she handled Ben, he figured she spent a good deal of her time getting the kid out of one scrape or another, although it was hard to understand why. Ben Ryan was nothing but trouble.

Hallie watched Ben a moment before reluctantly turning from her brother to the man who'd helped him. She supposed she owed him, but right then she wished he could have been anybody else.

From the look of him, she guessed she'd been right from the start, and he was the kind that made his living flipping cards in every saloon and hotel he passed through. But even if he wasn't, she immediately mistrusted that lazy, charming smile that seemed to be there in his eyes even when it wasn't on his mouth.

He reminded her of a phrase she'd once heard Tenfoot use to describe a rogue stallion: long, hard and fast. His hair, overlong and tousled, looked a hundred different shades of dark gold, as if the individual strands hadn't been able to agree on a color. It insisted on falling over one eyebrow, giving him a slightly rakish air that, combined with a wicked smile, Hallie was sure he used to his advantage.

"I'm Hallie Ryan," she said gruffly, sticking out her hand.

If he was surprised at her hesitation or her gesture, he didn't show it. "Jack Dakota," he said, taking her hand in a firm grip, at the same time studying her from her hat to her boots. From the look in his eyes,

Hallie got the impression he disapproved of every inch of her.

Why should she care? She'd thank him and he'd be on his way, and that would be the end of it. "I guess I owe you, Mr. Dakota. You saved my brother's life. Thank you."

"I hope you didn't hurt yourself sayin' that, Miss Hallie." Jack grinned when she scowled. Then, pulling out the wad of notes he'd taken from Redeye, he counted off several and handed the rest to her. "Ben's money. Don't bother thanking me for it, since he lost some of it fair and square to me. Most of it's there, though."

"How generous," Hallie muttered, thumbing through the notes, not about to give Dakota the satisfaction of seeing how much getting her money back meant to her.

Jack watched her, trying to figure her out. He'd known his share of women, but Hallie Ryan stuck out like snow in the desert. Then again, it was hard to tell she was female from the way she looked and acted.

Though tall for a woman and on the thin side, she might be pretty if she stripped off the dust and the cowboy garb, and stopped scowling. He couldn't tell the color of her hair with it haphazardly braided and stuffed under that twisted wreck of a hat. But she did have beautiful eyes, clear and direct, an unusual shade of soft green that reminded him of wild sage and sunshine.

Hallie shifted a little, uncomfortable with his scrutiny. "Look, Mr. Dakota—"

"Jack."

"Mr. Dakota, like I said, I owe you for helping Ben. If you're ever in Paradise again, you're welcome to call on us if you need anything."

"Well, Miss Hallie, I may be calling sooner than you think. You see…" Jack leaned against the wagon, thumbs hooked in his belt. "I plan on staying in Paradise."

"Staying?"

"Don't look so surprised. I can't leave until I collect on your neighborly offer, now can I?" Suspicion flared in her eyes and he laughed. "Don't get your fur ruffled, Miss Hallie. I was only thinking of asking for a little advice. Ben told me you know more about ranching than any man in the territory."

"Ben says a lot of things when he's had too much whiskey. Besides, why should you need advice on anything to do with running a ranch?"

"Because I'm now the proud owner of one."

Hallie barely stopped herself from laughing in his face. "Pardon me, Mr. Dakota, but you don't look anything like the kind of man who belongs on a ranch."

"I won't ask you where you think I do belong—I have a good imagination. But I plan on settling down and becoming a good citizen." Jack winked at her, laughing when she stared at him as if he was crazy. "I just bought what your friendly banker called one of the finest pieces of land in the territory. Eden's Canyon."

"You…" Stunned, Hallie could only gape at him. It couldn't be true. It just couldn't be.

"The bartender at the Silver Snake heard I was

looking for some land and told me it was for sale, and that it was a pretty fair piece of property. It seemed like a good gamble so now it's mine.''

Jack eyed her for a moment. The look on her face worried him. For the first time since he'd set foot in Paradise, he started to have second thoughts about how quickly he'd decided to try his luck at ranching rather than the dice table.

He couldn't blame Hallie Ryan for thinking he'd spent too much time in the desert sun. He'd surprised himself. But he had one very good reason for staying in this town, and because of that, he'd made up his mind to make this ranching business pay.

No matter what it took.

"Is there a problem, Miss Ryan?" he asked at last, when it looked as if she'd stand there for the rest of the day, staring at him as if he'd announced he'd come to town to turn the church into a house of wicked women and whiskey.

"A problem?" Hallie found her voice as the truth of what he'd told her finally hit and hit hard. "Oh, yes, there's a problem, Mr. Dakota. A big problem."

"Are you going to share it with me, or do I have to guess?"

"They should never have sold you Eden's Canyon. That land is mine."

All at once Jack's easiness slid away, leaving him tense. He straightened and slapped his hat back on. "I don't like to disagree with a lady—" the slight emphasis he put on "lady" made Hallie flinch inside "—but I've got the deed to prove it isn't."

"Eden's Canyon has been Ryan land for nearly

forty years. I would have bought it back if Ben hadn't taken my money to put in your pocket!''

Hallie could have bitten her tongue off the moment the words left her mouth. She hadn't meant to tell Jack Dakota anything about herself. But the shock and anger of losing Eden's Canyon to him, of all people, left her too furious to think straight.

''I'll buy it back from you,'' she said through gritted teeth. She thrust out the wad of notes he'd given her. ''I have more than half the money now. I'll get the rest soon.''

Jack ignored the money. ''I'm not selling.''

''You don't know the first thing about running a ranch! You'll lose everything before a year's over.''

''I wouldn't bet your last dollar on that, Miss Hallie,'' he said, smiling tightly.

''What I'd bet is that you've never stuck with anything longer than a week,'' Hallie said. Desperation began to spark the first twinges of panic in her. She couldn't lose Eden's Canyon. Especially not like this. *Oh, Pa, how could you have done this?* ''Why would you even want to try?''

''One very good reason.'' Gesturing to the porch of the saloon, he called over to one of the saloon girls. ''It's okay, Kitty, it's over. He can come out now.''

The girl leaned inside the door, beckoning with her hand until a fair-haired boy, about seven or eight years old, came out onto the porch. He stood by one of the posts, looking at Jack and Hallie with a mixture of curiosity and defiance.

''He's why I'm here,'' Jack said.

Hallie's face puckered in confusion. "Ethan Harper? What would you have to do with Ethan?"

"He's my son."

"Your—that's impossible. You couldn't be—I mean, when…how?"

"I do put the cards down once in a while, darlin'. And as to how, I'd demonstrate but I don't think you want to give the boys at the Silver Snake another spectacle."

Hallie flushed and opened her mouth to snap back at him, but Jack took a step closer so she could feel the heat of him. She faltered and stepped backward, uneasy with the expression in his eyes, which made her wonder if she'd misjudged his determination to suddenly become a rancher.

"Paradise is where Ethan's grown up, so Paradise is where he stays," Jack said. He looked straight at her. "And Eden's Canyon is mine and it's going to stay mine. Like it or not."

Hallie stood by the window in the front room of the ranch house, her hands fisted at her sides, and forced herself to look at the stretch of fine grazing land beyond the knobby wooden corral fences. The brilliant sunshine hurt her eyes, but at least it distracted her from thinking about Ben and what his latest escapade had cost her.

Outside her window, grasses knee-high and thick rolled in green, gold and brown over the flat plains of the Rillito Valley. On either side of the valley, the mountains, painted in reds and browns, jutted up in crags and peaks, guarding the rich grassland. Her grandfather had left behind a dirt farm in Missouri to stake his claim on this piece of wild Arizona territory. He'd built the sprawling cedar-and-adobe house near the river, started breeding Mexican cattle and made a modest fortune before Paradise was even a thought.

Hallie couldn't imagine living anywhere but here, or doing anything but ranching. She was good at it, if nothing else. She would never be the pretty, graceful, quiet kind of woman that men courted with their Sunday-best manners and sweet talk. But she told herself she didn't care. She didn't need nice ways and soft words to break a wild mustang or round up a herd of cattle.

She did, however, need Eden's Canyon.

A timid knock at the door turned Hallie from the window. The girl who poked her head into the room was not much younger than Ben, with smooth pale hair and round blue eyes that dominated her thin face. Hallie had given Serenity Trent a haven and a job at Eden's Canyon more than two years ago, and only regretted that the girl still crept around as if she expected someone to holler at her just for being in the room.

Hallie motioned her inside. "What is it, Serenity? What's wrong?"

Chewing at her lower lip, Serenity glanced over her shoulder. "It's—"

"Jack Dakota. Don't worry, sweetheart," he said, winking at Serenity as he pushed the door wide and walked inside as if he had a right to be there. "Miss Hal knows Ethan and me."

Serenity, her face bright red, appeared ready to

crawl under the rug. Ethan hung back, his face set in a sullen scowl as he clutched a ragged carpetbag close to his side. Only Jack smiled at Hallie, taking the whole mess in stride as if it were of no more consequence than an afternoon picnic. She ground her teeth together, feeling the itch to string him up the first opportunity she got.

"What are you doing here?" she demanded.

"Moving into my house."

"It is *not* your house."

"I thought we'd settled this."

"We didn't settle anything!"

"Well, the bank and I did," Jack said. Becoming slightly annoyed at her stubborn refusal to face the truth, he held the deed papers in front of her nose. "These look familiar?" He pulled the papers back when she made to snatch them away. "I didn't want to leave Ethan at the saloon any longer, and I didn't fancy staying in town after my little misunderstanding with Redeye. So I'm here, to stay, at *my* house."

They glared at each other before Serenity interrupted the charged silence by touching Ethan on the shoulder. "I've got some gingerbread in the kitchen. Would you like some?" She gave him a gentle prod in the right direction, and after a glance at Jack, Ethan left with her.

Jack nearly protested, but he didn't like arguing with Hallie in front of the boy. "Who is she?" He nodded toward Serenity.

"My housekeeper. And before you say anything, she might be young but she works hard, and she knows more about this ranch than you ever will."

"Is that a challenge, Miss Hal?"

"It's *Hallie,* and the only challenge I have for you is to see how fast you can ride out of here. You can't stay."

"Well now, darlin', I think it's the other way around," Jack drawled.

The color rose in her face and he smiled, slow and easy. She'd left behind her ugly hat, and her hair, a color somewhere between maple brown and honey, looked as if chickens had been scratching in it. He wondered if she knew it, let alone cared.

"If you just expect me to walk out of here and leave it all to you, you'd better be backing those papers up with a rifle," Hallie said, fighting to keep her voice level, when inside she felt like screaming at him.

"That's up to you. I came here ready to do some bargaining."

"Bargaining? Ha! Why do I get the feeling your idea of a bargain is what's best for you?"

Jack ignored her. "I've thought of a way you and your brother can stay at Eden's Canyon."

"You leave and sell my land back to me."

"You stay and work with me."

This time Hallie did laugh in his face. Work with him? Was he crazy? "I wouldn't work for you if I was down to my last dollar and starving."

"Good thing, because I'm not looking to hire you," Jack said. Leaning back against the wall, he looked her up and down with that infuriatingly smug smile. "I'm asking you to be my partner."

Chapter Two

"**Y**our *what?*"

"I think you heard me," Jack said, looking her up and down with a deliberate appraisal that made Hallie's cheeks burn. "Though judging from your face, you would've thought I'd asked you to be my partner in bed, not business."

"I'd rather bed a scorpion!"

"Suit yourself, darlin'. But unless you can die from pleasure, my bite isn't poisonous."

Hallie fought to keep from completely losing control of her temper. She'd worked with men all her life, but she'd never known any man who, after less than an hour's acquaintance, could aggravate her with just one look. "This is a home, Dakota, not a saloon. I don't allow talk like that under my roof."

"You don't strike me as the prim and proper kind, Hal." Jack pushed away from the wall. Pulling off his black Stetson, he tossed it onto a nearby chair with an insolent flip of his hand. "But it's my roof now," he said, slowly walking toward her, "and under my roof, I'll say and do as I please."

"Why, you low-down, good-for-nothing—!" After everything that had happened, Jack Dakota was one calamity too much. Goaded to the breaking point, Hallie swung a fist in the direction of his jaw.

Jack easily caught her wrist in midmotion, holding her at arm's length while she twisted to free herself. "If you'll calm down long enough to think this over, I'm sure you'll see it my way."

"Over your dead body," Hallie muttered at him. She stopped her useless struggle, and the moment he relaxed his grip, whipped her hand out of his grasp. Retreating a few steps, she rubbed her wrist, glaring at him.

Jack cautiously lowered his hands, not fully convinced the little wildcat wouldn't attack him again. "Look, Hal, before you go for your guns, consider that I could just tell you to pack your bags and get off my ranch." Fire flared in her eyes again and he held up his palms in warning. "But I'm trying to offer you a deal that's more than fair, under the circumstances."

"You expect me to believe you play fair?" Hallie said. She laughed, the sound grating and bitter even to her own ears. "You and I obviously have very different ideas of fair, Dakota."

Jack shrugged off the insult. "Whatever you want to accuse me of, lady, you can't call me a cheat. Everything I've won and lost, I've done so fair and square. I'm making you a straight offer. I've got the money to keep this place going, and you've got the experience. I'm willing to be your partner, and that's the best you're going to get from me or anyone else.

But it's your choice. You can stay or go, but right now, the boy and I are settling in.''

Before she could stop him, Jack strode past her and out the door in the direction Serenity had taken Ethan. Hallie stayed rooted in place and counted to ten, her hands flexing into fists at her sides as she tried to get some control of her stampeding emotions. Then she followed in his wake, catching up with him just as he stepped into the kitchen.

Serenity and Ethan, sitting at the kitchen table with plates of half-eaten squares of gingerbread in front of them, both looked up as Jack and Hallie came in.

"If you're finished," Jack said, walking up to Serenity, "I'd be obliged if you'd show us a couple of rooms we can bed down in.''

Serenity's eyes flitted between Jack and Hallie and finally settled on Hallie in appeal. "Do I...? Where should I put them?''

Hallie almost told her she could send Jack Dakota straight to hell, but for Ethan's sake, and the fact that Serenity would likely turn and run, she bit back the words.

What could she do? Her own home had been sold out from under her and Dakota was here to stake his claim. She supposed she could put a gun to his head and force him to leave. But she couldn't do that in front of the boy, and besides, Dakota would only come back with the sheriff. She didn't want to admit it, but he rightfully owned Eden's Canyon, and if she kept getting him riled up, he might send her, Ben and everyone else packing.

And they had nowhere else to go.

She had no choice. She had to let him stay. And damn him, he knew it. It was clear in the way he was looking at her now, with that self-satisfied expression in his eyes, a half smile curving his mouth.

Go ahead and smile, Dakota, she told him silently. We'll see who ends up staying. And it won't be you.

"Give Ethan the room next to Ben's," she told Serenity. "Ben's been using it to pile up what he doesn't want to put away, but we can clean it out soon enough." An idea struck her and she turned to Jack. "I'll take you to your room."

Not liking the sudden lift in her tone, Jack bent to take Ethan's tattered bag, but the boy snatched it up.

"Don't touch it," Ethan said. "I can carry it myself."

Jack opened his mouth to make a comment on Ethan's manners, but the flash of disapproval in Hallie's eyes stopped him. He wasn't going to give her something else to argue with him about.

Instead, he inclined his head and swept a hand toward the kitchen door. "After you, then, Miss Hal."

"This isn't a room, it's a stall." Unwilling to go through the doorway, Jack glanced around the tiny, cluttered space Hallie had led him to.

"You've just been spoiled by too many fancy hotels," she said, strolling to the window to lift the shade. "It's fine. It used to be the nursery for Ben and me. Now it just needs a little sorting through and sprucing up." She yanked the pull cord and the shade flew up, scattering dust motes in the rays of late-af-

ternoon sunlight streaming into the musty, long-ne-
glected room.

Waving away the cloud of dust, she turned and
smiled sweetly at Jack. "I wasn't expecting company."

Jack sighed. "I'm not company."

"As far as I'm concerned you are. So don't get too
comfortable."

A few long strides took Jack across the small room,
though he had to dodge a shabby wooden chest and
a rocking chair with no seat as he went. He stopped
when he stood less than a breath away from her.
Meeting her nose to nose, he was pleased to see her
false smile quickly fade, replaced by wariness.

He smiled, slow and easy. "Now, I think your joke
is real amusing, honey, but it's been a long day and
I'm ready for a shave and some dinner."

He was so close Hallie was forced to either tilt her
head and look directly at his face or stare at his shirt
buttons. She chose to meet his gaze squarely, immediately wishing she hadn't.

His eyes, a warm, golden brown, reflected his smile
and the laughter running through it. But she had the
feeling he was inviting her to share with him the humor of the situation they found themselves in.

For one crazy moment, Hallie wanted to. He made
it so easy and, she admitted, so tempting. She imagined he would be like that with a woman he wanted,
and that it would be hard to say no, especially if he
touched her.

The instant the thought registered Hallie sucked in
a breath, so suddenly she drew in a lungful of dust

and started to cough. What on earth was she thinking? She would never let a man like Dakota touch her, never.

"Are you all right?" Jack asked. He put a hand on her shoulder to steady her. "Can I get you some water? The dust in here is as thick as a dirt devil."

Hallie shook her head, swallowing hard. "I'm fine. It's nothing."

But it wasn't. It was definitely something. And she didn't want to have anything to do with it or with him.

"Let's get out of here before we both choke on the dirt," Jack said, steering her out the door with the hand grasping her shoulder. Outside, he turned her so both his hands held her, and he studied her face. "Can we at least settle the sleeping arrangements without a fight? I'm not asking for the master bedroom. I'm sure that's yours. I just want someplace bigger—and cleaner."

To Jack's surprise, the fight seemed to drain out of Hallie all at once. She wetted her lips, swallowed hard again and finally found her voice. It came out rough and uncertain, and strangely soft for her. "I don't use the master bedroom. After Pa died, I just... I left it the same as he and Ma had it. I have my own room."

Jack's hands tightened briefly on her shoulders. "Okay, not that room then. What's left besides it?"

Hallie tried to ignore the pleasing, disturbing warmth of his touch by telling herself Jack Dakota practiced charm as easily as he breathed. But she couldn't ignore the fact that he did seem to at least be trying to make some kind of peace between them.

''Oh, go ahead and take Pa's room,'' she blurted out, at the same time she pulled away from him. ''The moths and the mice are going to chew everything to shreds if someone doesn't move in there soon, anyhow.''

''Are you sure you don't want to have it yourself?''

''No, I like the way the sun hits my pillow at dawn. Somehow I don't imagine you'd appreciate that much.''

''Depends on who's sharing my pillow,'' he said, the rogue in him returning to tease her.

''No one here will, except maybe the cat,'' Hallie retorted.

Jack only smiled, thinking of an image of Hallie asleep, her wild mass of hair tangled around her, the early-morning sun kissing her face. She would look softer then, gentled by the night's rest. She might even be pretty, without her claws at the ready and her expression so serious.

''You'll be getting used to seeing the sun rise soon enough if you intend to run this ranch,'' she was saying.

''And I'll learn to like it—in about twenty years. But for now, if you'll just point me in the right direction, I'll get settled in.''

''Two doors down the hall on the left.''

''Two?'' Jack raised a brow at the flush creeping into her face. ''What's next door?''

Hallie wanted to look away, but instead found her eyes riveted to his. ''My room.''

''Well, now.'' He cocked his head slightly, a slash of afternoon sunlight catching every shade from pale

ale to brandy in his hair. "That's convenient, seeing as we'll be partners."

"Damn you, Dakota." Hallie turned her back on him, wishing he would just disappear. "Don't get used to it."

"Temper, darlin'," he said, laughing. He started past her in the direction she'd indicated, pausing to grin at her over his shoulder. "And watch your language. I don't allow talk like that under my roof."

After leaving Hallie, Jack found the bedroom she'd given him, then retrieved his bags from where he'd dropped them by the front door. Leaving them unopened in his room, he went in search of Ethan.

He found the boy in his new room, alone, curled up on the bed. He was toying with a worn-out shred of glossy yellow cloth. But when he noticed Jack in the doorway, Ethan clenched his fingers around the cloth and hurriedly sat up.

Jack hesitated before moving to sit down next to his son. "I came to see if I could help you get moved in."

"Nope." Ethan stared at his hands, clenched together in his lap.

Feeling awkward and uncertain of himself for the first time in as long as he could remember, Jack scoured his brain for something to say. His brand of charm wouldn't work with this kid. What would work to earn the boy's trust and confidence, he hadn't a clue.

"Nice room, don't you think?"

"It's okay. I guess."

Jack glanced around. Serenity had obviously been at work cleaning, changing the bed and moving Ben's possessions into the adjoining room. But a few things remained: a pile of clothes strewn over a chair; boots tossed in a corner; a lamp with what looked like a brightly colored scarf no lady would wear draped over the shade; a silver garter hung on the corner of a picture frame. Ethan ought to feel right at home, he mused ruefully, remembering the room he and Mattie had shared at the Silver Snake.

What on earth had convinced Mattie he'd be good for her son? Being a father had caught him completely by surprise. His relationship with Mattie had been brief, like most everything else in his life. He'd never taken it or any other dalliances with women too seriously. Women had been something to entertain him between card games.

But now the result of those few nights in Mattie's bed nine years ago was sitting next to him.

He didn't have the first idea of how to be a parent or make a family. He knew even less about ranching. But he did know one thing. Ethan wasn't going to grow up the way he had. His boy would have roots, a home, a real father.

Whatever those were.

Jack glanced at his son. When he'd told Ethan they were moving to the ranch, the boy had flatly refused to go. He'd only left Mattie's room after the woman who owned the saloon told him he couldn't stay.

Walking out of the Silver Snake, and all during the ride to Eden's Canyon, Ethan had said nothing. But Jack recognized something familiar in the way the boy held himself stiff and still. Ethan might have been the image of himself at eight years old, sitting on the porch of a San Francisco hotel while his father argued with his mother over which of them should keep him.

"Ethan?"

The boy kept staring at his hands.

"I want to talk to you about a few things. You don't have to answer, but I hope you'll listen, because this is important, for both of us."

No response.

Jack pushed on, determined to have his say even if he ended up talking to himself. "I'm sorry about your ma, Ethan. I told you before, I didn't know she was sick and I didn't know about you until I got the telegram a few weeks ago."

Ethan's shoulders shifted in what might have been a shrug.

"I know this isn't where you want to be right now, but we can't stay at the saloon. We need a home and this is going to be it. We're going to learn to be ranchers, and one day, this place will be yours."

His last words seemed to rouse Ethan. "Miss Hallie says it's hers," the boy said, without looking up. "She doesn't want us here."

That's an understatement, Jack thought. "Not now. But she'll get used to us. And she can teach us a lot."

"She ain't like Ma or Kitty or any of the other girls." His face pinching in a frown, Ethan twisted his fingers harder together. "Her skin don't look soft, her lips ain't red and she don't smell pretty."

"Uh, no, but—"

For the first time Ethan looked up at him, his mouth

set in a determined line. "She ain't gonna be my new ma and we ain't ever gonna be a family." It was both a plea and a decree. "I don't want no other ma. 'Specially one who ain't even a real girl."

"I didn't bring you here to find you a new ma."

"Why'd you come here then? You're a card player, not a rancher. I seen you. You're real good. Ma said so, too."

Despite the truth in them, Ethan's words made Jack uncomfortable. "Trust me," he said, his face hardening, "living in saloons is no life for a kid."

Ethan whirled away to face the wall. Tentatively, Jack touched his back. He was about to ask what the matter was when he caught sight of a corner of the yellow cloth Ethan still gripped, his thumb rubbing the edge of it.

"You miss your ma," Jack said softly, "don't you?"

Ethan sucked in a broken breath.

"Of course you do. And you're going to miss her a good, long while. I can't make that easier for you."

A shudder passed over Ethan and he stifled a sob, roughly wiping the back of his hand against his eyes.

Impulsively, Jack put his arm around Ethan's shoulders and drew the boy close against his chest, holding him awkwardly as Ethan finally let go of his tears.

It wasn't going to be easy for either of them. But Jack had to make it work.

Serenity, a wooden spoon in one hand and a crumpled dish cloth in the other, flitted about the kitchen like a skittish bird, checking a pan here, a platter there. "I started so late on supper, it'll never be ready on time."

"It'll be ready," Hallie said, not looking up from the cornbread batter she stirred with unnecessary force. "I'm here to help you. And we won't have Dakota underfoot in here. This is one place he's sure to stay clear of."

"You don't like him much, do you?"

Hallie stopped stirring and stared at the girl. "He practically stole my ranch."

"He bought it from the bank," Serenity pointed out, avoiding looking at Hallie as she began setting the plates on the long pine table. "He is letting us all stay. He can't be so bad, can he? Besides, he's awfully nice to look at. So clean and polished and all."

"What difference does that make?" Hallie said, irritated that Serenity would even notice. "And he's only letting us stay because he wants me to teach him how to run this place."

Serenity stopped in the motion of putting down forks, biting at her lower lip. "You mean he'll make us leave after he learns?"

Hallie heard the flood of fear in Serenity's anxious voice. At fifteen, Serenity had fled her grandparents' home to escape an arranged marriage. Orphaned as a toddler, she'd been raised by her grandparents and had always loved them. But the mere idea of marrying a man twice her age repulsed and terrified her, so she'd run away, ending up on Hallie's doorstep a month later, bedraggled, half-starved and looking for work.

Hallie knew part of Serenity still expected either her grandparents or the man she'd been promised to to one day show up and try to claim her, even after two years. She could see that the idea of being forced away from Eden's Canyon terrified the girl.

"Don't worry yourself, Dakota won't be around long enough to learn," Hallie told her. "He'll hit the trail just as soon as he figures out there's no excitement here. I know his kind."

She stopped short of saying she'd *lived* with his kind all her life—both her brother and her father. Serenity had a soft spot for Ben, and it was no good telling the girl anything that might be opposite the image she had of him.

"I don't know about that," Serenity said, her expression thoughtful. "He does have Ethan now."

"You wait and see." Hallie began scooping spoonfuls of batter into the square pan, slapping it so hard that yellow drops spattered over the worktable. "He may be the gambler, but I'd wager my stake in this ranch that Jack Dakota won't last here six months."

"I'd ask you to shake on that, but I can't win something that's already mine."

Hallie jumped at the sound of Jack's deep voice behind her. All at once she felt unsettled and annoyed, and angry at herself for letting him do that to her. She'd known lots of men—cowhands, ranchers, even a few gamblers Ben played with. But none of them ever made her feel like she couldn't move without tripping over herself.

She turned to look as Jack, with Ethan at his side, strolled into the kitchen. The man was clean-shaven, dressed in a fine white shirt that stretched across his broad shoulders beneath a black leather vest, and his pants clung to his hips as though they'd grown there.

Glancing at Serenity, she saw the girl's admiring look. But when Serenity turned and saw Hallie watching, too, the girl flushed scarlet and quickly switched back to setting the table. Hallie realized she had no ally there.

"We don't dress for supper," Hallie told Jack, as she went back to her chore, shoving the pan of cornbread into the belly of the iron stove. She wiped her hands down her pants, leaving a streak of yellow, and imagined she must look a right pretty sight compared to Jack's and Ethan's spit and polish.

"We didn't," Jack said. He leaned against the worktable, smiling at her rumpled hair and the smudge of flour on her nose. "We came to offer our help."

"Help?" Hallie looked him up and down. "With what?"

"You tell me."

Before Hallie could tell him anything, Serenity pushed a wooden pail into Jack's hands. "If you could get us some water from the barrel out back, I'd be obliged."

Jack took the pail with a smile. He looked to Ethan. "We'll do it together. You can hold the pail."

Ethan shook his head. "I'll dip it out."

"Fair enough."

No sooner had the two stepped down the back stairs than Ben, head hanging low, ambled into the kitchen with Tenfoot, followed by Eb and Big Charlie, the other two ranch hands. "Evenin'," they muttered more or less in unison as they moved to take their places on the benches at either side of the table.

Hallie noticed Serenity flash a sweet smile as Ben shuffled past her to his seat, but the smile faded when Ben seemed not to notice her. Best he didn't, Hallie thought. The last thing Serenity needed was to lose her heart to a boy who wouldn't know what to do with it even if he wanted it.

Jack and Ethan came through the back door just as the others settled in their seats. All eyes turned to the strangers. Hallie never invited guests to the ranch, making the men immediately suspicious of anyone new.

"This is Jack Dakota and his son, Ethan," Hallie murmured. She swallowed hard. There was no easy way to say what she had to say. "Mr. Dakota now owns Eden's Canyon."

Jack nodded and smiled at the rugged group of men. "Evenin'."

Silence fell over the table.

Tenfoot shot a look at Ben, but Ben kept his eyes fixed on his plate. Eb and Big Charlie exchanged glances, and Hallie easily read the surprise, doubt and concern that crossed their faces. Tenfoot sized up Jack with a long look, and Hallie could almost hear him wondering how a fancy stranger who obviously didn't know the right end of a cow had ended up with the Ryan ranch.

Edging slightly closer to Jack, Hallie whispered, "This is your doing. You'd better explain to them. And fast."

"My pleasure, Miss Hallie," he said, nodding his head to her. If she expected to scare him, he could have told her he'd faced tougher audiences than this one. At least none of these men had guns, with their fingers on the triggers.

While Hallie and Serenity served up supper, Jack briefly told his story, deliberately leaving out Ben's involvement, keeping the details vague and making it clear Hallie would be staying on, and everyone else, too, if they wanted.

"I hope you're shootin' straight, Mister." Eb Ryan spoke up from the far end of the table, where he always sat. Eb had a mortal fear of water and refused to go near it, even to wash. He was a cousin Hallie's pa had talked away from cowpunching on a Wyoming ranch, and because of that, and the fact that he worked harder than any cowpoke in the territory, everyone kept quiet about his one terror. "I been here a spell and don't fancy the idea of lookin' for work somewhere else."

"Things aren't going to change much around here," Jack said. "The only difference is I'll be around to help."

Big Charlie Dillon snorted. "How do we know you won't be changin' your mind the first time your hands get dirty?" he asked around a mouthful of ham.

"I won't," Jack said, glancing at Ethan.

Taking a place across from the boy, Hallie looked at him closely for the first time. She could easily see why Mattie Harper had no doubt who her son's father was. Instead of Mattie's red hair, Ethan shared Jack's coloring, and his face would one day be a copy of the clean, angular lines of his father's.

He watched Jack with quick sideways glances, partly curious, partly uncertain, but all uncomfortable, Hallie noticed. She knew that feeling all too well.

"Would you like some cornbread, Ethan?" she asked him as Jack sat down and the men concentrated on their food.

Ethan eyed her as though she were some new breed of varmint he'd never seen before. He reached for the thick square she offered, being careful not to touch her hand.

Hallie hid a smile. Considering Ethan's upbringing, she supposed she was like no woman he'd ever known. None of this was like anything he'd ever known, and she knew the boy must be feeling very alone.

Jack Dakota, on the other hand, had probably never spent a lonely moment in his life. He wouldn't know the first thing about being different, always on the outside. Even now he acted as if he'd sat down to supper at this table every night of his life.

"If you'd like, I'll show you around the ranch tomorrow," she told Ethan, trying to draw him out a little. "We've got a new colt you might want to see."

For the first time Ethan looked directly at her. He didn't say anything, but Hallie knew she'd at least stirred his interest a bit.

"We'll do it first thing after breakfast," she promised.

She turned in her seat to make sure everyone was getting enough supper, and found Jack watching her.

The appreciation warming his eyes flustered her. "He's got to learn his way around sooner or later," she said, as if her talking to Ethan needed some explanation. "Being here, having you around, is going to take some getting used to."

"Him as the boss is sure gonna take some gettin' used to," Big Charlie interjected, rousing laughter from the other men at the table. He scratched the black stubble on his jaw while he pretended to seriously consider Jack. "Somethin' tells us you ain't always been a rancher, Dakota."

Jack lifted a shoulder, letting the jab roll off with an easy smile. "I've done a lot of things when I needed the money. Now I've got the money and I've decided to do this."

"Ain't somethin' you can learn in a day or two," Tenfoot muttered.

"That's why Miss Hallie agreed to be my teacher."

Hallie glared at him. "Mr. Dakota and I agreed to be partners." She paused, then added deliberately, "For now."

Jack didn't bother to disagree with her. Instead, he only smiled and let her have her way. For now.

In time he'd prove to them all he was dead serious about keeping and running Eden's Canyon, whether one sassy lady rancher liked it or not.

Chapter Three

"Stroke his throat a bit. There. That's better." Hallie smiled in approval as Ethan coaxed the foal to take a few more swallows of the warm milk. On her knees in the straw beside him, she shifted slightly to give Ethan more room to work.

Like the boy, the colt was motherless. Hallie had taken over as substitute mother, ignoring the teasing from Eb and Big Charlie and their predictions that the foal didn't stand a chance. This morning, she'd prodded Ethan into taking over for her.

It hadn't been easy. After missing him at breakfast, she'd found him sitting hunched up in a corner of the porch. He'd refused to talk to her at first, and then balked at going with her to the barn. Only after she tempted him with seeing the horses did he begrudgingly follow her off the porch, dragging his feet in the dust the whole way.

But when the wobbly kneed colt repeatedly nudged his head against Ethan's leg, demanding to be noticed, the boy's eyes sparked with interest.

"He likes it," Ethan said, fascinated by the small,

smoky-gray colt pressed against his chest, now guzzling the milk from the makeshift teat Tenfoot had fashioned.

"He likes you," Hallie gently corrected. She stroked the colt's smooth head, not looking at Ethan. "He needs someone to take care of him. Maybe you could do it."

"Me?" Ethan looked astonished. "Not me. I never took care of nothin' before."

"Fine time to learn, since it looks like you're gonna camp here awhile," Tenfoot said, coming up beside them.

The boy's head shot up. "I'm not stayin' here! My ma and I always lived at the Silver Snake. I'm goin' back there as soon as I get the chance," Ethan finished defiantly.

Tenfoot scratched at his left ear. "Well, I think your pa sees it different."

"He ain't my pa!"

"That may or may not be," Hallie said quietly, "but you're here now. And the colt needs your help."

"You're doin' a fine job tendin' to him." Tenfoot gave the foal a pat and briefly clapped a hand on Ethan's shoulder. "A little more practice and you'll be doin' it better than the mares."

Ethan flushed and frowned as he stared hard at the colt half sprawled in his lap. But he didn't say no.

Smiling to herself, Hallie got to her feet and left Ethan to finish the job under Tenfoot's encouraging supervision. She still had a lot of work to get done before the heat made working outside unbearable. With her mind focused on the day's chores, she didn't see Jack standing in the doorway of the barn until she nearly walked into him.

"You're here," she blurted out before thinking. How long had he been standing there, watching? She felt an uncomfortable warmth creep up the back of her neck. "What are you doing here?"

"Good morning to you, too, Miss Hallie," he drawled, stepping back to let her walk out into the barnyard. He followed her a little way before propping a boot up on the first rung of the fence and crossing his arms over his knee. "I was looking for you."

"Why?"

Jack nearly smiled at the way she thrust her chin up, her jaw tight and her eyes narrowed. He was beginning to recognize that look, which meant Hallie Ryan intended to give him a fight if he gave her the slightest opportunity. "I see you've been keeping Ethan busy," he said, ignoring her question. "I'd been wondering where he'd gone so early."

"It's been light for three hours," Hallie pointed out, eyeing him meaningfully. "And Ethan needs something to make him feel like he belongs here. I thought taking care of the colt would help."

"You don't have to convince me. I think it's a good idea." Jack shrugged, straightening slowly. "Looks like so far you're better than me at being a parent."

"You haven't even gotten started. Why did you come back if you didn't want the responsibility?" Hallie asked bluntly.

Jack tugged his hat a little lower over his brow so

his face was in shadow. He didn't have an easy answer for that one, and he wasn't willing to let Hallie Ryan stand here and figure it out for him. ''The boy's my business.'' He waited for his meaning to sink in, then smiled and added lightly, ''As far as taking on this ranch, I needed a new game.''

''Raising a child isn't a game, Dakota. And neither is running a ranch.''

Refusing to wait for his response, Hallie turned on her heel and started back inside the barn to get her horse.

She couldn't remember when a man made her feel more stirred up and frustrated. Right now, all she wanted to do was ride as fast and as far away from him as she could.

He fell into step beside her. She sent him a glare. ''What do you want? I have work to do.''

''I'll go with you.'' Her eyebrows shot up and Jack smiled. ''I need to learn my way around. It is my ranch.''

''You may own it,'' Hallie said as she reached the corral and let herself in the gate. ''But it'll never be yours.'' She turned her back on him and kept walking.

''I'm not going away,'' he said, so close to her ear she jumped.

Hallie whipped around and found herself nearly nose to nose with him again. She took a hurried step backward. The heel of her boot skidded on a rock and she lurched, losing her hat and nearly her footing.

Jack quickly reached out and caught her upper arms, holding firmly until she righted herself, his hands lingering on her a few seconds longer than necessary. Their eyes met and Hallie felt an odd flutter inside, as if something buried within her had stirred in its sleep. Unsettled by it, she abruptly pulled back, glancing away. She bent and scooped up her hat. As she slapped it back on her head, she saw Jack grimace. "What is it now?"

"You have to admit that's a sad excuse for a hat, sweetheart."

Before she could stop him, he reached out and pulled her hat off, tossing it aside. Her braid fell down her back again. Jack wondered what she would look like if she ever took a brush to her hair, and if the idea even occurred to her.

Hallie snatched her hat back up again and jammed it on her head. "Looks like my hair offends you more than this."

"No, I've just never met a woman who cared so little about how she looked."

"Mister, I've run a ranch since I was seventeen," Hallie said, bristling at the implication in his voice. "I work with horses and cattle all day, make sure everything is moving along the way it should, and see to it everyone is cared for and stays out of trouble. I don't have time to worry about whether or not my ribbons match my eyes, or if there are enough curls in my hair. And I doubt satin skirts would last through the first throw from a wild mustang."

Jack couldn't help but smile to himself, though he turned slightly aside so she wouldn't see his amusement. The woman had pluck; that much he had to give her.

Hallie caught the hint of a smile teasing at the corner of his mouth, and it annoyed her. Either he didn't believe her or he wasn't all that impressed. She guessed the only thing about a woman that would impress a man like Jack Dakota was whether or not she knew how to use what Tenfoot called "feminine wiles" to please him.

She went into the tack room to get her saddle, anything to avoid looking at him. Whatever feminine wiles were, exactly, she didn't have them and she didn't care. The lack had never crossed her mind until now, and she wasn't about to let that kind of nonsense take root.

Pretending to adjust her hat, she stole a sidelong glance at the broad-shouldered man who insisted on walking next to her no matter how clear she made it she didn't want him around. Why did he make her feel so inadequate, so uncomfortable with herself? The smug, self-satisfied look still played about his mouth, giving him an air of having an advantage she didn't know about.

That along with his damnable good looks raised in her an impossible mix of anger and something she couldn't quite define. Part of her wanted to storm off and leave him Eden's Canyon so she'd never have to look into his laughing eyes again. But another part couldn't stop glancing at him, mesmerized for a moment by the way he moved as he reached to retrieve his bridle, the white cotton of his shirt stretched taut over his back and shoulders.

Jack looked up then, catching her gaze. "You must

like what you see, darlin'," he drawled, deliberately provoking. "You've been staring long enough."

Hallie immediately looked away. "You're wrong. Looking at you, I imagine you're nothing but trouble and always have been."

"Think so?"

"I know it. Ben told me what happened back in town during that card game. I wouldn't be surprised if most of it was your fault."

He laughed, the easy, deep-throated sound echoing into the heated stillness around them. "You're an ornery sort, aren't you, woman? Not at all like your brother."

Hallie stiffened. "Ben never needed to be ornery. He learned fast how to sweet-talk his way in or out of everything, just like you."

"It comes in handy, now and again."

"Don't you ever take anything seriously? Having to work for you isn't a game to me, no matter how amusing you find it." Hallie paced a few steps away, her back to him. "I knew Ben would get mixed up with someone like you sooner or later."

"I hate to break it to you, darlin'," Jack said slowly. "Ben *is* someone like me."

"He likes to gamble, but it's not his life. Not yet."

Jack looked up at her, the lightness gone from his expression. "Your brother is a born gambler," he stated, his tone suddenly serious. "Trust me, I know one when I see one. But I can't help that any more than I could stop him from getting in over his fool head with Redeye. He's old enough to make his own decisions, even if they're stupid ones."

"I don't trust you." Hallie spun around to face him. "And somehow I doubt you were too convincing when Ben wanted into that game."

"I'll say this one more time, Hal. I don't know your brother from Adam, but I'm well acquainted with his type. He might have a gambler's soul, but he sure as hell doesn't have a gambler's head. I warned him he'd lose his shirt in that game and he laughed at me. You should've kept him home on the ranch where he belongs."

To Jack's surprise her fierce scowl vanished and she jerked as if he'd struck her. "I've tried. Ever since Ma died, I've tried. It's only gotten worse, with Pa gone, too." She abruptly turned her head to stare blindly at the wall, her arms folded over her chest. "He wants things I can't give him." After a moment, she blew out a shaky breath and glanced at Jack. "And I told you, my name's not Hal."

The unguarded emotion he glimpsed on her face struck Jack like a fist to the chest. He felt a spurt of anger against Ben Ryan. Probably all his life the kid had let his sister shoulder his responsibility along with her own. Ben had no idea what he had. At one point in his life, Jack recalled he would have sold his soul to know Hallie's kind of love from anyone in his makeshift family.

He started to raise a hand to offer a comforting touch, then stopped himself cold. He wasn't about to make that mistake. She'd probably reach for the gun she had slung on her hip, thinking he intended to take advantage of her vulnerability.

"Hallie, I'm sorry about what happened with Ben," he said instead. "And your losing the ranch, too."

The gentleness in his voice made Hallie feel worse than before. She swallowed hard, wishing she'd kept her mouth shut and not let herself get upset in front of him. "But not sorry enough to give it up."

His expression hardened. "No. And you know why."

There was nothing she could say that would make any difference now. Without a word, she went and got her horse, Grano, from the stall, saddled the Appaloosa and led him outside. She mounted up, not bothering to check if Jack followed.

She started her horse into a gallop with a quick slap of the reins, wanting to pretend for at least a few minutes that everything she'd ever taken for granted hadn't been lost for good.

"Damn! Damn that good-for-nothing, smooth-talking—ouch!" Hallie yelped as the sharp pricks of cactus needles pierced the seat of her pants. She couldn't help blaming Dakota for this even though for all she knew he was still back at the ranch.

After her confrontation with him, she'd galloped her horse hard across the open grassland, relieved when she'd gotten to the edge of the cliffs to look back over her trail and find herself alone. After checking the grazing herd of cattle, she'd walked her horse along the rough path below the cliffs, taking a more leisurely pace back to the barn.

But as she'd started to turn the stallion toward the pasture again her horse had suddenly whinnied and reared back, throwing her bottom-first onto a patch of prickly pear. Stunned, Hallie didn't see the rattlesnake until it slithered off the path in front of her into a crevice in the rock. Grano she couldn't see at all.

Sucking in a shaky breath and letting it go in a whoosh, Hallie shifted slightly, then froze as pain sliced at her bottom.

All at once everything—the fall and her throbbing backside, Ben, Pa's death, losing the ranch—seemed too much.

"This is all your fault, Jack Dakota!" she said out loud. "Everything is your fault!"

Except it wasn't. No matter how much she wanted it to be. Angry tears stung her eyes. She was nearly as mad at herself as she was at him. How could she have let this happen, all of it? How could she ever put it right?

By getting yourself off this cactus for a start, she told herself. Sitting there sniveling wasn't going to change things. And it wasn't going to get the cactus spines out of her behind.

Hallie braced herself and pushed upward, jerking herself up onto her knees. For a moment, she hardly dared breathe for fear any little movement would make the pain unbearable.

Then, bent over in what felt like the most undignified position a woman could get herself into, she pulled off her bandanna, wadded it up and put it between her teeth to bite if the pain got too bad.

One by one, she began plucking out the cactus needles.

After the first three, she wanted to lie down and cry. But all she had to do was picture that roguish grin on Jack's face if he ever found her in this position, and it made her bite down and yank harder.

The sixth one stuck hard and Hallie let out a yell when she finally managed to yank it out.

Absorbed in her task, fighting the pain, she didn't hear the approach of a horse and rider coming fast across the open ground. Only when she lifted her face and found herself staring at a familiar pair of black boots did she realize she had an unwelcome audience.

She spat out the bandanna and looked up into Jack's face. "You!" Jerking to her feet, she gasped as the cactus needles sank deeper.

Jack knelt in front of her at once and grabbed her by the shoulders, preventing her from moving. "Keep still or you'll kill yourself before you get your shot at me."

"Just go away!"

"Right, and leave you by yourself, full of cactus needles. What were you trying to do here?"

"Oh, hush up. And leave me alone! I don't need your help."

"Oh, I can see that." Jack considered the situation and decided she'd been in the best position possible to get the needles out when he'd found her. "I think you'd better just bend over again and let me pull them out."

"I said I don't need your help!"

"Stop being so damned stubborn, woman. If you don't get rid of those soon, you're going to be begging me to shoot you just to end your misery." Picking up the bandanna, he rolled it tightly and offered it to her again. "Here, you're going to need this. Now turn around. You can plot my murder while I'm pulling them out."

With fury, loathing and humiliation swelling in her until she swore she'd explode, Hallie ground her teeth against the bandanna and bent over. Even accepting Jack Dakota's help had to be better than this pain.

Ignoring her provocative position and the small, heart-shaped curve of her backside, Jack forced himself to concentrate solely on the task at hand. One by one, with tender force, he tugged the needles from the seat of her pants.

At first she muttered curses in his direction, but by the time he finally wrested the last needle free, her anger had muted to whimpers.

"Okay, that's the last of it, sweetheart," Jack said.

Gently, he helped her straighten. Something twisted in his chest when he saw the unshed tears in her eyes. She held them back, keeping her pride intact. But he could see what the effort cost her and how much she was hurting.

"Hallie, I—"

"I hate you, Jack Dakota," she said, her eyes narrowed, her fists clenched. "I wish I'd never laid eyes on you. I wish Redeye had shot you when he had the chance."

"I never intended for you to get hurt."

She didn't know whether he meant the cactus or him buying her ranch, and she didn't care. She ignored the throb of pain in her backside and faced him squarely. "Well, you've said the words. Now get back up on your horse and ride off. I don't need you."

She started to turn away from him, but Jack caught her arm and pulled her to face him again. "Not without you."

For a moment they stared at each other, locked in a silent battle of wills.

Jack looked at her closely for the first time and realized she'd lost her ugly hat. Her braid had come undone and a wild riot of waist-long hair, a light honey-brown in the sunlight, fell over her slender shoulders, making her look more like a vulnerable young woman than the rough-riding ranch woman she pretended to be.

The intent way he looked at her only made Hallie feel more agitated. "Don't you ever listen to anything I say?"

"Every word. But I'm not leaving."

"I need some privacy to tend to myself. Go back to the ranch. I'll be there soon enough."

"Sorry, darlin'," Jack said, "but I can't do that."

Before she could protest, he slipped an arm around her waist, guiding her to a place in the rocks where she could rest her weight without leaning on her bottom.

Hallie glared at him. "What does it take to get rid of you?"

Jack only grinned and began rolling up his sleeves.

"You might as well get used to having me around. One day you might even like it. Now—" he eyed her with a glint in his eyes "—let's have a look at those holes the cactus left behind."

Hallie stared. He couldn't be serious. One thing was for sure, he was crazy if he thought she'd ever let him touch her again. Especially not *there*. But looking at him, Hallie knew he would.

And the worst of it was, right now she had neither the will nor the slightest idea how to stop him.

In fact, she almost said yes. That voice of his, deep, expressive, with laughter running underneath, and the way he looked at her, as if she mattered—it almost persuaded her.

Then he flashed a grin, as if he knew she was going to give in, and it jolted Hallie to her senses. What was she thinking to consider letting him see her half-naked, and then let him put his hands on her?

"I know that look," Jack said.

"Then you know I plan on tending to myself," Hallie retorted, pulling away from him.

Jack seemed as if he was about to argue with her, but after a few seconds he held up his hands and backed up a step. "You might try a mud pack with sage leaves. It'll help the pain enough to get you back to the ranch."

"You get stuck with cactus needles often?" she asked, eyeing him doubtfully.

"Once is enough, so don't get any ideas, Hal. Here…" He handed her his canteen. "Take a swig and I'll get you some sage leaves."

The temptation to set him straight about his inclination to order her around warred with the throbbing ache in her bottom. The ache won. Without a word, Hallie limped awkwardly away to find a place among the rocks out of Jack's view where she could pull down her pants.

She refused to think about him as she jerked the denim over her hips along with her drawers and used some water from his canteen to gingerly sponge the punctures in her tender flesh. All the while she tensed, listening for any sound of his return.

"Hallie?" he called after a few minutes.

"Don't come any closer!" she yelled, even as she heard the crunch of his boots on the rocky ground.

"Sorry, my aim's not that good. Here…" Reaching over the rock outcropping, he dangled a red bandanna filled with dirt and sage near her nose. "There wasn't much sage, but add some water and it should do for now."

Mixing the concoction with her fingers, Hallie dabbed it against her swollen skin, closing her eyes against the sting. On the other side of the rocks, she could hear Jack pacing, humming a little under his breath, and suddenly she felt hot and prickly all over.

He couldn't see her, of course. She'd made sure of that. The pacing stopped. She froze. He took a few steps, slower this time. Breathing fast, her heart thudding, Hallie yanked up her pants as quickly as she could, wriggling to get them over her hips and fastened.

When she finally emerged from behind the rocks,

Jack looked her up and down. "How are you doing?
You seem flushed. You aren't feverish, are you?"

"I'm fine, just great," Hallie muttered, wondering
how he could say that and look so innocent. In truth,
her bottom felt as if it was on fire, and she dreaded
even the idea of getting into the saddle. But she'd be
damned if she would tell Dakota that.

It would take a blind man not to see how much she
hurt. Jack grimaced as he watched her walk slowly
and awkwardly toward his horse. How did she think
she was going to ride like that?

"Hallie," he said, taking a few running steps to
her side and reaching out to grasp her arm.

She tugged free, glaring at him. "Let me go!"

"Not until we talk."

"I don't have anything to say to you."

"Maybe not, but if we're going to work together,
we've got to find a way to keep from strangling each
other. I'm only trying to help."

"Fine, you've helped. Thank you," she added with
an effort. "Now I want to go home."

"Then you're going to have to ride with me. I
don't see your horse."

Hallie cursed under her breath. She wanted to refuse. She wanted to say she would rather walk back
to the ranch than ride with him.

She did hurt, though, and it was hot and she didn't
think she could walk ten minutes, let alone hours.

Jack saw her wavering. But she was proud and
stubborn, and he guessed it would take a lot more
than a few cactus needles to overcome that. Gambling

she wouldn't shoot him, he moved quickly and scooped her up in his arms, being careful to avoid the slightest contact with her backside.

"Come on, sweetheart," he said softly when she started to struggle, "you can't do everything alone. Besides, if something happens to you, I'll have to start getting up early to do whatever it is you do at the crack of dawn. And I never get up at sunrise unless someone's shooting at me."

He grinned at her and Hallie found herself responding before she could think of a reason why she shouldn't. "I'll remember that when I have to roust you out of bed to round up the cattle."

"Sounds delightful," he murmured close to her ear as he carried her to his horse and gently put her sideways in the saddle. Mounting up behind her, he shifted her so her bottom was partly cushioned against his thigh.

"It'll have to do until we get back," Jack said when Hallie gave an awkward wriggle and winced.

She nodded, not looking at him. She could hardly tell him it wasn't the pain in her backside making her uncomfortable now, but the closeness to him. With her bottom snuggled up against his thigh and his arm firmly around her waist, holding her against his chest, she was more disturbed by the intimacy of their position than by the cactus pricks, in a way she'd never expected.

The feel of him against her gave her an unsettling sort of pleasure. She liked it. And at the same time, as the horse started a slow lope across the grass, she wanted to get away from him and the rhythmic press and slide of his body against hers. It didn't make any sense, but right now she hurt too much to try to figure it out.

One thing was for sure, she didn't need any more trouble, of any kind. But living with Jack Dakota, she had the feeling that was exactly what she was going to get.

Chapter Four

In all Hallie's memory, the ride back to the ranch house had never seemed so long. With each step Jack's horse took, a different part of her body reacted.

"Not much farther." Jack's low voice rumbled against her ear. "How are you doing?"

Hallie shifted, not sure which demanded more of her attention, the unforgiving saddle leather or the rub of his thigh against her backside. "I never knew sitting in a saddle could feel like torture."

"Ah, well, try riding for two weeks straight with only a few hours sleep every day."

"Mmm, that sounds like a story," Hallie said, glancing over her shoulder at him. "Take some poor fool's last dollar only to find out he had brothers, did you?"

Jack laughed. "Something like that. Let's just say it's hard to live on your luck for so many years without a few close calls."

Letting herself relax a little, Hallie found it easier on her bottom to lean against Jack's chest. He made it hard not to like him when he was doing his best to be accommodating. And the new feeling he gave her—of being protected, even coddled a little—Hallie discovered she didn't mind so much.

She could even get used to it. "Tell me your story, would you?"

"It's not much of a tale. It happened when I was too green and too full of myself to know when to bury my aces instead of laying 'em down. That was the first time I took Redeye Bill Barlow's winnings, and if he'd caught up with me it would've been my last."

"You knew Redeye before?"

Jack didn't realize his arms had tightened around her until Hallie wriggled a bit. He forced himself to relax his hold on her. "Longer than I want to remember."

She thought about that for a minute, and Jack wondered if she'd push him to say something more. Instead, she surprised him by murmuring, "I hope Serenity doesn't need help with supper. Standing at that stove doesn't sound too appealing right now."

"Don't worry, Miss Hal, I'll help her, if it comes to that."

"You?" Hallie started laughing. "Are you asking me to believe you found time to learn to cook between women and games?"

"Don't insult my cooking until you taste it." Jack paused a moment, then added in a voice he deliberately kept light, "My pa wasn't one to cook for or keep up with a boy he thought was old enough to fend for himself. I've got many talents that might surprise you."

"Rolling dice doesn't count."

"I'll have you know, darlin', I've had my share of respectable jobs in my time."

"This I would like to hear," Hallie said, deliberately teasing him because she wanted to know more about him. She'd pegged him as sweet-talking and shallow. But from the few things he'd said about his past, she was beginning to get a different picture of him.

He'd managed to smooth over and bury a good part of himself beneath layers of fine manners and fancy clothes. Except once in a while, the boy in him showed through, and Hallie guessed it was a boy with a rough and unstable start in life, perhaps much like his own son.

She closed her eyes a moment to concentrate on the rise and fall of his chest against her back, a pang of sympathy pricking her heart. There was more to Jack Dakota than met the eye, that was for certain.

"Let's see," he was saying, "I worked in a mercantile for a few months, I washed dishes in a restaurant and I played piano in several hotels. You should hear my rendition of 'Old Coon Zip.'"

"To do that, you and I would have to pay a visit to the Silver Snake."

Jack leaned over to look at her. "Do I want to know why?"

Hallie sighed and fingered a frayed edge of leather on the reins. "You know Lila Lee," she said, referring to the woman who owned the saloon. "I sold her my ma's piano after Pa died. She's sweet on Tenfoot, so I got a good price."

Jack didn't have to ask why. He knew Hallie had scraped together every dollar she had to try and buy Eden's Canyon back from the bank. It was obvious from the empty places in the sprawling ranch house that she'd sold most everything but the clothes on her back to pay off her father's debts.

He knew from the gossip in town that Jim Ryan had lost his money and his ranch at the card tables. It was no wonder Hallie resented Jack, a professional gambler, buying Eden's Canyon out from under her.

Ace lurched sideways over a patch of rough ground and Hallie grabbed for the pommel to keep her balance.

At once, Jack's arm swept around her waist, pulling her up out of the saddle and hard against him. His forearm brushed the underside of her breasts as Ace found his footing again.

Hallie angled herself away from Jack the moment she felt she wouldn't fall out of the saddle. The last thing she needed right now was more of his touch.

"Are you all right?" he asked. "Sorry, I didn't see that coming."

"It's not your fault. And the damage can't get any worse at this point."

"It will if you don't stay off your feet for a while."

Hallie's shoulders shifted. "Serenity can't do everything. Besides, I've had my share of scrapes and bruises. They never stopped me from doing what needed to get done."

"You're a damned stubborn female, Hallie Ryan," Jack said, and she could hear the smile in his voice.

"Stubborn I've been called many a time," Hallie agreed. "Female's the part they usually leave out."

She expected Jack to come back with some teasing retort. Instead his arm around her waist tightened a fraction.

"I don't know who 'they' are, but their eyesight's not too good. Look…" He gestured toward the barn and corral visible in the distance. "Your torture is nearly at an end."

Jack slid out of the saddle as soon as they neared the ranch house, knowing Hallie would throw her leg over the horse's neck and jump down on her own if he didn't hit ground first. She'd sooner suffer the pain than lose one more particle of her already wounded pride.

With one swift motion he was at her side, arms outstretched, leaving her no way off of Ace but into his arms. He looked up at her and saw a slight frown pucker her forehead beneath the brim of her ugly hat.

"And you call me stubborn?" she grumbled, glancing from side to side. Finding no witnesses, she hastily slid down against him.

For an instant, they stood practically nose to nose, his hands measuring the surprisingly small span of her waist. Hidden beneath her billowing shirt and loose pants, her shape was a curiosity of increasing interest to him, probably because she was so determined to keep any hint of her femininity hidden. A lopsided smile quirked his mouth. "That wasn't so bad, was it?"

"Compared to what—dancing a reel with a tumbleweed?'' Hallie asked, trying not to give away the effect being this close to him had on her.

She didn't like what he could do to her with a single touch. She liked it well enough, though, to stay still within his hold.

Despite her light quip, Jack felt her quickening breath, saw her eyes widen slightly. She might not look or act like any woman he'd known, but she couldn't help responding like one.

''Come on,'' he said, sliding his gaze down her. ''Let's get you inside and out of those britches.''

''You don't give up, do you, Dakota?'' Pulling away from him, she swung around and started toward the house, ignoring his call after her.

''I didn't intend to take them off you, darlin',''' he said to her back. ''Though I'd be glad to help, if you'd like.''

''Go away,'' Hallie yelled over her shoulder as she shoved open the front door.

She went straight to the kitchen, hoping Serenity would have some of that willow powder she used to make soothing teas. At the kitchen door, she heard Ben say something in a low voice, then Serenity's musical laughter.

She found Ben and the girl standing side by side near the table, Serenity's face aglow, Ben's hand at her elbow as she smiled into his eyes.

They turned in unison when Hallie stepped inside, their expressions changing at once. Serenity darted several uneasy steps away from Ben, keeping her eyes downcast.

Ben glanced at her, then scowled at Hallie. "I thought you were checkin' the herd."

"Obviously."

"What's wrong with you?" he asked, before Hallie could say anything more. "You're walkin' like you haven't been off a horse for a month."

Hallie opened her mouth, only to close it as Jack strode up beside her and shot Ben a look that clearly warned the boy to mind what he said. "I'm happy to see you here, Ben," Jack said. "You can help me and Miss Serenity with the cooking tonight."

"What...cooking?"

Hallie jerked her hat off and turned to stare hard at Jack. "I told you, I'm fine."

"You know, I might believe that, if you'd agree to take care of yourself." Trying to appeal to her in a way she might accept, as an equal, he laid a hand on her shoulder. "Listen, we're partners, and while I know you'd rather kiss a wild boar every morning than accept that, this is a chance for me to have some time alone with everyone."

Hallie shook her head, not willing to give him the slightest advantage over her. "I'm sure you mean well, but I told you earlier, thanks but no thanks." Stepping out of his reach, she turned to Serenity. "We'll use the spring peas and the rest of the ham from last Sunday's supper. Oh, and I moved the peas we put up early to the front of the top shelf of the pantry."

Not quite meeting Hallie's eyes, Serenity nodded and scuttled past them out the door.

"I'll give you a hand," Ben called after her, eager

to flee from his sister before she changed her mind about Dakota's idea and had *him* cooking supper.

Crossing his arms over his chest, Jack refused to back down. "Changing the subject won't make it go away. The men will have to accept me sooner or later, but I'd like it to be sooner, and on peaceful terms. Come on, Miss Hal," he coaxed, holding out his hands. "It's supper, not a cattle drive."

Hallie yearned to say no. While she knew it was stupid of her not to rest her backside and properly tend to her injuries, a small, jealous part of her didn't want to give up any of her responsibilities at Eden's Canyon to Jack Dakota.

Still, turning him down seemed more spiteful than anything. And she did hurt enough to cringe at the idea of standing up to fix supper and then sitting down to eat it.

"Okay," she said reluctantly. "This once, my kitchen's all yours."

Jack nodded and held the door open for her, watching as she slowly and painfully made her way to her room.

He supposed he should feel good about winning their latest battle. But he was left with the uncomfortable sensation that he'd done more damage to Hallie's dignity than he'd helped to heal her wounded backside.

"I can't believe I rode the biggest one. Can I do it again tomorrow?"

Hearing the excitement in Ethan's voice, Jack

turned from the griddle on the stove to see his son come into the kitchen, glued to Tenfoot's side.

"You must have talked your way onto one of the horses," he said, smiling at his son's happy grin.

It struck him that he'd never seen Ethan smile like that, and Jack found himself wishing from somewhere deep inside that it had been he, and not Tenfoot, who had put that smile on his son's face.

"You should have seen me," Ethan said. "I was ridin' that big brown stallion all around the corral, wasn't I, Mr. Tenfoot?"

"Just like you were born to it," Tenfoot answered. His eyebrows arched up as he took in the sight of Jack, a dishcloth slung over his shoulder, flipping eggs at the big black cast-iron stove. "Looks like your pa got himself a new job while we was out. Don't think I've ever seen the likes of you in this kitchen in my thirty-odd years here."

Jack didn't have time to explain as Charlie and Eb came in behind Tenfoot. Instead of taking their usual seats at the table, they, too, stopped to stare at Jack.

"Don't wait to be invited. Come on in and sit down," Jack ordered, waving them in with his spatula.

Serenity, working with Ben to get the table set, put a pile of plates into Ben's hands and let the men get settled as she went to fetch the platter of ham.

"Where's Hal?" Charlie asked, eyes narrowed as he looked around the room.

"She had a little run-in with an unfriendly cactus today," Jack answered over his shoulder, "so she's resting."

"Rest? Hal?" Eb shook his head doubtfully as he took his usual seat at the far end of the table. "That don't sound like her. She ain't dead, is she?"

Jack smiled to himself as he remembered Hallie and him together. "She's about as far from dead as anyone can be. Don't worry, she'll be back in the saddle tomorrow. But for tonight..." he bent to pull two trays of king-size biscuits from the oven "...I'm doing most of the cooking. And since the only thing I can cook worth eating is breakfast, breakfast it is tonight. How do you want your eggs?"

The men sat in silence while Jack searched their faces, one by one, for a response. At last Ben lifted his plate and handed it across the table toward Jack. "I'll take four, fried on both sides."

Jack reached for the plate. "Done."

One by one, hunger got the better of the others, and they surrendered their plates as well. As they ate, the tension in the room relaxed and Jack found it easier to ask them about the day's activities.

Even Ethan opened up enough to tell him a little about his ride on Tenfoot's horse. And he also managed to put away his share of eggs and ham.

Jack filled the biscuit basket for the third time, and Big Charlie reached for them before the basket hit the table. Glancing to the doorway and lowering his voice, the burly cowboy muttered, "Don't be giving me away to Hal, but I gotta say, these are some of the best durned biscuits I ever ate."

Eb, his mouth crammed with ham, nodded in agreement, giving Jack the first real sense of gaining ground since he'd come.

"I won't tell her because then she'll be having me in the kitchen all the time," he teased. "I'd better save a few for her, though."

"I'll take her a plate," Serenity said, shoving away from the table.

"No, I'll do that," Jack replied in a tone he knew she wouldn't question. "Ben will stay and help you clean up, won't you, Ben?"

"Me? Wash dishes?"

Serenity turned her sweetest smile on him. "You can dry, Ben. I'll do the washing."

He flushed from foot to forehead, and a round of raucous laughter filled the kitchen. When it died down, Jack turned to Ethan, who sat as close to Tenfoot as space would allow. "How was your supper?"

Ethan didn't look up from his nearly empty plate. "Strange havin' breakfast for supper."

"Well, I guess it's better than an empty belly." Jack didn't press Ethan any further. The fact that the boy had said anything to him this evening was progress. "I'm going up to give Miss Hallie her supper. When you're done, go on to your room and wash up. I'll come in a little while and check in on you for the night."

Crumbling the last bit of his biscuit between his fingers, Ethan only nodded.

Jack ignored Serenity's doubtful look as he pushed away from the table and went to fix a tray for Hallie. Charlie and Eb leaned back as they finished the last dregs of their coffee.

"Not half-bad grub fer a tenderfoot wrangler," Eb offered as he put down his cup and got to his feet.

Charlie nodded in agreement.

As they ambled out to the bunkhouse, Jack decided that was one of the best compliments he'd ever had.

Jack balanced the tray on one hand at Hallie's door and knocked lightly at first, then more firmly when she didn't answer. He waited a few more moments before deciding to risk going inside. She was probably sleeping, but he didn't want to leave without making sure she hadn't taken a turn for the worse.

Slowly, he eased the door open and stepped far enough inside to get a good look at her bed, expecting to see Hallie curled up in a nest of faded quilts and pillows. She wasn't there.

Typical of her, Jack thought, as he stalked back down the hall to the kitchen. Why should he be surprised at anything the bullheaded woman did?

Serenity met him at the door, glancing at the untouched tray. "Is she all right?"

"She's gone," Jack said shortly. He handed her the tray. "Where would she go this time of night?"

Chewing at her lower lip, Serenity hesitated, then said, "Maybe to the barn. She's been worried about that colt, the one Ethan's been helping with. But you probably shouldn't—"

"You're right. But shouldn't is what I do best. Besides, someone's got to talk some sense into her," he muttered on his way out the back door. "She doesn't have any business being out of bed."

She didn't have any business being in bed. Unable to lie there and stare at the walls a moment longer when there was so much to be done, Hallie had gotten up and made her way to the barn as soon as she heard the men come in for supper.

She'd checked on the horses, then gotten down the currycomb to take to the orphaned colt's stall to brush his curly coat.

The familiar rhythm and simply being alone with the animals soothed her. She was comfortable here, at ease with the feel and smells of the sturdy cedar-wood building. It was one of the few places she didn't feel awkward or out of place.

She loved the earthiness of it, the fresh scents of hay and corn, the soothing whinnies of the horses, the low moans and shuffling about of the milk cows. As she continued currying the colt, she absently hummed a soft little tune in time with the motion of her hands.

Somehow the simple task brought her upside-down world aright, and things didn't seem so terrible. She would get through this, just as she'd gotten through every other trouble the ranch had thrown at her over the years. She'd survived problems much worse than Jack Dakota.

The crunch of straw underfoot broke Hallie's peace. She turned to find Jack behind her, his long, lithe figure leaning lazily against the slats of a nearby stall, a piece of straw dangling from his lips.

With a sigh, Hallie went back to brushing the colt. "You've got this habit of sneaking up on me. I don't like it."

Though her words were short, Jack noticed the lack of heat in them. She sounded more as if she'd re-signed herself to having him appear where and when she least wanted him. "That's too bad," he said lightly. "If you gave it half a chance, you might find the unexpected can be exciting."

Hallie didn't know what to say to him. She didn't have any experience of men with silver tongues and teasing smiles, who did their best to make a person feel all twisted up inside. It seemed better to say nothing than to risk making herself look foolish.

Jack watched as she finished currying the colt, then gave the animal a final pat before getting up off her knees and unlatching the stall door.

She seemed different, somehow. As usual, his banter had made her ill at ease. But in the wavering lamplight, with the darkness wrapped around them, she looked gentler, softer around the edges. Though her hair was hastily braided, and she still wore a shapeless, mannish shirt and baggy pants, he'd seen a tenderness in the way she stroked the colt and the quiet way she spoke to it, a grace in the way she moved.

"How was supper?" she asked, reaching up to fasten the stall door behind her.

"No one spit it out," he answered distractedly, his eyes resting on the curve of her waist, visible through her shirt in the lantern light as she lifted her arm. "I left a plate for you. You can decide for yourself."

Hallie bent to lift a pail, unaware that her every move intrigued him.

"How are you feeling?" he asked abruptly, wanting to put a stop to the direction his thoughts were taking.

She shrugged as she reached to put the currycomb away. "I'll survive."

"Hallie…" Jack took her arm and gently turned her to face him. "I want to know."

The sincerity in his eyes disturbed her more than his usual mockery would have. "You make things so hard," she said before she could stop herself.

"Sometimes I do," he agreed, giving her a rueful half smile. Then he sobered. "I know it isn't easy for you, having Ethan and me here."

"Yes, well…" She looked at him, then away, very aware of his hand still holding her. "I'll get used to it. I'll have to if I want to keep Eden's Canyon running."

"Ah, work again. Tell me, do you ever think about anything that doesn't have to do with the ranch?"

Her head came up at that. "Like what? What color ribbons to wear in my hair or which dress matches my eyes?" Hallie gave an unladylike snort. "I figure that's the kind of woman you're used to. But I've told you, I'm not like that. I never have been, never will be. You'll have to get used to that."

"Well, darlin'," Jack drawled, his eyes roaming over her, "you may not be that kind of woman, but you are a woman. And a pretty one."

Hallie looked down at her boots to avoid seeing the teasing glint she knew must be in his eyes. She couldn't take him seriously. He probably tossed out compliments as freely as the wind blew, not meaning a one. "Staring too hard at all those cards must have ruined your eyesight, Dakota," she muttered. "I've got a mirror. I'm hardly a woman to tempt a man."

"Don't be too sure of that." Jack moved a step

closer to her. "Hasn't anyone ever tried to court you before? Kiss you behind the barn, maybe?"

"That's none of your business!"

He'd flustered her; that was clear from the confused emotion in her eyes and the patches of color on her cheeks. But Jack also noticed she didn't move away.

He narrowed the distance between them, standing so near her that the slightest motion would bring them together. "I think you're afraid of me, Hal."

"You're crazy," she said, the soft breathlessness of her voice at odds with her words.

"So you've told me. Maybe that's why you like me."

"I don't like you. You're everything I can't abide. You're—"

Jack cut her off by taking her face between his hands and kissing her.

For a moment, Hallie couldn't breathe.

She'd been kissed a few times, awkward, fumbling attempts by various hands who'd worked on the ranch, usually after they'd had a bottle too much to drink. She'd never liked it much and figured that kind of relationship with a man wasn't for her.

But Jack touching her, Jack kissing her made her feel as if she was waking up and seeing the sunrise for the first time, or standing atop the highest mountain peak, on the clearest morning God ever made. She found herself tentatively responding to him, seduced by the gentle caress of his mouth on hers.

Jack had wanted nothing more than to provoke her into answering him with something other than her usual antagonism. He'd made it a game, to see if he could stir the fire in her, to uncover some of the woman beneath those boy's clothes.

But he hadn't counted on her turning the tables on him by responding to his kiss. Suddenly his play became something warm and wild and sweet, and it jolted him hard.

He tensed and she pulled away. They stared at each other in silence, neither of them sure what to say. Hallie put her fingers to her mouth. "You shouldn't have… I never—"

"You're right. I shouldn't have." Jack abruptly turned away from her, pacing a few steps away. He rubbed a hand over his neck, took a deep breath and tried to regain his balance. "I'm sorry, I never meant…"

He stopped, not sure what he did mean or what he'd wanted.

"It's work, that's all. I said I would work with you. Nothing else. There's not—there can't be anything else." Hallie's words tumbled out and she sounded desperate to convince him.

"Work. Right. There can't be anything else." Jack repeated the words, but as he looked at her, he wondered if he'd just started lying to himself.

Chapter Five

Jack pushed his hat back and wiped a trickle of sweat from the side of his face with his forearm, grimacing as he flexed his shoulders. He couldn't remember using this many muscles in one day in all his life. He'd spent a good part of the time helping Tenfoot and Big Charlie round up a small group of mustangs and fix two holes in the barn roof and now all he wanted to do was wash the grit off and pour himself a long drink.

After nearly three weeks of living at Eden's Canyon, he couldn't call himself comfortable with the role of ranch owner, but he was beginning to learn the daily routine that was the foundation of the cattle business.

It was a start, Jack thought, as he walked around the barn toward the house, although he wondered if it would ever come as naturally—or feel as satisfying—as a game of chance. The cards might be golden and worthless by turns, but at least they didn't kick him.

Too tired to think about that for now, Jack turned

the corner of the barn just as Hallie and Ethan started inside. The gray colt followed at his son's heels.

Hallie stopped, looking as if Jack were the last person she expected to see there. She'd been like that ever since he'd kissed her in the barn—as skittish as a long-tailed cat in a roomful of rocking chairs.

Not that he could blame her. She made him feel the same way.

Jack smiled at them both. Hallie flushed and glanced away, but Ethan looked at him expectantly, obviously wanting him to notice the colt.

Jack obliged him, gesturing to the foal. "Seems you've done a fine job of taking care of him."

"Yeah, I guess," Ethan said, trying to look indifferent, though unable to hide the pride written all over him. "He follows me now."

Jack nodded and went down on one knee to inspect the colt more closely. "He's gonna be a fine stallion when he grows up. Have you given him a name yet?" If Ethan had, it would be more than he'd given Jack. It had been almost a month since Jack had found his son, and Ethan still refused to call him anything, even mister.

"I thought Storm, maybe. Because he's gray, and he's got that white on his face that looks like lightning."

Jack tried to hide his surprise. Those were more words than Ethan had said to him in weeks.

Ethan shrugged and prodded the dirt with the toe of his boot. He sneaked a glance at Jack, then quickly looked back down again. "Miss Hallie says it's good."

"She's right," Jack said quickly, "it is. I meant what I said. You've done a fine job taking care of him, Son."

An awkward silence fell between them. Jack studied the colt and Ethan stared steadily at the ground.

Hallie looked at them both, so alike, yet strangers in many ways. After a month, they still were uncomfortable in one another's company.

Jack, she had to admit, was doing his best to help the boy. She'd made it her business since Ethan and Jack had moved in to check on Ethan after he'd gone to bed, knowing he must feel lonely, and maybe even scared, to be sleeping alone in a strange room. Most times, she'd found Jack there, sitting with Ethan until the boy fell asleep. Occasionally, Ethan would cry over his ma, and Jack would just hold him.

In the light of day, though, they circled each other like two dogs trying to decide if the other was friendly or not.

Hallie hesitated to step in now, then decided to, anyway. Living with Jack Dakota might be the most frustrating, unsettling thing she'd ever had to do, but Ethan deserved a chance at a family, and that family was Jack.

"Ethan's showing a real talent with horses, and not just with Storm," she stated. She caught Jack's eye and held it, silently encouraging him to keep up the talk about horses. She'd discovered it was the one topic Ethan would actually have a conversation about. Anything else, and you were lucky to get a mutter or two out of him. "He's got good instincts. He shouldn't have much trouble learning to ride. He's done pretty well taking turns around the corral on Tenfoot's horse.''

To her satisfaction, Jack took the hint. ''Maybe it's time we got him a horse of his own,'' he said. He looked back at Ethan. ''One you could ride…just until Storm gets big enough for a saddle.'' He hid a smile at Ethan's sharply sucked-in breath and the flash of excitement in his eyes. ''What do you think, Miss Hallie?''

Hallie pretended to seriously consider the idea. ''Mmmm…well, it is a big responsibility—''

''I can do it!'' Ethan blurted out eagerly. Then he flushed and scowled a little. ''I can learn. I already know a lot. Mateo Chavez has a pony and he's only six,'' he added, as if his eight years gave him a lifetime's more experience.

''Well, if your pa agrees, we'll go look over what we've got tomorrow, see if we can find one that suits you,'' Hallie said. She glanced at Jack to get his approval and found him smiling at her.

Getting to his feet, Jack gave her a look that made Hallie feel warm all over. ''How could I say no?''

For a moment, their gazes locked, then Hallie deliberately looked at Ethan. ''It's settled then. Why don't you take Storm to his stall now and give him a good brushing? Then you can give him his oats.''

Jack waited until Ethan and the colt had disappeared inside the barn before touching Hallie's shoulder. ''Thank you.''

She shrugged off his gratitude, refusing to acknowledge the pleasure it gave her. ''It's time he learned to ride properly, that's all,'' she said. ''Besides, they are your horses now. He can have his pick.''

"They're ours. We're partners, remember?"

"None of this is *ours*. None of it belongs to me anymore."

"I have a feeling it'll always be more yours than mine," Jack said. The corner of his mouth twisted up in a half smile. "If I didn't have the deed, I'd have a hard time convincing myself it belongs to me."

There was an easy reply to that, but Hallie held her tongue. Instead she walked over to the corral and rested her hands on the fence. Ben and Tenfoot were watching Eb try to sweet-talk one of the young mares into accepting a halter.

Jack followed and leaned against the fence post next to her. "What are you thinking?"

"I was wondering if that deed—or even Ethan—is going to be enough to convince you that you belong here." She eyed him thoughtfully, then added, "It's not exciting, it's hard work."

"Are you trying to scare me? I have worked before, and not just playing cards."

"Really. Is that where you got the money to buy this place, working an honest job?"

"No, actually I won a pocketful of silver nuggets from two men in Albuquerque who claimed their business was poker, but who should have stuck to mining." Jack shifted to look out at the men at the far side of the corral. "The next day I got Mattie's letter, telling me about Ethan."

Hallie's eyes narrowed as she tried to decide just how much of his story to believe. The letter, maybe.

But making his fortune in one night of poker? Even Jack, with his silver tongue, couldn't convince her of that.

"So you just decided to give up that life and come here?" she asked. She shook her head. "You know what? I think there's more to you than that. And I don't think you'll be able to walk away from that life so easily. I don't think this will be enough."

"Wanna bet?"

Hallie opened her mouth to snap at him, but he laughed, and despite herself, she couldn't resist laughing with him. It felt a lot better than fighting with him.

Jack held out his hand to her. "Truce? For now at least?"

She hesitated, then put her hand in his. "For now. But don't get too comfortable, Dakota." She added with a hint of a smile, "You know it won't last."

"Maybe not," Jack agreed easily. He caught her fingers when she tried to slide them free of his grasp. "But I plan to enjoy myself while it does."

"I'm planning on doing that myself," Ben said, sauntering up to them, a rope slung over his shoulder.

Hallie pulled her hand out of Jack's, but not before Ben saw it there. She dared him with her eyes to say anything.

He only raised a brow. "I'm headed into town, Hal," he told her. "There's a dance tonight at the hall. I told Serenity I'd take her."

"You're going to a dance," Hallie said flatly. "With Serenity." She didn't believe him, and from the way Ben colored and shifted his feet, he knew it.

"She needs a ride. That's all."

"And what about you? After what happened—"

"It's a dance, Hal! Just a dance. And you can't keep me penned up here like one of your damned horses! I don't need your mothering. And I sure as hell don't need you telling me what to do."

Before Hallie could answer him, Ben stomped off to the barn. She made a move as if to follow him, but Jack's hand on her arm stopped her.

"Don't," he said.

"I need to. I have to—"

"You can't stop him. You'll only make it worse by trying."

"And if I don't try and something happens?"

"Then it happens. Let Ben get himself out of it for once."

It was an echo of the advice Tenfoot had been giving her for months now. But Hallie didn't want to hear it from Jack. "That's easy for you to say. You've never had to be responsible for anyone but yourself." She pulled away from his hand. "I'll remind you of this conversation when you have to stand there and watch Ethan do something stupid you know is going to hurt him."

Jack was saved from coming up with an easy answer to that one when Tenfoot came over to them after finishing with the mustang.

"We've had enough of that girl for one day," the cow puncher told her, wiping his face with his bandanna as he propped a boot on the fence rail. "She's about as friendly as a new-made steer. I don't know if we're ever gonna get a saddle on her."

"Maybe I can try her tomorrow," Hallie said. She turned toward Eb, who was heading for the bunkhouse. "I'll be right back." Calling after Eb, she left Jack and Tenfoot at the fence.

Jack watched her, curious, then looked back when he heard Tenfoot chuckle.

"Hal thinks she's bein' clever, but we all know her secrets," he said, with a wink at Jack.

Jack made himself look uninterested. "I didn't think she had any secrets."

"Oh, Hal doesn't want anyone to know she's got any soft spots."

"And she's got a soft spot for Eb?"

Tenfoot thumbed back his hat and laughed. "You might say that. Eb's got a widowed brother with two young'uns, and Hal makes sure Eb doesn't go visitin' him empty-handed. She's the one puttin' supper on their table most days."

Somehow that didn't surprise him. Seeing her with Ethan, knowing how she took responsibility for her brother and Serenity, Jack suspected she went out of her way to help anyone she thought needed it.

"Now she may not look it, but Hal's got a real tender heart," Tenfoot added.

The innuendo in his voice was so heavy, Jack figured Tenfoot could've used it for a club. "I've guessed that," he said.

"Be a shame if she got it hurt by someone who thought she was all spit and fire, don't you think?"

"It would be a shame. But Miss Hal's pretty good at taking care of herself."

"Don't be too sure of that. Hal is—"

"Ready for a bath," Hallie interrupted, coming up beside them. She smiled at Tenfoot, who looked unrepentant about being caught talking about her. "You could use a night off, too. Hasn't Miss Lila Lee been pestering you all week to visit her?"

"The woman's nothing but trouble." Tenfoot grumbled something about supposing he needed to take a trip into town, anyway, and stomped off toward the bunkhouse.

"Sounds like a good idea," Jack said.

Hallie looked at him. "Tenfoot going into town?"

"Not just him. How about us, too?"

"Us?"

Jack laughed at the astonishment on her face. "Why not? We can't work all the time."

"I…" He sounded serious, and Hallie didn't know what to say. For one crazy moment, she wanted to say yes. She wanted to forget her responsibilities and worries and spend time with a man who wanted to be with her—if for no other reason than she'd never done it before.

Then again, she could imagine the looks she'd get in Paradise if she showed up at her first dance in her boots and britches, with Jack at her side. It wouldn't be Jack they'd be laughing at.

"I can't," she finally managed to say.

The note of regret in her voice prompted Jack to press her. "Why? The ranch can do without you for a few hours."

"I just— I have things to do."

"Why, Hallie Ryan, if I didn't know you better—"

Jack cocked his head and looked her up and down "—I'd say you were afraid."

"I'm not afraid!" She tried to sound good and riled, because she wouldn't admit to him he was right. She was afraid. But she doubted handsome and charming Jack Dakota, who treated life as if it had been made just for his amusement, would ever understand that. "I don't have time for that kind of nonsense."

Jack gently lifted her chin, searching her eyes. "It's not nonsense when a pretty woman wants to enjoy herself once in a while."

"Probably not," Hallie said, stepping away from him. "But I'm not a pretty woman and I've got things to do here. You go ahead. I'm sure you can find something to entertain you for the evening."

He said nothing for a moment, then shrugged. "Suit yourself."

Hallie figured he was probably relieved at not having her tagging along. He'd find a game at the Silver Snake and waste the night at the card table.

For some reason the idea of Jack gambling again disturbed her, although it was hardly a surprise. She'd known all along what he was. And she knew he wasn't going to change.

"Just don't lose all your money," she called over her shoulder as she turned to head back to the house. "You'll need it to keep those fancy boots shined if you keep on riding the range with me."

She couldn't see his face but knew he was smiling as he called after her in that smooth, deep voice, "Don't worry, darlin'. I'll have plenty for my boots and still have something left for you when I get back.''

Hallie resisted the temptation to throw something at him.

Near the front porch of the ranch house, Jack was getting ready to leave for town. He'd started to drape the saddle blanket over Ace's back when Ethan rushed up to him.

''Let me. I'll help.''

Surprised by the offer, Jack stepped back. ''Thanks.''

''I fed and curried Storm,'' Ethan said, hefting the blanket into place. ''I'm ready to go into town with you.''

So that explained Ethan's sudden burst of generosity. Jack should have figured the boy would have his heart set on going back to the Silver Snake.

Jack picked up his saddle and swung it over Ace's back. ''You can't go to town with me tonight.''

Ethan stiffened. He frowned up at Jack. ''Course I can. I just told you, my chores are done and everyone's goin'.''

''Not Miss Hallie. I want you to stay here with her. I'll be out late and you need your sleep.''

''I ain't been to town since you made me come here!''

''That's a fact, and I'll do something about it. But not tonight.''

''It ain't fair! Everyone else gets to go.''

''Everyone else is grown-up,'' Jack pointed out. He

laid a hand on Ethan's shoulder to offer some consolation, but the boy jerked away.

"You can't tell me what to do."

Jack took in a slow, deep breath, giving himself time to think without reacting hotly to the boy's anger. Ethan's eyes were aflame with defiance. Somehow, Jack knew he had to be firm without provoking his son's outright hatred.

Although how the hell he was supposed to manage that, especially over this issue, Jack didn't know.

"I'm sorry, Ethan," he said finally, "you can't go into town tonight. I know you miss your room at the Silver Snake, but that's no place for a boy."

Standing rigidly, hands clenched at his sides, Ethan stared Jack down. "I don't like you."

"You don't have to like me. But you do have to stay here tonight."

Ethan continued to glare at Jack a moment longer, frustration, rage and a hint of tears welling in his eyes. Then, abruptly, he whirled around and ran headlong back to the barn.

Guilt pricked at Jack, but he still couldn't regret what he'd done. The farther away from the Silver Snake and his past he could keep Ethan, the better for them both.

Hallie squinted in the dim lamplight, straining to make out the last column of numbers in her ledger. She had no idea how many hours she'd been sitting hunched over her desk. But from the little oil left in her lamp, now casting barely enough light to finish her task, she knew it must be long past midnight.

Pausing to rub her knuckles against her eyes, she leaned back in her father's old leather chair, letting the late-night breeze from the window behind her caress her tired, aching head. The house was silent except for the ticking of the mantel clock.

Until from outside, far up the road somewhere, the clattering of wagon wheels broke the quiet, drawing Hallie to the window.

Who on earth would be coming to her ranch in a wagon at this hour? Whoever it was, she doubted they were up to any good.

Grabbing up her shotgun from the gun cabinet, she headed to the front porch.

As the wagon neared she saw the shadowy outlines of two men sitting on the bench, and a horse tied to the rear. Something huge bulged atop the wagon, the shape vague and looming against the starry night sky. One of the men whistled a cheery tune. Drunkards who took a wrong turn, Hallie thought, hoping the explanation was that simple.

"Who's there?" she called out, raising the shotgun to her shoulder.

The whistling stopped. "Why, hello, Hal!"

"Jack?" Hallie stepped out onto her front porch, keeping her shotgun aimed.

"One and the same!"

"Jack, are you drunk?"

The wagon rattled to a stop at the front steps of the plank porch. "Drunk? No, ma'am. Just feelin' happy."

"Happy?" Hallie let the shotgun slide to her side as she walked over to the wagon. "So happy you couldn't find your way back here in your own saddle?''

Jack jumped down from the bench, pulled Hallie into his arms and spun her around. "Now, Hal, don't spoil such a fine night."

"Let me go. You are drunk!"

"I am, am I?" He released her and strode to the back of the wagon. "Well, I'm not so soaked in whiskey that I didn't have the winning hand."

Hallie rolled her eyes. "Drinking and gambling. And to think only hours ago I was telling myself there was hope for you."

Jack grabbed the heavy canvas covering the huge object in the wagon. "Hopeless, that's me," he said, whipping the canvas back from the wagon.

"What have you…?" Hallie walked to the wagon and peered through the dark to look at Jack's prize. "A piano?"

He swung his hat from his head and took a deep, if slightly wobbly, bow. "Your piano, ma'am."

"My piano! But…how—?"

"Señor Dakota won it fair and square from Miss Lila Lee herself," the wagon driver interjected. "He said he would beat her in one hand, and Miss Lila did not believe he could do it. She took him up on the gamble, and *caramba,* if he did not lay down a royal flush!"

Hallie gaped at Jack. "You won it?"

"For you."

"I—I don't know what to say."

"Then don't say anything, just go on inside and clear a spot for it while I go round up Tenfoot to help us get it inside. Poor Juan here is barely going to pull the covers over his head before sunrise as it is.''

Jack turned and headed to the bunkhouse, leaving Hallie stunned. The man was downright crazy! How on earth had he convinced Lila to risk the piano in a poker game, of all things?

Then she thought of the mischievous sparkle in Jack's eyes and that irresistible lopsided smile of his when he turned on the charm. How indeed.

She waited in the doorway as Jack and a bleary-eyed Tenfoot returned to move the piano to its former home against the parlor wall. Luckily, she'd left the spot vacant, unable to face replacing her beloved piano with a dull, silent piece of furniture.

As soon as the piano was square against the wall, Jack set the stool in front of it. With a playful spin of the top, he took his seat there as though he'd done it a thousand times. Setting his fingers to the keys, he picked out a rowdy Irish tune, whistling along as he played.

Hallie couldn't help but laugh. ''You are full of surprises, Jack Dakota.''

''That's the song I used to play up in a little mountain town called Cimarron over in New Mexico. It was always a crowd pleaser.''

''You mean you were telling the truth when you said you actually worked for a living?''

Continuing to play, he glanced over his shoulder and flashed her a wide grin. ''Only when I was down to my last dollar. Lady Luck's a fickle lover, you know.''

''I can't say as I do,'' Hallie teased, his infectious

joy tugging at her. ''You're going to wake Ethan and Serenity, you know.''

''Good! Let's go get them and we'll have us a little party.''

Tenfoot yawned. ''I've had all the party I want for one night. I'm goin' to sit this one out.''

Jack laughed, the rich sound adding to his festive tune. ''Thanks for the help, and sorry I had to drag you out of bed.'' Tenfoot waved the thanks away and lugged himself out the door.

Jack whirled around on the piano stool and took Hallie by the hand. ''C'mon, let's go get Ethan.''

Caught up in his lighthearted mood, Hallie grabbed a lamp and let him fairly drag her down the hallway. She followed him into Ethan's room and held the lamp aloft over Ethan's bed.

But when Jack threw back the covers, the bed was empty.

Chapter Six

"Damn him, he's run off."

"Wait a minute...." Hallie caught up with Jack at the door, grabbing his forearm to keep him from striding out of the room. "You can't be sure of that."

Jack turned on her. Anger hardened his face, erasing any remnants of the charming rogue who had gambled for her piano and then hauled the prize home in a wagon. "I'm sure. He's headed back to the Silver Snake. He wanted to go with me earlier. I should have...."

Should have what? Jack raked both hands through his hair, resisting the urge to put his fist through the wall. He didn't have the first idea what he should have done. That was the problem.

He was angry with Ethan for running off, and at himself for not knowing the right things to say to the boy to keep him here. Worse, he felt guilty because he'd refused to take Ethan into town all these weeks, telling himself it was better that the boy get used to thinking of the ranch as home.

He felt Hallie's hesitant touch on his arm again.

"I've felt the same about Ben. More times than I can count. I don't know what the right thing is, but we'll find Ethan and then maybe we can get it sorted out."

Jack looked at her and Hallie saw him struggling for words. Finally, the corner of his mouth twisted up in a shadow of a smile. He briefly brushed her cheek with his knuckles. "Thanks."

"I don't need thanks for helping you find Ethan. I care about him, too."

"I know, but the thanks is for not pointing out I still have no idea what I'm doing."

Before Hallie could answer, Jack strode out the door, leaving her to follow him outside and to the barn.

"Your saddle is missing," Jack told her, after a quick look into the tack room.

"So is Eb's mare." Hallie chewed at her lower lip. "She's small, but..."

They exchanged glances, both of them knowing that Ethan didn't have the experience to ride a pony any distance, let alone the temperamental mare.

Jack swore violently and went to saddle up Ace. He didn't have to say anything for Hallie to know worry was eating him up. She worked silently saddling her own horse, and rode up beside him as he headed Ace in the direction of Paradise.

They'd been gone less than ten minutes before they came upon Eb's mare, meandering in the direction of the ranch, stopping every so often to crop at anything soft and green.

"He can't be far," Hallie said. She slid off her

horse, taking her rope with her, and quickly hitched the mare to her saddle.

The late-night air, cooled quickly by the darkness, raised gooseflesh on her arms and neck. It was the howl of a lone wolf in the distance, though, that sent a chill down her spine. The open plains were no place for the young and unprotected, especially after sunset, when predators roamed.

Jack said nothing but waited until she'd finished with the mare before urging Ace to a trot again.

A few minutes later, they both spotted Ethan. Limping slightly, he was tromping through the heavy grasses, still heading toward Paradise, his eyes fixed straight ahead.

Jack wanted to shake some sense into his son as much as he wanted to hold him and make sure he was all right. He didn't like the feeling but he couldn't stop it.

Right now, he didn't try. He was off his horse and in front of the boy before Ethan had time to turn around.

"Are you all right? Where did you think you were going?" He grabbed Ethan by the shoulders, looking him over. The scrapes he could see gave him a jolt, but he didn't think the boy was too seriously hurt.

"I'm going home," Ethan said. He brushed his overlong bangs from his eyes and raised his chin defiantly, daring Jack to argue.

"You're headed the wrong way." Ignoring Ethan's yelp of protest, Jack hoisted him in his arms and plopped him down on the front of Ace's saddle.

Swinging up behind him, he turned Ace back in the direction of the ranch.

Hallie clamped her mouth shut and said nothing, tempting though it was. This was Jack's battle, and she couldn't fight it for him.

She kept quiet all the way back to the ranch. Jack bundled Ethan off to his room, supervised his scrubbing up and watched with his arms folded over his chest as Serenity tended to Ethan's scrapes and bruises.

When Serenity slipped out of the room, Jack sat down on the edge of the bed and looked hard at his son. "I thought we had this settled. You don't live at the saloon anymore. No one there wants you. I do. Your home is here."

"I don't want to be with you! And this ain't my home!"

"You don't have a choice. Your ma wanted me to take care of you and that's what I aim to do, whether you like it or not."

"I don't like it!" Ethan yelled back. "I'm not going to stay!"

"Because you don't like it, or because you're afraid?"

Both Jack and Ethan jerked around when they heard Hallie's softly spoken words. They'd obviously forgotten she was there, but she couldn't stand by any longer and watch them hurt each other.

She looked straight at Ethan, challenging him to look back. "I know you don't think you belong here. But you don't belong at the Silver Snake, either. It's just what you're used to. This scares you because you don't know what tomorrow's going to be like.''

Ethan didn't say anything. He hung his head and plucked at a thread on the worn quilt.

''I understand,'' Hallie said quietly. ''I'm afraid, too, sometimes, because I don't really fit anywhere, either. But if you don't give the ranch a chance to feel like home, you'll never know if it can be or not.'' She drew in a deep breath, not wanting to hurt the boy, but hoping to help him face the truth. ''Your pa is right. There's nothing left of your ma at the saloon. The people that care about you now are here.''

Ethan lifted his head and stared at her until Hallie's steady gaze made him drop his eyes again.

Hallie could see how tired he was, and she thought about suggesting Jack finish his talk after Ethan got some sleep. Before she could say anything, Jack took Ethan by the shoulders and gently eased him down against the pillows.

''You look like you could fall asleep standing up.'' Drawing up the quilt over his son, Jack hesitated, then stroked back an unruly lock of blond hair from Ethan's forehead. ''Wherever home is, you aren't going to figure it out tonight. We'll talk it over tomorrow.''

Ethan mumbled something even as his eyes drooped and he curled up on his side, snuggling under the quilt.

Jack doused the lamp and sat down on the edge of the bed. Hallie quietly left the room, glancing back once to see Jack gently touch Ethan's head as he watched his son fall asleep.

Half an hour later, Jack found her in the parlor, sitting on the couch with her legs stretched out in front of her.

Hallie stifled a yawn as she watched Jack poke at the logs in the fireplace, then pace to the windows and back. He returned to the windows to stare at the open land spread out around them, at the shadows that moved in time with the wind.

He looked so lost that Hallie got up to stand next to him, lightly touching his shoulder. "Jack…"

"I always hated living in saloons and hotels," he said, not looking at her. "I figured Ethan would be the same."

"He's never had a chance to know anything else, and he's missing his ma. Give him some time."

Jack's shoulders shifted. He glanced at her with a faint, rueful smile. "You're a lot better at this than I am."

"I'm not trying to compete with you," Hallie said. "I just understand how it feels when someone you care about is suddenly gone. My pa…" She made herself gaze at the darkened landscape to avoid looking at Jack. "It's hard."

Jack didn't say anything, and after several moments, Hallie asked, "You know what I'm saying, don't you? I mean, surely there's been someone—your parents, or…?"

"I have no idea where either of my parents are. I haven't for a long time," Jack said shortly. "And to answer your question, no, there hasn't been anyone I've cared for like that. Ever."

"I'm sorry," Hallie whispered, stricken by the underlying bitterness in his voice.

"Don't be. I found out very early where I belonged, and it wasn't in one place, with a family around me."

"And now?"

Jack finally turned so they faced each other. "Now there's Ethan."

"Yes, but Ethan doesn't know where he belongs right now. It's hard for him, especially with his past. Even here on the ranch. This town's so small it's going to be hard for people to forget where he came from. And who you are."

"Who I am. You think that matters?" Jack shook his head. He walked back to the piano. Sitting down in front of it, he ran his fingers lightly over the keys. "People forget soon enough who you are if you look respectable, have money to spend, and know how to tell them what they want to hear."

"That's the gambler talking," Hallie scoffed. "You said you didn't want that kind of life for Ethan."

"It's the only way I know how to make us being father and son work. Only he's determined to fight me every step of the way."

Hallie had to laugh. "He's just pigheaded, like his father. I must say, you two are quite a pair, Dakota."

Glad of her teasing tone, Jack smiled at her. He wasn't good at baring his soul to anyone, with the exception of Ace now and then, when they were alone on the trail.

"I only got to play one song for you," he said,

with an attempt to lighten the conversation. "What would you like to hear now?"

"The sound of my head hitting the pillow," Hallie answered. She didn't try to hide her yawn this time as she sat down again, curling her arm against the chair back and resting her head on the makeshift pillow.

"A lullaby, maybe?"

"How about just 'good night'?"

Jack grinned at her. "Come on, darlin', one song to give you sweet dreams." Before she could protest, he turned back to the piano keys, flexed his fingers and started playing an Irish ballad.

Hallie hadn't known what to expect, but she sure hadn't expected anything like the tender, bittersweet, almost haunting music he created with his fingers. She hadn't guessed he'd be able to make music with such feeling in it. It was so different than the man she thought him to be that she wondered, not for the first time, just how much of himself he kept hidden.

When he finished, he let his hands rest on the keys for a moment before turning to her. "You're still awake. Is it the music or me?"

Hallie tried to tamp down the sudden awareness of him that shot through her, and keep her manner light. "Definitely you. I don't trust you enough to fall asleep. I never know what you're going to do next."

"Don't you?" Jack got to his feet and walked over to where she sat. He stood looking down at her for a long moment, then reached out and slowly stroked a hand down her tangled hair. "Guess."

Her breath lodged in her throat. She thought from

the gleam of intent in his eyes that he was going to kiss her, as he'd done in the barn, and the idea made her feel anxious and trembly inside.

Instead, he bent and brushed a kiss against her forehead. "I hope you have those sweet dreams," he whispered.

He turned to go before she could respond. Although, sitting alone in her chair, watching that broad back move as he strode away, Hallie didn't know if she could have found her voice to answer.

Hallie rolled over and pulled the quilt up over her head. What was that confounded noise? With her mind groggy with sleep, the faraway sounds registered as mere annoyances.

She tried to ignore them, bunching her pillow up around her ears. But whatever it was began to grow louder and more insistent, finally jerking her out of the comfortable, snug nest of quilts and sheets.

"What now?" she muttered. She rubbed at her eyes as she looked toward the first tentative light of dawn filtering through her window shade, trying to figure out the sound.

It was familiar, like the rumbling of thunder in the distance, and yet...

The howls and barking of her dogs, and what sounded like coyotes, and the low, anxious moans of cattle brought her at once to her feet. Tugging on her wrapper, she ran to her window and yanked up the shade. At the same time, all around her the house began to tremble.

"Oh no. It can't be."

Bolting out of her room, Hallie dashed toward the front door. She yanked it open just as Tenfoot, his fist raised, started pounding on it.

"Stampede!" he shouted.

"Eb? Charlie?"

"Already on their way to try and steer 'em away from the house."

"If we don't do something, we aren't going to have a house." She raised her voice over the approaching din, which was growing louder by the second. "You go on, I'll do what I can from here."

Tenfoot whipped around and was on his horse, heading in the direction of the stampeding herd, when Jack came up behind Hallie, Ethan at his heels.

With his shirt gaping open, and still buttoning his pants, Jack looked from her to the dust cloud that seemed to be heading straight for them. "What's happening? What is that?"

"Is it a storm?" Ethan asked, peering between Jack and Hallie.

"Stampede," Hallie said. "Come on, I need everybody's help."

She ran into the kitchen and started grabbing up pots and pans and shoved them into Jack's hands. Serenity, awakened by the clamor, came into the kitchen, and before she could ask what was happening, Hallie gave her a pan and a wooden spoon.

"They're heading for the cover of trees by the river, where they'll feel safe. Take these and make as much noise as you can. We have to distract them and scare them away from the house. They'll storm right over the front porch and damage the walls, if we don't.''

Jack glanced doubtfully at the pans he held, looking back at Hallie. ''You think we can do any good against a herd of two hundred stampeding cattle with these?''

''Pray they don't all come, and yes, we can. Just come on!'' Hallie urged, not wanting to take time to explain to him. ''Not you Ethan,'' she said, as the boy made to follow them. ''You stay inside where it's safe.''

Ethan frowned. ''I don't want to be safe.''

''Oh, Lord, I do.'' Serenity clasped the frying pan Hallie had given her to her breast. ''Won't they stomp all over us?''

''Not if we can scare them worse than whatever it was that set them running in the first place,'' Hallie told her.

She headed for the door and nearly slammed into Ben. He squinted at her, wobbling a little from the night's indulgence as he made his way to a chair.

''What's all the racket down here? You all are makin' enough noise to wake a dead man.''

''You might *be* a dead man if you don't take this and get outside this minute.'' Hallie grabbed up the largest frying pan and a lid and pushed them at her brother.

Ben stared at her as if she'd gone mad.

''Come on!''

Shouts from the cowhands outside told Hallie they had only seconds to avert disaster.

Jack grabbed Ben by the sleeve and pulled him

along as he followed Hallie out into the front yard, Serenity trailing behind.

The girl froze, though, when she caught sight of the chaos of dust and cattle careening their way.

Taking immediate stock of the approaching disaster, Jack left Serenity to Ben and joined Hallie in shouting and banging on their pans to create as much noise as possible.

"Come on," Ben yelled over the racket as he took Serenity's arm, "Hallie's right. The more noise we make, the better chance we'll have of steering them away from the house."

Reluctant still, Serenity inched forward until she stood shoulder to shoulder with Ben. Taking a deep breath, she closed her eyes and began beating on her pot with every ounce of strength in her.

Hallie ran straight into the oncoming fray, knowing they had to try to force the herd to split and go around the house.

Cursing, Jack fought the urge to drag her away from danger. Instead, he sprinted into the middle of it with her.

His attention taken up with helping Hallie pound and yell, he didn't notice Ethan running out of the house, pot and spoon in hand, limping slightly from his earlier escapade, but making more noise than any of them.

For several seconds, it seemed to Jack they didn't have a chance of stopping the cattle from heading straight for them, especially armed only with pans and spoons. He judged the distance between himself and Hallie in a quick glance, weighing the chances of being able to shield her from the onslaught of a charging herd.

He didn't like the odds.

Then, like an answer to a prayer, the cattle started to change direction.

With Eb, Tenfoot and Charlie on horseback, coming at the mad rush of cattle from three angles, and Hallie, Jack, Serenity, Ben and Ethan making a wild uproar in front of them, the confused and terrified herd split apart in a Y. Swerving past the people and the house, the animals barreled onward to the safety of the brush and trees near the river, crushing everything in their path.

The earthshaking sound of hundreds of hooves reverberated through the air. Like a rush of storm-driven wind, the cattle's passing whipped up a frenzy of noise, dust and confusion.

Hallie reached out blindly to keep her footing. Jack caught her hand and pulled her back against him, holding her tightly, his legs braced apart to keep them both standing.

Serenity screamed, dropped her pot and latched on to Ben's neck with both arms. Ethan lost his balance and fell nose first into a clump of grass.

When the last of the herd ran past, pursued by Tenfoot, Charlie and Eb, and the earth stopped shaking, everyone stood there for a moment as if frozen in place.

Then Hallie sucked in a noseful of dust and started coughing. Jack plucked the pan from her hand, flung it aside and turned her so her face was pressed against his chest, protecting her from some of the thick, billowing dirt.

Trembling inside, Hallie let herself stay in the protective circle of his arms, taking the comfort he offered. It wasn't her first stampede, but she didn't think anybody ever got comfortable standing up against a herd of terrified cattle.

A few minutes later, kneeling in the grass and still clutching his pan, Ethan blurted out, "That was fun!"

Hallie twisted to look first at the boy, then back at Jack.

All Jack could do was shrug. He cleared his throat, grinned a bit sheepishly and lifted his hands. "Don't look at me."

"Well, I doubt he got that streak of insanity from his mother."

Hallie turned to where Ethan had resumed banging on his pot as though hoping to repeat the stampede. He even danced a silly little jig, favoring his wounded ankle all the while, as he drummed his spoon on the soup kettle.

Though still white-faced and shaking, Serenity started laughing, leaning on Ben for support. Hallie and Jack exchanged a look before they both burst out laughing, too, at Ethan's antics.

"So, Ethan, if we arrange to have a stampede every so often, do you think you'd like living here any better?" Jack called out over the clatter.

"Yeah! That was great. Can we get 'em to do it again?"

"I don't think you're going to get Miss Hallie, or

anyone else, to show you how it's done,'' Jack told his son, winking at Hallie.

She smiled back and shook her head. Now that it was over, she felt almost giddy with relief.

That would pass soon enough, though, once the full morning light showed all the damage around the house.

As if he could read her thoughts, Jack put a hand on her shoulder, squeezing briefly. ''We're alive and the house is still standing. The rest will wait.'' He beckoned to his son. ''Let's go back inside. I could use a cup of coffee after that.''

''I think we all could,'' Hallie agreed. She looked around her, already eyeing the wreckage. ''It's going to be a long day.''

Chapter Seven

They walked back to the house together, Jack dropping a casual arm around Ethan's shoulders. "I guess you're too excited to go back to bed, aren't you?"

"'Course I am. Can I go and see where they stopped? Tenfoot and the others will be there."

"You can, after breakfast, but you might at least want to put your boots and pants on first," Jack said, looking pointedly at Ethan's bare feet.

"Oh yeah, I forgot." With that Ethan wriggled out of Jack's reach and ran into the house, letting the door slam shut behind him.

Jack looked after his son and wondered if he would ever figure out what interested the boy. "Maybe I should have taken up cattle rustling, rather than ranching," he said, half to himself. Catching Hallie's questioning glance, he added, "More exciting."

"Ah, well, Ethan probably won't be quite as excited when he sees the mess we have to clean up. Right now, though, I need some breakfast."

"I'll start on the biscuits," Serenity offered.

The tremulous note in the girl's voice made Hallie

turn toward her. Serenity managed a small smile, but Hallie could see she looked pasty, her hands knotted together and quivering.

Hallie put a hand on her arm. "Your first stampede is always bad. It feels like the earth's going to fall out from under your feet, doesn't it?"

"I can attest to that," Jack affirmed lightly with a smile for Serenity. "Don't feel badly. It was my first stampede, too, and I'd just as soon make it my last."

"Oh, it was terrible!"

"Why don't you go on back to bed? I'll help Miss Hallie with breakfast," Jack offered. He looked to Hallie, half expecting her to protest. Instead she nodded in approval. "Remember, that's the one meal I can cook," he said to Serenity. "You'd be doing me a favor. It would calm my nerves to keep busy right now."

Serenity seemed to believe him, but Hallie seriously doubted anything could shake Jack's nerves, honed as they were from countless hours of trying to outwit his opponents at various high-stakes games. He seemed to have taken in stride being tumbled out of bed by a stampede. Even half-dressed and dusty, he kept that easy control intact, as if he regularly risked being crushed by a rampaging herd of cattle.

She doubted she looked as collected. More like dirty, rumpled and rattled. She appreciated his effort to help Serenity, though, and that was all that mattered right now.

Serenity looked to Hallie in wide-eyed appeal. "May I?"

"Of course. I'll bring you a tray." Hallie shot Jack

a teasing smile. "I suppose you've proved you can at least fry up an egg or two."

"You forgot about my biscuits," he bantered back. "And I'm also pretty good at—"

"I can guess." Hallie cut him off before he could say something to reflect that wicked gleam in his eyes.

"I'll take Serenity her food," Ben said.

They all turned to look at him as he came up to them. Hallie and Jack exchanged a quick glance.

"Will you?" Hallie asked.

Ben ducked his head a little. "Well, I thought I'd go on back to bed, too, for a spell. I'll take it to her on my way to my room."

Before Hallie could protest, Serenity smiled at Ben and said, "Oh, thank you, that's awfully nice of you."

"Very generous," Hallie said dryly. "In the meantime, Ben, you can help with breakfast by cutting down that length of sausage in the smokehouse."

Ben looked as if he might refuse, before falling in with Jack, who was walking behind the women. After a few hushed words from Jack, Ben veered off toward the smokehouse before they reached the front porch.

Her cheeks flushed with excitement at Ben's show of attention, Serenity scurried ahead of Hallie into the house, heading toward her room.

Hallie shook her head and said something to herself Jack suspected he'd rather not hear. Besides, his attention had shifted from what she had to say to how she looked. As she stepped into the doorway, a patch of early-morning light clearly showed the gentle outline of her body beneath her thin wrapper and night-gown.

Jack couldn't stop himself from staring, and as he indulged his eyes, letting them wander over the indentation of her small waist and the gentle sway of her slim hips, it occurred to him he'd never seen her in anything but pants before, and therefore hadn't realized how pleasing her shape was.

The tantalizing image stayed with him when he followed her to the kitchen. In the soft sunlit glow, he saw that her figure had every curve and angle a woman should have, in all the right places.

Oblivious to his growing admiration, Hallie was already absorbed in her work. "Will you set this on the table, please?" she asked him as she turned from fetching a stack of plates.

She found him only inches away, looking at her with a strange, intent expression. A rush of warmth spread over her.

"Anything else you want me to do for you?" he murmured. Jack didn't move, but instead kept looking at her with that odd glint in his eyes.

Nervous all of a sudden, Hallie thrust the plates into his hands. "Nothing. Thank you."

His eyes still on her, Jack stepped over to the table and set the plates down. Then, with slow, deliberate strides, keeping her in his sights, he came back to her. "You know, Hal, you look real nice with your hair down and wearing a dress."

"What?" Hallie started. She fumbled with the wild mess of her hair, which she knew must look like a mustang's tail after a storm, whipping it into a sloppy braid. "I didn't have time to dress or comb my hair."

Jack took a step closer and gently reached out to undo her handiwork. "I'm glad."

She knew she should stop him, or at least protest, but his touch felt good and she didn't want to. Instead she ran her hands down the front of her wrapper to the tie at her waist, cinching it a little closer to her body, trying to prod to life some sense of modesty.

Modest wasn't what she felt, though.

"What are you doing?" she asked when Jack made no move to take his hands away.

"Just touching your hair. Do you mind?"

"Y-yes. I…no. I don't know."

"Well, does it feel good or bad?"

Hallie looked straight into his eyes, searching for mockery. Finding only frank approval and a tenderness that made her heart leap, she answered honestly, "Good. Mostly."

Jack smiled and stroked his fingers through her hair. "I'm glad. This feels good to me, too."

Drawing the heavy mass of her hair forward, around her face, he let it fall over the swells of her breasts. "You look pretty this morning."

"Pretty if you like dust and tangles."

"Pretty like I always thought you would."

Hallie shifted uneasily, uncomfortable with his compliments, more uncomfortable with the warm pleasure they gave her. She crossed her arms over her breasts. "You thought about me like this?"

"Guilty, darlin'. The first time I saw you here, I wondered what you'd look like in your nightdress,

with your hair all tumbled around your shoulders.''
His smile curled up one corner of his mouth. ''I ought
to be ashamed of thinking it and worse for telling you,
but to be honest, I'm not.''

She knew that lopsided smile well. In it she saw
his lady's-man charm and his gambler's glibness. But
this morning it didn't raise her dander the way it usually did when he teased her. This morning it made
her smile, too. This morning it made her feel like a
woman who knows a man admires her.

For a long moment they stood still, simply looking
at each other. Slowly, Jack eased his hand from her
hair to brush his knuckles gently down the side of her
cheek.

She shivered and he smiled again. She didn't move
away, and he moved closer.

Jack slid his hand down her neck, over her shoulder
and down her back, to cup her waist and pull her to
him.

Hallie didn't resist. She pressed against his hard
chest, her face lifted to his. He meant to kiss her and
she meant to let him.

Jack bent close to her, his warm breath brushing
her lips.

''I don't smell any cookin' yet!'' Tenfoot's voice
boomed from the front hallway.

Jack and Hallie froze.

Boots clomping against brick sounded from just
around the corner, breaking them apart.

Jack retreated to the table, making a show of laying
out plates. Hallie stepped quickly to the stove to light

the fire, and tried not to spill the entire box of matches as she did it.

When Tenfoot surged into the kitchen, she cleared her throat and said over her shoulder, "Ben's out getting the sausage."

"No coffee yet, either?" Tenfoot observed as he pulled off his hat. "What've you been doin' in here? We've already been to the river and back. And where's Serenity?"

Hallie couldn't think of a thing to say that didn't sound ridiculous or betraying.

"Serenity's resting and it's been a busy morning," Jack answered for her, acutely aware of how lame that sounded. He grabbed a basket from beside the worktable. "I was just on my way to the henhouse."

Tenfoot stared hard at Jack, then Hallie. "The henhouse, is it?" He snorted. "My guess is you've already been to the henhouse."

Jack hadn't felt this awkward since he was fifteen and his father had caught him kissing a saloon girl behind the stables. There didn't seem to be any reply worth making to Tenfoot, so he headed out the back door to make good on the promise of eggs.

Hoping vainly that Tenfoot would think it was the heat of the stove making her flush bright pink, Hallie hurried to start the coffee just as Charlie and Eb, with Ethan beside them, came into the kitchen.

"Don't say it," she warned, as they looked at the empty table and started to echo Tenfoot's questions. "It'll be ready soon."

"Not soon enough for me," Charlie grumbled. "That stampede cheated me out of two hours' sleep."

"What do you think spooked them?" Hallie asked as she began searching amid the jumble for a usable frying pan. Finding one, she started it heating and left it to find yesterday's biscuits and corn muffins to reheat them. "A wolf or a mountain lion, maybe?"

"Mighta been," Eb said, looking doubtful.

"And might not've," Charlie said.

Ethan filched a biscuit while Hallie pretended not to watch. "Maybe it was rustlers," he said around a huge bite.

"Well, now…" Tenfoot rubbed a hand over his whiskered jaw. "Almost brandin' time, you know."

"My thoughts exactly," Hallie said, setting out the forks, knives and coffee cups.

They were interrupted by Ben and Jack, returning with the sausage and eggs.

As Ben handed the rope of sausage to Hallie, he jerked a thumb over his shoulder. "It's a mess out there. The washtub's in slivers, garden's trampled, clothesline's down—"

"Don't tell me the rest," Hallie said. "I don't even want to know right now."

Jack took his basketful of eggs to the workbench and, after checking the pan Hallie had started heating, began breaking eggs into it. "It'll take days to get it all cleaned up and repaired."

"Days we don't have." Hallie slapped the sausage down on the cutting block. "We're doing roundup and branding this week."

"Stampede's a good way to move some calves to someone else's property just before brandin' time," Ben said.

''That's what we were talking about.''

''Come to think of it, someone over at the saloon said something about selling off some calves a few nights ago.'' Ben stopped and seemed to search the air for his memory. ''I can't recall who, though, or what exactly they said.''

''Why doesn't that surprise me? Although I can guess who they were talking about.''

''Now, Hal,'' Tenfoot interrupted, ''don't get started accusin' people of things till you get all the facts.''

Hallie scowled as she set a cup of coffee in front of him. ''I'm not accusing anyone. Yet.''

''Who do you have in mind?'' Jack, flipping eggs at the stove, asked her.

''Oh, no,'' Eb protested. ''Don't get her started.''

''Ever since Whit Peller bought the old Tyler place Hal's got it in her head he's after her cows,'' Charlie explained.

''Is that true?''

Hallie refused to look at Jack and instead busied herself with pouring coffee for the rest of the men. The rich aroma of the strong brew mingling with the smell of sausage frying made her stomach growl.

''That parcel's always had water problems,'' she said. ''Everyone who's owned it's been after Ryan land. Our water runs pure and strong, rain or shine.''

''That's only part of it, Hal,'' Ben said. ''You know old man Peller's just waitin' for you to whine and throw up your hands like that prissy wife of his would have from day one if she had to run her own place. Then he could more than double the size of his spread.''

''Don't remind me.''

Jack slid eggs onto plates, added sausage and passed a plate each to Ethan and Tenfoot before turning to Hallie. ''Maybe we ought to go on a ride after breakfast and see if we can turn up any clues to what happened this morning.''

Tenfoot grinned approvingly at Jack. ''By golly, Hal, you might just make a puncher out of him yet.''

Hallie tried to shake a case of the jitters as she rode out with Jack and Tenfoot to look over the herd. Charlie and Ben had set off in the opposite direction, acting on Jack's suggestion and hoping to find some clue as to what had spooked the cattle, although Hallie doubted they'd turn up much. Stampedes weren't uncommon.

This one, though, had left her feeling uneasy. She put it down to too little sleep and too many worries, and told herself not to be such a fool. She didn't want Jack thinking she turned soft every time there was trouble. She had the sinking feeling he already knew she went soft every time he looked at her with that glint in his eye that said he wanted to touch her.

Slanting a sideways glance at him, she smiled a little at Ethan, perched in the saddle in front of Jack. The boy had insisted on riding with them. He'd balked at first when Jack flat out refused to let him ride alone, giving in when Jack gave him the alternative of riding double to staying put at the ranch with Serenity and Eb.

Now, Hallie thought, Ethan seemed content to just be with them, part of what he'd decided was an adventure.

"There they are!" Ethan suddenly shouted. He pointed to the river, where the herd was bunched along the bank.

Hallie frowned as she looked them over. The cattle seemed restless, shifting and bumping against each other nervously, their lowing more frequent than usual.

"I'll circle around, take a look there," Tenfoot called to her.

"What are we looking for?" Jack asked, reining in Ace to pull alongside Hallie's Appaloosa.

"Any missing cattle, especially calves."

Jack and Ethan exchanged a look. "How can you tell if they're missing? There must be over a hundred here," Jack said, squinting into the morning sun as he looked out at the herd. "Don't tell me you know them all individually."

"Maybe I do," Hallie said, laughing when it looked as if both Jack and Ethan half believed her. "We're going to look for any cows who had calves that don't have them now. If someone was trying to cut out part of my herd, depending on who it was, they'd go for the calves first."

"I don't know how you could tell if a cow is supposed to have a calf or not," Ethan said. "They all look alike to me."

"I'm with you," Jack said. "I don't think we've quite got the hang of this cowboy stuff yet."

Ethan twisted to look over his shoulder at Jack. "You should have kept playing cards."

His son's grin and obvious teasing caught Jack off guard. He returned the grin, feeling a rush of unexpected pleasure. "But if I had, think what you would have missed. A stampede knocking you out of bed, and the chance to learn how Miss Hallie knows one brown cow from another."

Hallie took their teasing with a smile as she began searching the herd for calves. By the time she and Tenfoot finished, they'd discovered at least four missing.

"Was it rustlers?" Jack asked when Tenfoot joined them again.

Tenfoot scratched at his ear. "Maybe. Strange kind of rustlers if it was. They didn't take enough to make it worth their while."

"Maybe they got interrupted. Something spooked the herd and started the stampede before they could finish the job." Jack looked at Hallie and caught her staring out over the herd, a frown on her face. "What is it?"

"She thinks it's Peller," Tenfoot answered for her.

"Do you really think he had something to do with this?" Jack pressed her.

Hallie sighed, scowling a little at Tenfoot. "I don't know. But I don't trust him. Like Ben said, he's been pestering me to sell to him since Pa died."

"Well…" Tenfoot seemed reluctant to go any further until Hallie stared straight at him. "Okay, Hal, you don't have to look a hole in me. Maybe I could ride up there and take a look, see if any of those calves have showed up in his herd. Although it ain't exactly gonna break us, losin' four calves.''

"It's not exactly going to help us, either.''

"I have a better idea,'' Jack said before Hallie could go any further. "Let's pay Mr. Peller a visit.''

Hallie raised a brow, giving him a clear idea of what she thought of that suggestion. Jack just looked back and smiled. "What's the problem, darlin'?''

"We can't just…go and visit him,'' Hallie said, suddenly uncomfortable.

"Why not? It's a good chance for us to know him better. What've we got to lose?''

"This isn't a game, Dakota!''

"Sure it is.'' He winked at her. "The rules are just a little different.''

Tenfoot recognized the warning signs of Hallie's temper and turned in the saddle to Ethan. "How'd you like to ride with me down to the river's edge? I got a trick or two with a rope I've been wantin' to show you.''

Moving his horse close to Jack's, Tenfoot helped Ethan slide from one saddle to the other. He shifted his eyes from Hallie to Jack before he nudged his horse into a trot in the direction of the river.

Hallie didn't waste time turning back to Jack. "I don't think it's a good idea to confront Peller now. We can wait until roundup. All the ranchers in these parts are together then and we can get a good look at their stock.''

Jack got the message that Hallie would rather be hog-tied and horsewhipped than put herself in any situation that called for the barest social skills. But he was just as determined to show her there was life outside the fences of Eden's Canyon.

Why, he couldn't have said. She was as prickly as a porcupine and about as approachable most times. Still, he'd made it his own private game to see how many times he could tempt her to think and experience something beyond the ranch.

"You know, Hal," he drawled, "you might be right." The relief that started to relax her face vanished when he added, "But I think this is a good time to meet some of these ranching neighbors. Someplace where everyone is sure to be, where we can talk to people without raising suspicion."

"Trust me, Dakota, me showing up at any social event would make everyone immediately suspicious," Hallie muttered, staring hard at the pommel of her saddle.

"You let me worry about that, honey. I may not be good at telling brown cows apart, but I can talk my way in and out of most anything."

He grinned at her, inviting her with his smile to share his amusement. Hallie shook her head. "It won't work."

"It will. Where can we go?"

"Jack…"

"Where?"

Rolling her eyes, Hallie gave up. "There's going to be a social after church tomorrow."

"Well, now, I think that's a fine way for me to meet my new neighbors," Jack said. "You do go to church, don't you, Miss Hallie?"

"Probably a fair sight more than you ever have,

Dakota.'' She didn't tell him that while she regularly attended Sunday services, she always made sure she got to the little clapboard church a moment or two before the preacher started, then hid in the back pew and hightailed it out of there before everyone else started to leave.

She never thought too much about wearing her pants those times. Now, if Jack insisted on dragging her to the social, she'd have to wear a dress.

"You'll be the prettiest one there," Jack said softly, as if he could read her thoughts.

"I hope you don't expect me to believe that," Hallie retorted. "But it looks like I'll have to go with you. Otherwise, there's no telling what you might say to people."

Jack thought of several answers to that one, but held his tongue. He didn't want to make her any more nervous than she already was. Instead, he gave her his best innocent expression and said, "Nothing you haven't heard before, darlin'. Trust me."

"Not for a second." But even as she said it, Hallie knew she'd have to trust him enough to help her through an afternoon social in Paradise. Compared to that, an early-morning stampede looked good.

Chapter Eight

The moment Hallie stepped down from the wagon and nearly tripped over the hem of her skirts, she knew this was a mistake. It took her all of five minutes enduring the surprised stares and whispered comments to decide she'd rather be dragged backward through a patch of prickly pear than face most of the residents of Paradise in a dress.

Why had she let Jack talk her into this? Sitting in church had been bad enough, but now, with everyone gathered on the grassy side yard of the chapel for the early-afternoon social, they had plenty of time to look their fill at the sight of Hallie Ryan gussied up and on the arm of the disreputable gambler who'd bought her ranch.

The last time she'd worn a dress was for her pa's funeral, and then she'd only put on the dark skirt and blouse she'd dredged out of her ma's trunk as a sign of respect. It had been one of the few times she'd worn anything womanly, and she'd felt like a rattler with fur.

This time was even worse. Serenity had offered one

of her own dresses, but she was several inches shorter, so Hallie resorted to digging in her mother's trunk again. She'd picked the dress with the fewest ruffles, and after airing it out, had let Serenity nip in the waist and full sleeves and iron out the wrinkles.

It now fit her a bit better, but the pale orange disagreed with her hair and washed out her skin, and the outdated style hardly flattered her. She looked ridiculous and she knew it, even without the amused and disapproving looks she kept getting.

"If you keep pulling at that dress," Jack's voice whispered in her ear, "it's going to end up in pieces around your ankles. Then they'll really have something to talk about."

"You've already given them that," Hallie muttered back. She made herself stop twitching the sleeve of her dress, however. "This was a bad idea."

"Well, it's obvious you and Ethan think so. The two of you look about as happy as the main attractions at a public hanging." Jack gave his son's collar a gentle tug.

Ethan shifted his shoulders, but didn't look up, his eyes fixed on a grass clump he was pushing around with the toe of his worn boot. "Why are we here, anyway?"

It was a variation of the same question Ethan had asked a dozen times since last night, when Jack had told him they were going to take Hallie to the social. Clamping down his irritation, and noting his son's need for new boots, Jack said evenly, "To show we belong here."

"We don't," Ethan said.

"We will." Before either he or Hallie could protest, Jack steered them toward where Big Charlie stood talking to a thin, dark-haired woman dressed in faded brown-and-cream calico.

Hallie inwardly sighed as she walked alongside him. She was annoyed with Jack for insisting they come here, but she couldn't fault him for his attention to both her and Ethan since they'd arrived. He'd sat between the two of them during the church service, then afterward, with a hand on Ethan's shoulder, and Hallie's hand tucked in the crook of his arm, he'd stayed with them as they mingled with the families there.

Hallie expected even Jack's charm might fail him this time, though, when it came to convincing everyone he belonged on a ranch in Paradise. But he had the power to beguile people into forgetting who he was. She couldn't help but envy his ability to smoothly ease into the midst of any group and conversation. He made it seem the three of them had been a part of social life in Paradise all along.

"Why, Hallie Ryan!" Rosa Bellweather intercepted them before they reached Charlie and his companion, drawing Hallie into her circle of family and friends.

Hallie's stomach clenched when she saw Whit Peller and his wife, Rachel, among the group, but catching the warning glance Jack slanted her way, she worked at keeping her face and voice polite. It wouldn't do either of them any good to get on Whit's bad side right before roundup, especially when she had no hard proof he'd stolen her calves.

"We are so surprised to see you here," Rosa said, briefly touching Hallie's hand. "Why, you hardly ever come into town. Even before your papa died we never saw much of you."

"Except when she was chasing after young Ben," her husband added. Rosa nudged him with her elbow and Joe Bellweather shrugged, while the rest of the group exchanged glances. Ben's reputation was well known in Paradise.

"Don't listen to him," Rosa said. "We know what a time you've had keeping up with that ranch. But surely now…" She slanted a meaningful look at Jack.

Jack felt Hallie stiffen beside him and knew she wanted to walk away, get in the wagon and run the horses back to Eden's Canyon. But he wasn't going to let her give up that easily.

"Oh, Hallie's still very much the boss at Eden's Canyon," Jack answered. "She does the work of three men and puts us all to shame when we can't keep up with her. Although—" he smiled and winked at Rosa, inviting her to laugh at his cheek "—I have been trying to convince her of the benefits of a little less work and a little more play. But so far my efforts have failed me."

"Somehow I doubt that," Rosa said, her eyes crinkling at the corners.

She looked at Hallie, and something in her expression made Hallie squirm a little. Her face was already warm, she knew, from Jack's unexpected praise, but surely Rosa didn't think Jack admired her or that…that she and Jack—

Hallie immediately stomped on that thought. If fate

hadn't shoved her into his life, a man like Jack Dakota would never have looked her way. Not even Jack and his silver tongue could make anyone believe he'd choose her for anything other than a business partner.

Then she thought of them standing close together in the kitchen after the stampede, the expression in his eyes, and the way he'd touched her, tenderly and with anticipation, as if he'd wanted to do so much more. Did he? Did she want him to?

"You know, Mr. Dakota," Rosa was saying, "you have been the talk of Paradise for a month now."

"Yes, we were so surprised to find out Ethan had a father," interrupted Allison Danvers. Her gaze swept him coolly even as she touched a hand to her soft, honey-colored curls.

Jack's pleasant expression didn't change. "Well now," he drawled, "I think you'd have been even more surprised if you'd found out he didn't." Allison flushed and looked away as he gazed at her steadily. "I'm glad to have found my son after all these years and I'm grateful to his mother for the job she did raising him. Ethan's a fine boy."

Ethan started, as if Jack's remark had caught him by surprise, and Jack tightened his hold on the boy's shoulder for a moment. Then, before Allison could come up with any reply, Jack turned to Miguel Cortez, who owned one of the largest spreads next to Eden's Canyon. Jack asked a question about the upcoming roundup, drawing Hallie into the conversation when the man turned the talk about a breed of Texas longhorns he wanted to expand his herd with.

"I hope you haven't added Allison Danvers to the

list of neighbors you want to get to know,'' Hallie said, after they'd moved away from the group.

"Jealous, darlin'?" When she flared up, Jack laughed. "The answer's no. You're more than enough woman for me to handle right now."

Hallie ignored his attempt to rile her. "Good thing. You'd be disappointed. She's going to marry Whit Peller's son next month."

"Good luck to him. She doesn't strike me as the kind of woman that would make a good rancher's wife. Those pretty curls of hers wouldn't last through the first throw from a wild mustang," he added with a grin, echoing her own words to him.

"I don't think Cord Peller is marrying her because she'd be good at breaking horses and rounding up cattle."

"No? I wonder why, then? Why, Hallie Ryan," Jack teased, when she didn't answer, "I do believe I've made you blush."

Charlie's greeting saved Hallie from thinking of something to say to Jack that wouldn't scald Ethan's ears.

Face-to-face, she recognized the woman Charlie was introducing to Jack as Elizabeth James. Elizabeth worked as a seamstress, and although Hallie hadn't much use for her services, she'd always felt a sort of kinship with her. Elizabeth's husband spent more time in jail than out, and when he wasn't warming a cot in a cell, spent the rest of his time on a bar stool at the Silver Snake.

Charlie had taken a shine to her, too, and was always making some excuse or other to ride by Elizabeth's small house and offer her a hand at fixing or patching. Seeing them together, though, never failed to make Hallie smile to herself. Elizabeth, small and dark and quiet, seemed an unlikely match for rough and brawny Big Charlie.

Charlie had just finished his introductions when a little girl in a bright pink calico dress and with Elizabeth's black hair came running up and took the woman's hand. "Mama, there's apple pie. Could I have some? Please?"

"Jessica, remember your manners," Elizabeth murmured, touching her daughter's hair. She glanced to the rest of the little group.

"Oh, you're the gambler who bought Miss Hallie's ranch," Jessica said when her mother introduced her to Jack and Ethan. Her dark blue eyes brightened with a spark that looked suspiciously like mischief. "Miss Lila at the Silver Snake told Mama you were the finest-looking man ever to come in her place."

"Jessica!"

Elizabeth looked mortified, Charlie rubbed a hand over his mouth and tried to look sober, Ethan stared at Jessica as if he couldn't decide what kind of creature she was, and Hallie flushed, imagining what else the girls at the Silver Snake had said about Jack.

Jack only laughed and shook the hand Jessica thrust at him. "It's a pleasure to meet you, Miss Jessica. I've always liked a woman who could speak her mind."

Jessica grinned at him, then turned to Ethan. "Would you like some apple pie? Pastor's wife made it so it's sure to be good."

Ethan stared at her, then at Hallie, and finally appealed to Jack with an expression that left Jack in doubt as to whether his son needed rescuing or wanted encouragement to go ahead.

Jessica made the decision for him. "Come on," she said, grabbing Ethan's hand. "If we hurry and get some, no one will have time to say anything about it."

Ethan looked once more at Jack before reluctantly allowing Jessica to tug him in the direction of the apple pie.

"Your daughter is quite a girl," Jack said, watching as Jessica put a plate of pie in Ethan's hands.

"I'm afraid I've not been much good at curbing Jessica's high spirits," Elizabeth said with a rueful little smile. Her smile faded when she added softly, "She's too much like her father in that way."

At the mention of Jessica's father, Charlie abruptly started talking about the start of the roundup. They stood chatting a few minutes until Elizabeth began to wonder where her daughter had gotten to, and Charlie offered to help find her.

"I could use some of that lemonade," Jack said, when Hallie started to look uncomfortable at being left alone with him. "How about I go and get us some?"

Hallie nodded and tried not to fidget as she stood by herself. She guessed Jack had probably figured she was nervous at finding herself alone with him, so had made an excuse to leave her.

But as soon as he walked away, she wanted to call him back. It made no sense, but out of everyone here, she felt most comfortable with him. At least with Jack she didn't have to pretend.

Several people walked by and nodded to her in greeting, but no one stopped to talk. Hallie was just congratulating herself on escaping meeting anyone without Jack when Winifred Shelby strolled up to her, shadowed by her two daughters, Grace and Charity.

Hallie managed to greet them politely, although she would rather have been confronted with anyone else. Winifred Shelby was the worst busybody in Paradise.

"This is the first we've seen you alone all day, Hallie," Winifred began. "You and this Mr. Dakota seem to have formed quite an attachment."

"It's nothing of the sort," Hallie said, feeling both her face and her temper getting hotter. "We're business partners, that's all."

"Well, I wish Pa had business partners that looked like him," Grace said. "All the hands Pa has look more like your cousin Eb."

Her sister giggled and Winifred frowned at them both before fixing Hallie with a stern eye. "You might not like me saying so, but it doesn't seem proper, a young girl like you living alone with all those men. Your brother is hardly any chaperon."

Grace and Charity looked at Hallie, then exchanged a glance. They didn't say anything, but Hallie easily read their thoughts: *the way Hallie Ryan looks, they probably don't even notice she is a girl.*

It might be true, but she didn't need to be reminded of it. "Thank you for your concern, Mrs. Shelby, but I can look after myself. Proper or not, I've been doing it long enough. Now if you'll excuse me..."

Without waiting for her reply, Hallie hurried away from them as fast as her skirts would allow. She headed for the wagon with a mind to hitch up the team and get back to the ranch and out of the infernal dress as soon as possible.

Jack's hand on her arm stopped her flat. He'd seen the woman and her daughters head for Hallie, then Hallie stalk off, and had abandoned his attempt to get lemonade. "Were you leaving without the rest of us?"

"No—yes!" She thought of Ethan and Charlie, and Serenity and Ben, whom she'd seen neither hide nor hair of since they'd left church. "No, I just…" She chewed at her lower lip, looked away and back again. "Could we just please leave now?"

Jack studied her for a long moment. Then he took her hand and led her a little way from the church grounds to where a stand of cedars sheltered them from view.

"We shouldn't be here," Hallie said, glancing nervously in the direction of the church. "Someone might see us and think—"

"I don't care what they think, and no one can see us. What did they say to you, that old hen and her daughters?"

"Nothing." When Jack raised a brow and eyed her skeptically, Hallie sighed. "It doesn't matter. It's not that. I—I'm just not good at this sort of thing." She indicated her old-fashioned dress with a jerky motion and tried to laugh. "You can see I'm much better at dressing and acting like one of the boys."

Hallie when she fought him, Hallie being too se-

rious, stubborn or outspoken, Jack could handle and
even admit he liked. But Hallie with hurt in her eyes
and a smile that trembled twisted him up inside until
he didn't know what to feel for her.

"You may dress like one of the boys, but that
doesn't make you less of a woman," he said softly.
"I will say, though, that dress is the most god-awful
color I've ever seen. I'd like to see you in green like
a meadow and without that braid."

Even as he said it, Jack slipped his hands into her
thick plait and began loosing it until he could freely
comb his fingers through her hair. It rippled softly
against his skin, the sprinkling of sunlight through the
cedars dappling the maple brown with honey.

Hallie couldn't have moved if she'd wanted to. The
feel of Jack's hands in her hair and brushing lightly
against her neck seduced her into stillness. But it was
the look on his face that made her want more than
that gentle touch. He looked at her as if she were
pretty, almost beautiful, and seeing herself reflected
in his eyes, she nearly believed she could be.

Jack's hands slid to her shoulders, his thumbs making caressing circles that started Hallie's insides flut-
tering. "This isn't a good idea," he said, his voice
low and rough.

"No… You can't—I'm not…" Hallie didn't know
what she meant to say, but seeing the intent in Jack's
eyes, she knew it didn't matter.

"I can and you are. That's the problem, sweetheart.
But I'm damned if I care right now."

Before she could even form a thought, let alone

resist him, Jack gathered Hallie into his arms and kissed her.

He kept it tender and light until she made a small sound of pleasure and leaned into him. Then, ignoring every good common sense reason he had to stay away from her, Jack pulled her closer against him and deepened his kiss until her lips parted under his and he couldn't think of anything but the taste and touch of her.

A sudden loud burst of noise—of voices shouting—broke them apart. They stared at each other, both breathing fast and hard.

Jack, his hands still on Hallie, glanced behind her, half expecting to see a group of Paradise citizens ready to descend on them. Instead, through the trees, he glimpsed some sort of commotion at the edge of the church grounds.

Hallie followed his gaze. "What is it?"

"I don't know. But I have a feeling I should find out."

Hallie's hands went immediately to her loose hair and she started to rebraid it. Jack stopped her and gazed at her for a long moment before brushing a kiss against her forehead. "I'll go and see what's happening."

"Not without me," she said, with more firmness than she felt inside. Fumbling with her hair, Hallie followed after him, trying not to look as flustered as she felt.

Jack was walking fast, but when they got closer to the disturbance, he broke into a run. Hallie didn't understand why until she saw him push past several people and grab his son by the collar, separating Ethan and the youngest Peller boy.

Whit Peller trotted up and pulled his son up off the ground. He scowled as he took in his boy's torn shirt and the bruise just starting to darken under his right eye. "What are you doin' here, Brett, rolling in the dirt like a Saturday night drunk?"

"He started it!" Brett shouted, pointing a finger at Ethan.

"That's enough!" Jack snapped, when Ethan twisted to free himself, his hands still clenched. "What's going on here?"

Ethan wiped a streak of blood off his lower lip and glared at Brett. "I didn't start it. He did."

"I did not! He jumped on me! Everybody saw it."

Jack deliberately ignored the frown Whit now directed at him, and took his son by the shoulders, making Ethan face him directly. "You tell me what happened."

"He said Jessica and I didn't belong here because her pa is a drunken outlaw and my ma was a—a..." Staring down at Jack's boots, Ethan swallowed hard.

"Well, now." Whit stepped in before Jack could say anything. He put one heavy hand on his son's shoulder and gestured to Jack with the other. "I'm sure Brett didn't mean anything by his teasin'. Sometimes he goes shootin' off his mouth before he uses his brain. No harm done, I'd say."

Jack gave him a hard look. "I'm sure you would." Suddenly aware of the people grouped around them, all watching and making whispered comments to one another, Jack took Ethan by the arm and steered him away from the onlookers in the direction of their wagon.

Hallie met them halfway. "I rounded up the others. I figured we weren't staying."

"You figured right," Jack said. His mouth set in a grim line, he waited until they'd reached the wagon before turning to Ethan again. "Are you okay?"

Ethan nodded, refusing to look up.

Jack rubbed a hand over his jaw. He didn't know what to say to the boy. On the one hand, he couldn't blame Ethan for taking a swing at the Peller kid. In Ethan's position, he'd have probably done the same thing. But on the other hand, Ethan was never going to fit in here if he swung a fist every time someone brought up his past.

"I'm sorry about what Brett called your ma," Jack said at last. "He had no call to say something like that. But—"

"You think it's my fault, don't you?" Ethan blurted out.

"Ethan, I didn't say—"

"Well, I don't care if I ever belong here like you want. He shouldn't have said that about Jessica, and nobody is gonna say that about my ma!"

Evading Jack's arm, Ethan scrambled into the back of the wagon and sat huddled up in the corner, staring hard at the wooden floorboards.

"Don't," Hallie said, when Jack started to go to him. Irritation flared in his eyes, but she stood her ground. "You can't help him right now. You'll only make it worse."

"Yeah, I seem to be good at that," Jack said with

unexpected force. "While you, on the other hand, seem to always be right."

For a moment Hallie was taken aback by the flare of anger in Jack. She'd never seen him this angry; he always appeared to be in control, to handle everything with a shrug and a smile. "I didn't mean to interfere," she said softly. "It's just that I understand what he's feeling."

"And I don't."

"I didn't say that. It's just that you fit in. You probably always have."

"And who am I to argue with Hallie Ryan?" Jack said, in a tone that had undercurrents of bitterness and hinted at a past hurt. He glanced at Ethan, then back at her. "Since you seem to have everything in hand, I'll let you get everybody back to the ranch."

His attitude both confused and exasperated Hallie. "And what are you going to do?"

Jack smiled, but only with his mouth, not with his eyes. "I'm staying in town for a while. There's one thing I do understand very well, and that's a handful of aces. I'm going to find me a few."

He strode past her in the direction of the Silver Snake, leaving Hallie looking after him with the feeling she'd just stumbled onto something important about Jack Dakota.

If only she understood what it was.

Chapter Nine

Lord, it felt good to be back in denims and chaps. Hallie breathed in the crisp morning air as she swung herself into her saddle, cursing the invention of petticoats and laced-up ankle boots. Surely those were meant for the torture of women. Other women. One afternoon in prissy clothes was enough to remind her of the merits of male attire.

Taking up the reins, she muttered, "I'll take my pants and a Stetson on my head over skirts and a bonnet any day of the week."

With the ordeal of the social behind her, Hallie itched to get back to doing what she did best, and today that meant starting the roundup. Anxious to set out, she called back to the stragglers just coming out of the barn several feet behind her.

"Are you ready yet?" she asked, watching as Jack, Ethan and Ben went about the business of saddling their horses. "Slow as you're moving it'll be suppertime before we even get started."

Somewhat irritated, since Jack had stayed out half the night playing cards when he knew the next days were going to be the busiest he'd yet spent on the ranch, she kept herself from telling him he probably deserved to be suffering this morning. To be fair, though, it wasn't only him. Ben and Ethan were also moving about as fast as lizards in winter.

Ignoring her jab lest he start the day off arguing with her over his supposed sins of the night before, Jack kept his mouth shut as he saddled Ethan's horse. The sturdy chestnut mare still looked too big for the boy, in Jack's eyes, but Ethan had taken to her and to riding easily. Tenfoot had assured him the boy was ready to ride alone, so Jack had made himself stop worrying.

He boosted his son into his saddle, Ethan still rubbing sleep from his eyes. Then, with no great show of enthusiasm, Jack slung his saddle over Ace, tightened the leather strap under the stallion's belly and hoisted himself up.

Ben yawned, stretched and grudgingly followed suit. "We could have at least waited till sunrise," he grumbled as he caught up with Hallie.

"Not today. You know we have twice the work we usually have to get ready for branding because of the stampede. The corral fences are down and they have to be fixed before we can bring in the extra saddle ponies."

Hallie gave Grano a swift kick in the flanks and headed out ahead of the others toward the open range. Ethan hung back with Ben, so Jack, deciding he might as well face her wrath and get it over with, caught up to her, Ace falling in with her Appaloosa's easy canter.

Hallie glanced over. Jack's black Stetson was pulled low over his brow. Low enough to keep her from seeing how bloodshot his eyes were, she guessed. "Feeling fine this morning, are you?"

"Not particularly. Are you happy?"

"It helps to know you're regretting last night."

"I'm sure it does, Miss Early-to-bed-early-to-rise."

Hallie couldn't help but smile. "You ought to try it sometime. Maybe your life would be a little easier."

"Sleeping another hour would have made today a lot easier. What's the rush to fix those corrals, anyhow?" he asked. "We already have our horses."

Hallie looked sideways at him. Even out here amid the grassy plains and cattle, under the wide-open sky, he seemed to have his own special brand of style. From the tilt of his black Stetson to the knotted red kerchief at his neck, to the cut of his black leather vest, he had a definite flair. As handsome as it made him look, it also made him look equally out of place. As out of his element as his question showed him to be.

Amusement flickered in her eyes, and Jack figured he'd asked another of those stupid questions. "So, this time my question is so ignorant it doesn't even merit an answer?"

Hallie laughed aloud then, pulling on her reins to slow her horse to a trot to make it easier to talk. "No, I'm sorry. It's a fair question. It really wasn't that. I was just thinking how you looked so right at the social the other day and how I looked so wrong. But out here, it's the other way around."

Jack hung back a little in his saddle, pondering her comment.

They hadn't really spoken since the social yesterday, but now was a good time to try to talk without constraint. After several unproductive hours at the Silver Snake's card tables, he'd come back last evening expecting to be confronted by a furious Hallie.

But he'd seen nothing of her until this morning. And she'd been distant, saying very little and seeming almost subdued around him, as if she were trying to hold back her thoughts.

That left him feeling rather ridiculous about walking out on her at the social, while at the same time irritated that she felt the need to guard every word for fear of upsetting him.

Apart from that, he didn't have a clue how she felt about their kiss. He hadn't intended to get that close to her. But after seeing her confidence get kicked out from under her, he'd given in to the sudden desire to show her that, ugly dress or no, she was as much a woman as any of those pretty little things in their lace and curls.

Hallie didn't need those kinds of trappings to be attractive. In fact, he was beginning to develop a real appreciation for those pants of hers.

"Well, darlin'," he said at last, "in spite of that unbecoming dress, I thought you looked pretty in skirts."

Finding none of his usual teasing in his dark eyes or serious tone, Hallie felt the heat of embarrassment rise to stain her cheeks a bright pink. "Well, you can't say that today, can you?"

"Sure I can. Today you're a different kind of pretty. Out here, on your land, you're a comfortable pretty. Then, you looked nice, but you weren't relaxed, and I could see it hurt you to smile." He flashed her that familiar grin. "And you didn't have the sparkle in your eyes you do now."

Hallie didn't know whether he was teasing or honestly complimenting her.

She wished she could figure the man out. One minute he was doing his best to make her mad, and the next he made her feel things, made her want things, that—

She shook off the disturbing thoughts. Right now, she had work to do, and work didn't include mooning over Jack Dakota.

Avoiding Jack's eye, she checked on Ethan and Ben behind them. "Pick up the pace, you two! We don't have all day."

Ben clicked his tongue and gave his horse a light slap on his backside. With Ethan trailing him, he rode up beside Hallie. "Hal, in case you forgot to notice, the sun's just now peekin' over the mountains. The day's not even started yet."

"Oh, that's right," Hallie teased. "I forgot, this is about the time you're usually hitting your pillow, isn't it, little brother?"

Ethan rode up beside Jack. "It feels like the middle of the night to me."

"That makes two of us, Son. But if we're ever going to be real ranchers, I guess the first thing we have to do is learn to put our boots on before noon."

"You're starting to get the hang of it," Hallie said,

directing her smile to Ethan. "How's that saddle feel, Ethan? Looks like it suits Cinnamon there just fine. Did we let out the length all right in the stirrups?"

Ethan straightened a little, grinning proudly. "The saddle feels fine," he said. He gingerly touched his swollen lower lip. "Better than this does."

"That Peller boy took quite a swipe at you, didn't he?"

"Yeah, and I'd 'a knocked him flat, if I could've." He stared pointedly at Jack.

"Fighting's not the answer, Ethan." Jack tried to muster a stern tone, but found he didn't have the heart for it. "Aw hell, I'd have probably flattened him too, after what he said to you."

Ethan stared at him in surprise. "You would've?"

"And I would've been spitting mad at anyone who told me it wasn't right," Jack said, holding Ethan's gaze with his own. "Just like you."

Ethan's smile reappeared, this time just for Jack.

Jack returned it, satisfied he'd been able to make peace with his son, at least over this.

"You know," Ben said, riding at Ethan's side, "I broke a kid's nose in a fight when I was about your age."

"Oh no." Hallie groaned. "Please, don't encourage him."

Ben winked at Ethan. "Yep, I was sittin' right there in that saddle when I did it. That used to be my saddle, you know."

"You were fightin' on a horse?"

"Sure enough was. Billy Jay Clamp was tryin' to yank me down off old Crow and I let him have it between the eyes, hard and square right up the side of his nose. It's crooked to this day.''

''It's not something to be proud of,'' Hallie said, noticing Ethan's awestruck expression.

She didn't make the slightest impression on the youngster. Ben had just gone up about ten notches in Ethan's estimation, she figured.

Jack said nothing, his eyes and expression still hidden beneath the low tilt of his hat. She wondered what he thought of Ben's story, and how that and other tales of Ben's exploits might affect his son.

''Anyhow, that saddle's good luck, I'd say. It ought to suit you for a couple of years.''

''Then I'll be needin' a grown-up one. Like you got.''

Ben laughed. ''Well, you'll be needin' a bigger one, that's for certain.''

As the foursome rode out across the wide expanse of grass, the easy, almost brotherly comradery between the two boys struck Jack with an odd combination of happiness and concern. It pleased him that Ben had taken to Ethan and Ethan to Ben, since they'd be living together for a while yet.

But he worried that Ethan might begin to idolize Ben, as he'd seen many a younger sibling do to an older one, and begin to copy Ben's bad habits.

Jack had moved Ethan out of the Silver Snake to get him away from gamblers and drunkards. And Ben, for all his gentleness, had a reckless, rebellious side Jack understood all too well.

Just then, Ben tempted Ethan into a game of chase, and the duo shot out ahead of Jack and Hallie.

"They look like two tumbleweeds caught on the wind," Hallie said. When Jack didn't answer, she reached across Ace and flicked the brim of Jack's hat a little. "Penny for your thoughts?"

"Just thinking about the boy, that's all."

"I could have guessed that much all on my own."

At last Jack pried his eyes from the boys to look at her. "Don't tell me you've got me all figured out, too."

"You were thinking Ben has his good points, but he might be a bad influence on Ethan, weren't you?"

"I was thinking that loud, was I?"

"Afraid so."

"Ben's been good to Ethan. Ethan thinks a lot of him."

"Ben does have a good heart." She caught and held Jack's gaze. "But the way I see it, most everyone does, if you just give them a chance to show it."

Jack knew what she was driving at. "And Eden's Canyon is my chance, right?"

"You tell me. I don't know what you were trying to find before you came to Paradise."

"Well, if I wasn't trying to find a new way of life here for Ethan and me, I sure as silver wouldn't be stuck in a saddle before the rooster's even crowed, now would I?"

"Mmm...I suppose not."

"Go ahead and ask," he told her, grinning when she looked embarrassed. "You were obviously fishing."

"I was not!"

"You were. I'm not promising you any answers, though."

Hallie didn't like the notion that he could read her so easily, yet she couldn't resist the opportunity to learn something more about his past. "I was just wondering why you seem so set on changing everything about your life. Most men I've known who live at the gambling tables don't find it that easy to give up, whether they have a family or not."

"I remember what it was like being hauled from saloon to hotel by my father," Jack said. He didn't look at her, instead staring out over the landscape ahead of them. "I don't want that for Ethan."

"Your father was a gambler?"

Jack flashed her a tight smile. "How do you think I got to be so good? I played my first game when I was about Ethan's age. I won two dollars with a handful of diamonds, and I thought I owned the world."

"Your mother must have hated it," Hallie said.

"I have no idea what she thought about anything," Jack said, his voice hard. "When I was about eight, she and my pa decided to part ways. They ended up tossing the dice to see which of them would keep me." His shoulders shifted in a jerky motion. "I suppose I should be thankful to my father that he did teach me one useful skill."

"I'm not sure that's something to be grateful about." He hadn't told her much, leaving Hallie to try to imagine the things he'd left out about his growing up. Her own pa had had his faults, but she always knew both her parents loved her.

She hurt for Jack and the boy he'd been. She

couldn't help wondering, too, after being weaned on the illicit thrill of a winning hand, if he could ever truly put his past behind him.

"Tell me honestly," she asked, "after so many years of it, doesn't it eat at you now, the itch for excitement, the risk?"

"I'd be lying if I said it didn't now and again."

"You must miss it. This isn't exactly the most exciting place to be."

Jack veered Ace closer to Hallie and leaned toward her. He put on his best ladies'-man smile. "But I'm counting on you for excitement nowadays."

Taken in as always by that smile, Hallie let herself simply bask for a moment, staring at his devilishly handsome face. Then, annoyed at herself for being such easy bait, she gave his shoulder a playful shove. "If I'm your best bet for fun, Dakota, your luck's gone sour."

"I'm wagering you sell yourself short."

"Well, I can promise you the next few days will bring you lots of excitement, but it's a far cry from the kind you're looking for."

With that she gave Grano a swift kick and darted ahead of Jack.

When she was out of earshot, he smiled to himself. "We'll just see about that, Miss Hallie, now won't we?"

"Ever seen one of these?" Hallie wiped sweat from the midday heat off her brow with the back of her shirtsleeve and pulled a hammer out of her saddlebag.

"Very funny." Jack swiped it from where she dangled it annoyingly close to his nose.

"Well, I didn't know whether you could handle anything but a deck of cards."

Jack expertly twirled the hammer in a neat circle. "You might like to learn what else I know how to handle, Hal."

"Actually, I wouldn't." She wasn't about to give him the satisfaction of provoking her today.

Plunging her hand into her leather pouch, she drew out a handful of nails. Taking his free hand, she turned it palm up and placed the pile of nails there.

"If the corral doesn't hold, I'll know who to blame," she said, turning toward Ethan and waving him closer. "Ethan, come on over here and help your pa."

Ethan dropped the rope he'd been using to practice lassoing a tree stump, and scampered to Jack's side.

"Here," Jack told him, "you can put the nail in place for me to hammer it in."

Ethan's smile immediately vanished. "But that's boring! I want to ride out on the roundup."

"You can ride with us, and you can help with the branding, but we can't start any of that until this corral is fixed," Hallie explained.

Ethan kicked the grass. "That don't make no sense to me. Ben said you ain't gonna put no cows in there."

Hallie knelt down to look the boy in the eye the way she remembered her father doing when she'd gone out on her first roundup. "No, but we need it for the extra horses. We have to keep changing horses because they get tired chasing down all those cows. Roundup's hard on punchers and horses alike.''

Jack brushed his hand over his son's hair, ruffling it a little. ''Guess that means our job's real important, doesn't it?''

Ethan scrunched up his nose and pondered the idea. Finally, he shuffled over to the scattered and broken fence rails and picked one up. ''I s'pose so, but it still sounds boring.''

''Here's the nail pouch,'' Hallie said. ''I'll be over there by that stand of mesquite trees, setting up camp with Eb, if you need anything else.''

Jack took the pouch, slung it around his hips and tied it on. ''We'll have these rails back up in no time.''

Hallie walked away from him toward the chuck-wagon, silently struck by Jack's simple acceptance of the job she'd given him. Most men she'd known would have balked at being reduced to mending a fence after the usual winter fixing-up time had passed.

But Jack seemed to have a genuine willingness to learn the ranching trade from the fence posts up. Though he had plenty of pride, she admired the fact that he knew when humility would serve him best.

Glancing back at him now as he leaned over Ethan, painstakingly showing him step-by-step how to hold a hammer, place a nail and slam it in square, a warm feeling welled up in her. He truly did care for the boy. Ethan's face lit up from serious to smiling when he pounded his first nail and it took.

Jack was teaching Ethan a new skill, one of the first practical skills the boy had probably ever learned.

Hallie knew instinctively that Jack hoped to give Ethan the chance to feel a sense of pride and accomplishment. Something to keep the boy on the straight and narrow when temptation struck. Something she was sure Jack's father had never done for him.

"Looks like the boy's startin' to take to his pa after all, don't it?" Eb commented as he threw back the flap on the chuckwagon.

Hallie puttered about with pots and pans, all the while keeping one eye on the pair over at the corral. "Ethan is sticking by him today, that's for certain. Let's hope it lasts."

And hours later, Hallie paused in her chores to drizzle water from her canteen onto her kerchief and wipe her face.

About the same time, Jack stopped and laid his hammer aside. She watched as he unbuttoned his vest, then pulled his shirt from his pants and unbuttoned that, too.

Peeling them both off of his shoulders, he tossed them over a fence post. Hallie scarcely noticed Ethan copying the move, for her eyes stuck to Jack.

"Oh my," she whispered, unaware that Eb was listening. She hadn't realized how much strength Jack kept hidden under all his fancy clothes. He hefted up a heavy post, the muscles in his chest and shoulders stretching and flexing with the effort. Sweat darkened the edges of his hair and put a fine sheen on his skin.

"What's that?" Eb asked, looking over at Hallie. He followed her line of vision and whistled. "Well, I'll be. Ain't like you never seen a bare-chested man before, Hal."

"I'll finish up here," Hallie said, to stop Eb from going any further. She reached for the closest thing she could, a big black kettle, and made much of moving it to the cook fire. "You go ahead and ride on out with the others," she added, avoiding Eb's eyes.

"You sure?"

"Go on ahead. Serenity will be along soon. She only had a few things to finish back at the house."

Eb shook his head. "Shame we had to let old Jed go. He wasn't much on variety, but he made one mean pot of beef stew."

"I didn't want to send him off, either, but I couldn't pay a cook anymore. Besides, Serenity does just fine."

"Well, it just don't seem right havin' a scrawny girl out here doin' our cookin', that's all," Eb said. He hoisted a length of coiled rope over one shoulder, his saddle blanket over the other.

"She can cook everything Jed cooked and more."

"Maybe, but she ain't safe here. 'Course, with us she's fine, but all manner of ramblin' punchers who've hooked up with the other ranchers will be out here, too. And we're gonna have one new man ourselves."

"I'll keep watch over her," Hallie promised, "don't you worry."

"Who's worried?" Eb muttered to himself, ambling off toward his horse.

When he'd gone, Hallie darted another look at Jack, watching him pound one of the fence posts into the ground.

The man was blessed, that was certain. For all she

knew, he'd scarcely done a hard day's work in his life, yet the breadth of his shoulders and chest and the hard muscles in his arms were a match for any cowboy's she'd ever seen.

As though he sensed her watching him, Jack stopped and turned. Smiling, he waved, then set his hammer aside, tapping Ethan on his shoulder and saying something Hallie couldn't hear.

Ethan nodded, and Jack let his hand rest on the boy's shoulder as the two began heading toward Hallie.

"Could we talk you out of a drink of water?" Jack asked when they'd drawn near.

"Yeah, I'm mighty thirsty," Ethan seconded.

Struggling not to show the effect Jack was having on her, Hallie backed away, hastily averting her eyes.

"I guess we're not fit for company right now," he teased.

"No, I didn't mean…no, that's not it."

Jack cocked his head to one side, trying to figure her out. He'd forgotten he was half-dressed, and wondered why she seemed suddenly uncomfortable and nervous around him. Baffled, he took a step toward her.

Hallie took a step back. "I'll get you a drink."

"Are you all right? You're as skittish as a rabbit with a coyote on its tail."

Her back to him, she gulped the first drink of water herself. "I don't know what you're talking about. I'm fine."

Turning, she carried two tin cups brimming with cool water over to them. Ethan grabbed for his, but

Jack reached out slowly, meeting her hand as she gave the cup to him. Their fingers brushed, and when she dropped her eyes to look away, she found herself staring at his chest.

"Ah," Jack murmured, "now I understand."

"No, no you don't."

"Look, I didn't mean to break any roundup etiquette rules, but it's hotter than blazes out here."

"You didn't break any rules," Hallie said, her voice low and breathless.

For a long moment Jack studied her. What an intriguing puzzle of a woman Hallie Ryan was. Just when he'd decided to accept her as rough-edged, too serious, and demanding when it came to work, she showed her soft side to him.

This time, though, that side, the vulnerable part of her he'd glimpsed at the social and on a scant number of other occasions, held a sensual appeal.

He had affected her without intending to, provoking something in her he'd have called desire in any other woman. The idea of Hallie wanting him at once aroused and perplexed him.

What should he do about it? Did he want to push it further, to tempt her to want him? Did he want her? Up to this moment, he'd made a game of teasing her. He'd told himself it was nothing serious, mostly play.

Mostly. But the look in her eye now wasn't playful. It was the look of a woman who wanted more from a man. A look he'd seen a thousand times, and run far and fast from almost as often when it got too serious.

He didn't want to run from Hallie. But he wasn't sure he was ready to face what he did want from her.

"We'd better get back to work," he said at last.

"Yes, work. There's still so much to be done." Her voice sounded distant and vague even to herself.

Jack patted Ethan's head. "Come on, Son, duty calls."

"I'm hungry. I'm tired. I don't want to work no more."

"I'm not too excited about it myself. But as Miss Hallie says, some things just have to be done, that's all."

"We'll be serving up supper before you know it," Hallie said. "And after all this work, I'll bet you it'll taste better than any supper you ever had."

"You're right about that." Jack wiped the sweat from his face and neck, shoved his bandanna into his back pocket and looked straight at Hallie. "I know I've never had an appetite like the one I have now."

Chapter Ten

Hallie watched the flickering flames of the campfire, listening to the wind whispering through the grasses and the stand of mesquite trees, paying little attention to the talk around her. She was tired, but satisfied. It had been a good day, and now she allowed herself a few minutes to savor the pleasures of being out on the range, with the cool darkness wrapped around her and a million stars glittering overhead, all perfumed with the sweet, wild smell of grass and earth.

A hand reached out and took her half-empty cup of coffee from her hands. Startled out of her reverie, Hallie looked away from the fire to see Jack smiling at her.

"You nearly had a lapful of coffee," he said. "Although the way you were staring at the fire, you probably wouldn't have noticed. Maybe you should bed down early."

Eb laughed as he worked at mending the bridle in his lap. "Now that ain't likely. Hal can outride and outlast us all. Times we wonder if she beds down at all."

"I can believe that." Jack shifted, giving Ethan more of his shoulder to rest against. The boy had practically fallen asleep over his supper, and shortly afterward leaned against Jack, his eyes drifting closed. "At least we didn't run into any trouble today."

Hallie frowned a little. "Were you expecting any?"

Jack answered her with a shrug. Looking back to the fire, he rested his arm on his knee as his fingers played with a couple of stones, turning them over and juggling them like a pair of dice. "After what you said about Peller, I wasn't sure what to expect."

"Hal expects more outta Peller than the rest of us do." Sitting across the fire from them, Tenfoot drained the last dregs of coffee from his cup and got to his feet. "I'd say he's one of them fellars who thinks the sun comes up just to hear him crow. But that ain't the sort that usually causes the kind of trouble you're talkin' about."

"You don't think he took the calves," Jack said flatly.

"Can't say as I do. Hal, here, though, is likely to have the skin off my rump for sayin' it."

Big Charlie gave a guffaw. "Ain't that the truth?"

Hallie rolled her eyes and they both grinned at her.

Tenfoot then turned to Charlie and the two men sitting a few feet apart from the rest of them, and offered to refill their coffee cups before he took his own cup over to the chuckwagon.

Of the newcomers, Hallie knew one, a vaquero from the past several roundups and cattle drives. The other she'd reluctantly hired after another of her regulars broke a leg while trying to saddle train a mustang. She didn't like relying on strangers, especially this one, who seemed to be always watching one or the other of them. She hadn't had a choice, though. Good cowboys were hard to find during roundup.

As Tenfoot stomped around them toward the chuckwagon, Hallie could hear Serenity and Ben behind them, working on the supper dishes and setting the chuckwagon to rights for the night. Ben had raised everyone's eyebrows when he'd offered to help Serenity with the cleaning, but it hadn't taken much to figure out his reasons.

Serenity and Ben suddenly burst out laughing over something, and Hallie bit her lower lip.

The expression on her face told Jack everything. "Serenity can take care of herself," he said quietly, touching Hallie's hand so she turned to him. "Besides—" he winked at her "—maybe a good woman can reform young Ben. Look what you've done for me."

"If you're supposed to be reformed, Dakota, I've done a miserable job," she retorted. But there was a smile in her voice and eyes that took any sting out of her words.

Jack smiled back and then glanced at Ethan when his son mumbled something and tried to nestle closer to Jack's chest. "I think it's time to get you into your bedroll, partner," Jack said softly.

Ethan muttered as Jack let Hallie support him for a moment while he spread out Ethan's bedroll just the right distance from the fire. Finished, he tugged off his son's boots, then carried Ethan to his makeshift bed and tucked him up in the woolen blankets.

Hallie watched Jack as he hesitated before stroking a hand over Ethan's hair and leaving his son to his dreams.

Despite his past, and his never having known a loving parent, she could see in his face how much Jack cared for Ethan. In the beginning, she'd doubted that he could ever truly care for another person. Now she found it easy to believe him when he said all his efforts with the ranch and the people in Paradise were for his son.

A gentle quiet stole over the camp as the night deepened. Eb, done with his bridle, brought out his guitar, and after plucking a few notes, began strumming a soft ballad.

Tenfoot stayed by the fire, sipping at his coffee. Serenity and Ben, done with the dishes, came to sit side-by-side near Eb, listening to him play. Charlie and the other hands began shaking out their bedrolls.

Jack stood by the fire a minute or two, listening to Eb, before he strolled to the edge of the camp. He stood in the shifting shadows, leaning against the largest of the mesquite trees as he looked out at the moonlit vista.

Hallie fidgeted a moment, then, trying to look at ease, got to her feet and walked over to where Jack stood.

He glanced at her as she came up beside him. "Not tired yet?"

"Yes, but not enough to fall asleep." She shifted

in the darkness, then said, ''I just wondered what you found so fascinating out here.''

''Oh, nothing in particular,'' he answered. ''It's different than what I expected, that's all. Peaceful. It makes me wonder why I ever liked sleeping in hotels.''

''The feather beds?''

Jack chuckled. ''Oh, yeah.''

They stood next to each other in comfortable silence for a few minutes before Hallie felt a light prickle of awareness chase up her spine.

She knew without looking that Jack was watching her. She could feel his eyes on her as surely as if they were his hands instead. At the same time, she was also very aware of the people behind them. She and Jack might be hidden by the darkness and the shadows of the trees, but they weren't alone.

Hallie's quick glance over her shoulder betrayed her thoughts to Jack. He smiled to himself as he moved behind her and slid his arms around her waist, gently pulling her backward until she fitted against him. She tensed at first, but he held her close, his cheek resting against her hair, and gradually she relaxed.

''Much better,'' he murmured in her ear. ''Don't you think?''

''I—oh, yes...'' She trembled at the brush of his breath against her skin.

The slight tremor stirred up the embers of a banked fire in Jack, and he felt his body responding to her, even as a voice in his head whispered that here and now might not be the best of times. He ignored it, pushing her braid over her shoulder so he could kiss the sensitive place on her throat where her pulse quickened for him.

The hardness of his body pressed to hers coupled with the caress of his mouth on her skin made Hallie forget they stood within yards of the campsite. Jack made her restless with wanting more from him than just a taste of pleasure.

For once, she pushed aside responsibility and common sense. Here in the darkness, with the wide-open range spread around them, she could pretend, if only for a few minutes, to be the kind of woman who knew how to take what Jack freely offered, without expecting anything more.

She shifted restlessly against him and he responded instantly, turning her in his arms.

"Do you have any idea what you're doing?" he said in that low, rough voice that seemed to have a touch of its own.

Before Hallie could put together a sensible reply, Jack kissed her, a slow, hot kiss that mocked any attempt to quell it. The fever in his lips made her head spin.

She never so much as attempted to resist, and Jack found her innocent response more arousing than any practiced seduction. He deepened their kiss at the same time he pressed her closer so he could learn every curve and valley of her body against his.

Hallie started, unprepared for how intimate being this close to him would feel. A few layers of clothing made very little difference, she discovered. They didn't stop the heat burning through to her blood, or keep her from imagining exactly how his body would feel if there were nothing at all between them.

Her own brazenness astonished her, but not as much as she guessed it should have. Never, in her most secret dreams, had she ever thought she could feel like this.

All reason melted like butter in the desert sun, all the familiar voices in her head fell silent, and she found all she wanted was for this feeling to go on. She wanted more. And she wanted it with Jack.

Jack felt the need blossoming in her, as strongly as his own. It had been too long since he'd been with a woman, and he couldn't remember any of them as sweet and full of fire as Hallie. Not one woman in his memory had responded with the open innocence Hallie offered him now.

It would be so easy and so right to lay her down here, in the starry darkness, and show her just how a man loves a woman.

He almost convinced himself it could be that simple. But even as the thought formed, Jack felt a cold uneasiness intrude.

Hallie Ryan wasn't a saloon girl he could love tonight and leave tomorrow with a kiss and a smile. She wasn't like any woman he'd ever known.

Hallie deserved more than a quick loving behind the trees with a group of people near enough to discover them. That much he knew for certain. Exactly what she did deserve had never occurred to him before this very moment. Maybe she needed something he wasn't sure he even knew how to give her. Or worse, something he wasn't sure he had it in him to give.

Reluctantly, Jack kissed her mouth one last time, lingering long enough to drive himself crazy with the ache to do more. Then he let her go and stepped back.

"I—we can't," he said softly. He caressed her cheek, his chest tightening when he saw the confusion and hurt in her eyes. "Not here, not now. There'll be another time, sweetheart."

After a moment's realization, Hallie stiffened. "Don't count on it," she said, trying to twist away from him.

Jack caught her around the waist and hauled her up against him again, kissing her soundly. "I'd bet everything on it, darlin'," he said with a lightness he was far from feeling. "But right now, I don't want every cowboy on this range telling tales about how Hallie Ryan never bothered with her bedroll."

She only glared at him.

"Dammit, Hallie," he said hotly when she continued to look at him with reproach in her eyes, "it's your reputation I'm trying to protect. I'm sure as hell not worried about mine."

"Maybe you should be." Angry, frustrated and baffled by her jumbled feelings and Jack's swift change of heart all at the same time, Hallie took advantage of their closeness and pressed her mouth to his, kissing him hard.

Jerking out of his hold, she took a few steps, turned around and looked straight in his eyes. "And maybe I don't care about my reputation, if I'm with you."

Jack stood very still, caught completely off guard

by her words. Hallie looked bravely into his eyes until she began to feel more than a little self-conscious at her boldness.

Without another word, she whirled about and hurried back to the campsite.

Jack followed her, nearly an hour later. As he bedded down on the hard ground, he couldn't stop thinking about Hallie, and knew his dreams would be filled with her.

Hour after sleepless hour, he wondered if she were thinking about him.

Hour after sleepless hour, Hallie wondered if Jack was thinking about her.

But what did it matter if he were? Hallie asked herself over and over, finally laughing inwardly at her own stupid question. The fact was it mattered, more than she ever expected and more than it should.

The question wasn't what did it matter. The question was what was she going to do about Jack Dakota?

Jack, with Ethan at his side, took in the spectacle awaiting them. Father and son rode special saddle ponies trained for the roundup that Hallie had assigned them to. For as far as he could see to the right and to the left, circle riders, stationed yards apart in a line, waited for the roundup boss to signal.

Hallie had taken a spot just within Jack's view, but far out of hearing range. She could have ridden close by, but after last night, he guessed she'd decided to steer clear of him.

Over breakfast, she'd given Ethan and him a run-down on the day's activities and what their roles were to be. But she'd avoided looking Jack in the eye throughout. Maybe he'd gone too far, gotten too close to her. But she'd certainly responded, practically demanding his affections. Hell, what should he have done?

Jack shook his head and tried to shrug off his odd mood. There was neither rhyme nor reason to women. Especially a woman like Hallie Ryan.

Who would have expected she'd be willing to give herself to the likes of him? He knew without her saying it that she'd never done anything with another man nearly as intimate as the little they'd shared. Why on earth would she choose to offer herself for the first time to a man with a history of making first encounters last encounters?

Too many questions. Spending the day chasing down hundreds of cows was sounding better and better.

"You ready, Son? How's that saddle feel this morning?" Jack leaned over and tugged on Ethan's saddle to make sure it wouldn't budge.

"It's fine. But I ain't too sure I want to do this, after all."

"Why's that?"

Ethan chewed at his lower lip, then blurted out, "I didn't know there'd be so many of 'em! It didn't seem like there were that many of 'em before, even during the stampede."

"Cows, you mean?" Jack swallowed a chuckle. "They are a sight. Remember, though, there are cattle out there from neighboring ranches, too. But we know what to do, right?''

At least I hope we do. Jack had thought the whole process sounded easy enough when Hallie explained it. But then, to Hallie, who'd started rounding up cattle about the time she could walk, it *was* easy.

''We wait for that rotten Mr. Peller to give the signal, then we circle around and close in on them. Then we just follow along and keep 'em quiet and slow till they get to the corral.''

''You got it. But you could leave out the rotten part.''

''Well, he is, ain't he?''

''He's not one of my favorite people, that's for sure.''

''Like I said, rotten.'' Ethan's face fell a little and he stared hard at the ground. ''I still wish Miss Hallie was ridin' with us.''

Jack looked over to where Hallie was reining in a restless Grano. As the horse quieted under her coaxing, she lifted her eyes and turned toward him.

For an endless moment, he watched her and she watched him.

Finally, Hallie tore her gaze away, pretending she'd only turned to place her palm on her horse's mane and stroke him. The last thing she wanted today was to be distracted by Jack Dakota. But after last night, the only way she had any hope of accomplishing that was to ride far enough away from him so she didn't have to speak to him, feel the power of his presence, but close enough to keep an eye on him so he and Ethan didn't get hurt.

Darned if he didn't have a way of twisting her all up inside, until she didn't know if what she felt was right or wrong or even what she ought to be feeling. Last night she'd hardly slept. Dreams of him, of them together, of feelings she'd never had before Jack touched her, but had wanted every moment since, kept her tossing and turning until nearly dawn.

Today all she wanted to do was avoid him.

He knew it, too. She could tell from the way he kept looking at her, trying to catch her eye. But as determined as he was to get her attention, she was just as determined to keep a good-size distance between them.

Jack resisted an exasperated sigh as Hallie deliberately refused to look his way. All he wanted to do was to be near her so they could talk and straighten things out. After all, had he done anything last night that she hadn't wanted for some time now?

And he would have given her far more, if circumstances had been different. He'd only stopped for her sake. All night and into the morning he'd told himself as much, but the reasoning wasn't working. He felt ill at ease about the whole damned thing, and it was her fault.

Why did she have to make it so difficult?

Ethan reached over and tugged at Jack's sleeve. "Look! We gotta go!"

"What?" Jack didn't realize he'd drifted off again. "Oh, you're right, that's the signal."

Slowly, Jack and Ethan joined the huge circle of horsemen advancing on the herds, gradually bringing them together toward the branding corrals. The gentle lowing of cattle drifted on the breeze, adding to the strangely peaceful scene of cows, calves, horses and riders.

Jack leaned back in his saddle and relaxed. "You know, Ethan, I think I could get to like this ranching business. There's something soothing about it. How about you?"

"It's kinda slow if you ask me."

Jack laughed. "We have to ride slowly because any sudden movement might make the cattle break and run, remember?"

"Yeah, that's what Miss Hallie told us."

Hallie, again. He couldn't forget her, even if he wanted to.

He looked for her again, this time straining in his saddle to catch sight of her over the backs of hundreds of head of cattle.

While he was searching for her he noticed an errant animal cutting out of the mass and heading for a nearby grove. Another cow followed, and two more followed that one.

"Ethan, there's trouble up ahead. Do you see those cows?"

Ethan nodded to where Jack pointed. "What do we do?"

"We have to turn them back into the herd, or I think the rest of the stupid beasts will follow. Ready?"

Suddenly Ethan's face lit up. "Ready, Pa!"

Pa? As he kicked his pony into a gallop, Jack could hardly believe his ears. The boy must have slipped up in his excitement, but mistake or not, Jack would never forget the sound of the name he'd yearned to hear coming from his son's lips.

Ethan rode beside him, and Jack discovered that the sense of working together, father and son, side by side, must be the most gratifying feeling on earth.

The two rode out ahead of the wayfaring cows and began coaxing them back into the herd. A minute later Hallie appeared from behind the dense shrubbery dragging a single cow with a lasso about its neck.

More than a little surprised to find Jack and Ethan away from the others, she spoke before thinking. "What are you two doing here?"

She instantly regretted her abruptness.

"We thought we ought to get them back into the herd before they started a trend," Jack said flatly.

Hallie softened her voice. "Well, you've done a mighty fine job. This one here is the culprit. She's one of ours. She used to lead a herd and still doesn't like to follow."

"How do you know her from all the others?" Ethan asked.

"When a cow turns up as a leader, I mark her with a special cut on the ear. Then I can find her easier if I need her. We'd better get a move on before they leave us behind."

"Will you ride with us?" For Ethan, it was almost a plea.

This time Jack wasn't going to let Hallie avoid his eyes. If she was mad at him over last night, she'd have to show him face-to-face. He rode over to her, his horse butting up against hers. "We'd both like it if you would."

With his dark eyes forcing her to acknowledge they had something unsettled between them, Hallie felt cornered. She had no justifiable reason to avoid him. She'd wanted everything he'd given. Still, she felt awkward about it all.

"Sure, of course I will," she said finally, and was rewarded by Ethan's beaming smile. "But we have to hurry up."

Jack tipped his hat and waved her on. "Lead the way."

Chapter Eleven

The rest of the ride to the branding corral, Ethan managed, unknowingly, to ease the tension stretched so tightly between her and Jack that Hallie thought it wouldn't take much more than a word or a glance for something to snap.

Grateful for the boy's endless questions and idle prattle, Hallie also felt encouraged that the start of the roundup had perked his interest in ranching. And today, at least, he also seemed to be glad to be with Jack. Important beginnings if Ethan were ever going to call Eden's Canyon home and mean it.

By the time they neared the corral, the sun beat down mercilessly. Hallie took out her canteen and offered water to the others. Taking a long draw on it herself, she wiped her mouth with the sleeve of her shirt and slung the canteen back across her shoulder and chest. "Okay, you two, now's when you learn why you're wearing those kerchiefs around your necks."

Jack looked to Ethan and shrugged. "You mean they're not just to make us look dashing?"

"Fishing for compliments already?" Hallie teased back. "You'd both be dashing even without your kerchiefs. Now hurry up and pull them over your mouths and noses or you'll be eating dust for weeks."

Jack and Ethan followed Hallie's example none too soon. Someone up ahead shouted, "Throw open the wing fences!" and moments later the earth beneath them seemed to come to life, shaking from the thunder of hundreds of pounding hooves.

In moments the world around them went dark in a thick cloud of dust.

"This is what we do for excitement out here in cattle country!" Hallie shouted at the top of her lungs over the mayhem.

"Yippee!" Ethan's gleeful cry rang out in response.

When the living flood of flesh and hide had finally passed, and the gates were securely closed, wild hoots and hollers shot up all around, Ethan's voice loud and clear among them.

Hallie led Jack and Ethan to the pony corral once the flurry died down. She slid off Grano and patted him on the rump. "The fun's just starting around here. Wait'll you see what we have waiting for you next."

In one swift move, Jack swung off his horse, then helped Ethan down. "It's all pretty exciting for us, but these fellas look ready for a break," he said, patting his horse's nose, now damp with sweat.

"I'm sure you two are, too," Hallie stated. "After you take their saddles off and lead them to their corral, you can go on over and sit a spell at the branding

fire. You might learn a thing or two before supper. I'll start setting up camp for the night.''

''I'll help you,'' Jack volunteered.

But Hallie backed away. Somehow she still wasn't ready to be alone with him. If he asked anything at all about last night, she knew she'd just blush and garble her words and embarrass herself.

''No—I mean, go on, you and Ethan sit and watch the others lasso and brand the calves.'' She ruffled Ethan's hair. ''You'd like to see that, wouldn't you?''

''Yeah.'' Ethan looked up at Jack and bumped him playfully with an elbow. ''We been practicin' our ropin', haven't we?''

''You could say that,'' Jack said, laughing. He could imagine Hallie's expression if she'd seen their first dismal attempts at lassoing. ''We nearly hog-tied that old stump out by the water pump a time or two, didn't we, partner?''

''Then you'll have to take your turn roping a calf.''

''Ah, well, we might not quite be ready—''

''When? Now?'' Ethan cried, hopping from one foot to the other. ''Can we, Miss Hallie?''

Hallie smiled indulgently and touched a hand to his shoulder. ''Tomorrow. Go on now and watch how it's done so you'll be ready when your turn comes.'' With that she turned and walked off, not giving Jack another chance to protest.

She was glad for the walk alone to the campsite, glad for a little time to herself. Yet it seemed lately even when she was alone, Jack was with her. Immediately, her thoughts turned to moments they'd shared, to the way he made her feel.

And those feelings, she had to admit, though jumbled and contradictory at times, were almost all good. Too good for her. The idea of a man like Jack Dakota choosing to lavish his attentions on *her* was too good to be real.

To think otherwise would be to set herself up for rejection and a hurt she didn't know if she could bear.

And she wouldn't have to, if she kept her mind on her work and off a certain gambling man.

The next morning Hallie waited to rise until after the others, and went straight to work. Last night's supper around the campfire had been spent trading stories of the day's exploits, with much teasing and exaggerations all around.

But she'd retreated early and bedded down as far from Jack as possible. His constant presence had become unnerving to her, especially when there was so much work to be done.

By the time she reached the fire pit, branding was already in full swing. Several irons belonging to neighboring ranches glowed red-hot, and Hallie felt a surge of pride. Every time she saw the branding iron for Eden's Canyon in the fire alongside those of the larger, wealthier ranches in the valley, she knew she was right where she belonged.

Tenfoot grinned at her as she came up to where he was heating their branding iron. "Made it to another spring, didn't we, Hal?" He grabbed the handle of glowing iron and turned it over in the coals.

"By the skin of our teeth this year."

"S'pose you have Dakota to thank for that."

Hallie didn't know how to answer. On the one hand, Jack had come into her life at a fortuitous time. And yet she was hardly convinced his ownership of the ranch was a positive thing in the long run.

What if he did stay, after all? Where would that leave her?

Then again, what if he left?

Where would that leave her?

Nowhere and nowhere. Either she'd own nothing and wind up Jack's ranch hand, or she'd own it all again and end up...

Alone.

Alone as she'd never felt before. Alone the way she felt when he was no farther away than the corner of her eye.

With a shrug, Hallie tossed off the unsettling notion. Motioning to Tenfoot to hand the iron to her, she lifted the brand out of the fire possessively.

"We'd have made it without him," she muttered, almost to herself. "One way or the other."

Tenfoot cocked a brow at her, then shook his head. "Sure we would have."

"No doubt." Jack's voice sounded behind her.

Startled, Hallie swung around and found him a few paces from her, his expression telling her nothing. "I would have found a way to hold on to Eden's Canyon."

Jack took in the defiant lift of her chin, the challenge in her stance and the mix of bravado and uncertainty in her eyes.

Part of him was irritated by her possessive love for her land. Despite their moments of closeness, his ownership of her ranch remained a sore subject between them.

But one thing Hallie never did was bore him. Every woman he'd been with in the past had been predictable in her wants and desires, and in the way she calculated what would please him.

With Hallie, he never quite knew how she felt about him. She never pretended for his sake, but told him straight out how she felt. And just when he thought he was becoming expert at knowing how she played the game, she changed the rules and left him scrambling to get to know her all over again.

"Are you ready to get to work?" she asked, obviously impatient with his silence. She handed the iron back to Tenfoot.

"I've been waiting on you, darlin'. You bedded down early and slept late. I thought for sure you must be sick."

"I'm fine," she said, avoiding his eyes now. "I hope you learned a thing or two watching the others cut out the calves at the corral yesterday."

Jack fell into step beside her as they walked back to the roundup corral together. "Not as much as I would doing it."

"You're right," she agreed, climbing up on the fence and waving Eb out of the ring. "I'll take over here for a while," she told him. "You go and help Tenfoot with the branding."

Eb pulled his hat off and wiped his sweaty and dirt-covered brow. "Sounds fine to me. I'm ready to git out of this dust hole."

On the far side of the corral, Hallie spied Ethan

crawling along the fence railings, holding the top rail and stepping along the bottom in a game Hallie recalled playing as a child. The goal was to get all the way around the corral without touching your boots to the ground.

She smiled to think how similar children were, after all. The same little joys delighted them all, no matter where they came from or who their parents were.

She darted a sideways glance at Jack and found him smiling at his son's game, as well.

"I did it!" Ethan cried gleefully when he caught up to where Jack, Hallie and Eb waited by the big wooden gate.

All three of them applauded Ethan's balancing skill, and the boy surprised them by taking a deep bow.

Something Jack would have done at that age, Hallie mused. Evidently, Ethan had inherited his father's flair for drama. Would he develop his charm, as well?

"You two saddle up now while I go on in and start roping them down," she told them. "Then I'll let you both in to try your hands. You first, Jack."

"Yes, ma'am," Jack answered with a tip of his Stetson. His hand on Ethan's shoulder, he headed off for the pony corral with his son.

"She's nice most of the time, but she sure can be bossy, can't she?" Ethan said when he figured they were out of Hallie's hearing.

"Sometimes. But then, she has to be a little bossy to get things done. She's a woman, and that makes it harder for her to win the respect and attention of the men."

''Well, once you learn it all, you'll be the one boss-ing *her* around, won't you?''

Miss Hallie's greatest fear, Jack thought. ''Some-how, I can't imagine anybody bossing Miss Hallie. And for now, you and I have a lot left to learn.''

Jack helped Ethan saddle up, and they rode back to the corral. Through thick dust and a confusion of cattle, horses and humans, he spied Hallie.

He could only have described the look on her face as fiercely beautiful. She rode bending low over her saddle, her slim body graceful, yet strong. The way she dodged among the cattle, keeping her sights set on her prey, seemed as natural to her as walking.

Her every movement captivated Jack. Raising her arm like the single flame of a fire, she swung her lariat, circling it high, then tossing it out to lasso her prize. Gestures so typically male looked smooth and rhythmic when she executed them, full of power, speed and accuracy.

When she finished, she rode over to Jack and Ethan. With her face damp, her smile beaming, her eyes alive with the thrill of what she obviously thought of as more sport than work, Jack decided that here in her element she was also in her glory.

''What's wrong? Do I have dirt on my nose?'' Hal-lie caught him staring, pulled her kerchief from her neck and opened her canteen.

She felt suddenly self-conscious. Jack had been practically gaping at her for what seemed an eternity. She knew her face was covered with sweat, but until this moment, in all her years of roundups, she'd never cared. Drenching her bandanna, she wiped her face, but gave up trying to actually make it clean. The dirt would only become a muddy plaster.

"Oh, to heck with it," she muttered to herself, retying the kerchief around her neck. "All right, Dakota, it's your turn. I'm going to make this easy on you. I'll ride ahead and cut the mother away from the calf. When I head her off, you ride in and lasso the baby."

Jack pried his eyes from her and tried to concentrate. "I'll give it my best shot."

Ben strode up and opened the big gates for them. "Good luck, partner," he offered with a slap to Jack's horse's backside.

Jack rode in after Hallie, working to keep up as she dodged in and out among the cows. She rode with lightning-quick switches of direction, forcing a cow apart from her calf, clearing the way for Jack to do his part.

Jack readied his rope, but just as he was about to grab the lariat, his pony abruptly stopped in its tracks. Jack flew forward in his saddle, much to the amusement of the onlookers now gathered around the corral.

"Come on, you can do it." He heard Ethan's voice above the laughter. "Remember our stump!"

Gritting his teeth, Jack jabbed his spurs into his pony's flanks and dove after the squalling calf. The pony bounded forward while Jack readied his lariat. Quickly, he managed to twirl it in a large circle, and when the circle became an oval, let his hand shoot forward to release the noose.

He didn't realize he'd closed his eyes until groans from the onlookers told him he'd missed. Thinking it was one hell of a lot easier to learn poker than roping, he ground his teeth harder and pulled his rope in to try again.

Another useless toss. At least this time, though, he kept his eyes open.

"Get up more speed before you throw," Hallie called out. "And let your right shoulder fall back."

Heeding her advice, Jack also decided to ride in a little closer. As he did, he whirled the rope high and fast, until it made a high-pitched whirring sound, then he flung it out hard. Dust clogged the air to the point he could scarcely see in front of him.

But he felt the rope hit something—and this time it wasn't simply the unforgiving ground. Immediately he jerked the lariat. The downed calf cried out, and on cue, his well-trained pony stopped short.

Cheers went up all around. Jack let out the breath he'd been holding. When the dust settled, he slid off his horse. He saw he'd roped the calf by a leg. He'd been aiming for the neck, but decided he'd keep that fact a secret.

Hallie came over to him and put her hand on his shoulder, squeezing lightly. "Nice job, puncher."

Jack shrugged. "You know what they say about the third time…"

"I can't ever recall seeing a greenhorn down a calf on his third try. You did well." She grinned up at him. "But then, it might just have been beginner's luck."

"Oh, I don't know. I think maybe I'm a natural."

Hallie gave a little guffaw. "Maybe with cards in your hand."

Outside the corral, Ethan rode over to them. "I knew you'd get him. I just knew it! Now it's my turn, right?" he asked, appealing to Hallie.

"Tell you what, why don't you tie your pony and come climb up with me for the first couple of rounds?" she offered.

Ethan frowned and turned his pleas to Jack. "You did it by yourself."

"I'm a little taller. And remember, Miss Hallie's the boss. She doesn't want you hitting the dirt head-first your first time out."

"I can stay in the saddle," Ethan grumbled, but he followed Hallie, and working together, the three of them cut out several more calves.

Each time they took a calf down, Hallie taught them a little more. She decided Jack's deftness with his hands served him well for more than poker and piano. And Ethan's squeals of delight, whoops and hollers made it clear he reveled in being a part of it all.

Before they called it a day, Hallie led them to the branding pit and showed them step by painstaking step how the deed was done. Jack and Ethan knelt beside her as she applied salve to a newly branded calf.

"You have to put this on the wound to keep flies from laying eggs in it," she explained.

Jack followed her lead, plunging his fingers into the vile-smelling salve and gently dabbing it on the seared hide. Ethan copied his father motion for motion.

The sight warmed Hallie's heart. She was enjoying being with them, working with them.

Even if it meant that one day they'd no longer need her.

Suddenly, a dragging tiredness hit her hard and fast. Hallie got to her feet, excusing herself to take a break from the sweltering heat of the fire.

Jack and Ethan, absorbed in their work, scarcely noticed her walk away.

At the chuckwagon, she took a long cool drink of water, relieved to find that Serenity had supper well under way, although the campsite was deserted. Succulent smells of chili beef and potatoes wafted up from the kettle simmering over the cook fire, and somehow the scent of a good meal to come helped ease a little of Hallie's weariness.

She squinted at the sun, and finally spotted Serenity draped over the corral railing, watching Ben ride. Almost envying the pair for the simplicity of their attraction, she bent over the hodgepodge of supplies and began rummaging through crates at the back of the wagon for a new pot of salve.

Serenity had no reason to stop herself caring for Ben, except his recklessness, of course. But Hallie continued to hope her brother would eventually settle down, and Serenity's unflagging devotion might be just the motivation to inspire him to do so.

Hallie delved deeper into the back of the wagon, certain she'd packed more salve in there somewhere. Preoccupied with her thoughts, she didn't sense she was no longer alone until someone grabbed her from behind.

"What in the—"

Hallie tried to jerk around, but a man's arm gripped her waist and a hand at her mouth shoved her head back.

A days-old beard scraped her cheek, the sour smell of whiskey and sweat nearly choking her.

Trying not to panic, Hallie struggled, kicking and clawing at her captor when he started dragging her away from the wagon toward a stand of scrub pine.

She tried for her holster but his arm blocked her reach, his hand finding her gun first. He yanked it from the holster and tossed it aside.

"Quit yer squirmin' or I'll keep you quiet with the butt of my gun," he growled against her ear.

Hallie recognized the voice immediately.

It was the new cowboy she'd hired for the roundup. Damn it, but she should never have taken on a stranger.

"I'm gonna teach you a lesson, rancher lady. You're gonna learn a woman's got her place and it ain't the range."

Managing to kick him in the shin, Hallie jerked to the side, dislodging his hand from her mouth. She seized the advantage and bit down hard on his thumb.

"Damn you, bitch!"

Hallie wrenched away from him and grabbed a thorny branch from a brittle bush nearby. She swung fast and swiped the side of his head.

The puncher fell back a couple of paces, cursing a blue streak as he stumbled, groping for balance.

He fumbled for his gun just as Hallie spotted hers in the grass a few feet away.

She dove for her Colt, and as she landed facefirst in the grass, saw a pair of familiar black boots.

"Jack!"

She looked up in time to see him draw.

A shot rang out into the dead heat of the day.

Chapter Twelve

Hallie instinctively grabbed her gun out of the grass. At the same time, her stomach clenched in fear. Who had fired the shot? Jack? Or had the cowboy reached his own gun?

She raised her head to look, tense because she expected more shots. None came. "Jack?"

"Over here. Damn." A few yards from her, Jack pushed himself to his feet, cursing and holding his upper arm.

"What happened—" Hallie broke off when she saw the blood staining his shirt and fingers. Scrambling to her feet, she ran to him. "Jack..." Her hand trembled as she reached out to him, needing to know how badly he'd been hurt.

"It's not bad," Jack said. He briefly touched her cheek with his free hand, grimacing as pain stabbed his arm, before looking around them. "Who the hell took a shot at us?"

"I thought..." Hallie stopped, swallowed hard. "I thought it was that cowboy." She glanced at the bushes, at the land round them, but didn't see any sign of the puncher who'd attacked her.

Jack didn't look convinced. "He took off before my gun cleared the holster. At least whoever it was didn't have a very good aim," he said, spreading his fingers to look at his arm. He gave Hallie a twisted smile. "Hurts like the devil, though."

She didn't say anything, and for the first time Jack realized how much the shooting, coming so soon after the attack, had shaken her. He'd never seen Hallie afraid, but her white, pinched face, the stiffness of her body and the way she stared at him told him she was scared now.

Ignoring the pain that came with the motion, Jack let go of his shoulder and wiped his hand down his pant leg before pulling her against his chest. Hallie, warm and whole in his arms, felt good. A knot of tension in his chest loosened, releasing a surge of relief.

He'd acted on instinct, finding her in trouble, and with the unexpected shooting happening so close after that, he hadn't had time to recognize his own fear. Fear for her, and what could have happened.

"It's okay," Jack said softly, stroking her hair, as much to soothe himself as her. "It's over. And the way you fought off that cowboy, I don't think he'll want a rematch anytime soon," he added in a lighter tone, hoping to draw a smile from her.

Hallie's fingers tightened on his shirt, but she didn't reply.

Her silence worried him. Drawing back from her enough to look into her face, Jack searched her eyes for a clue to what she was thinking. The blankness of her gaze told him nothing, so he gave up.

"Let's get you back to camp." He got her to take a few steps before Hallie suddenly stopped and turned around. Slowly, she eyed him up and down, color and expression gradually returning to her face.

The worried look Jack gave her made Hallie feel foolish. She was gaping at him like an idiot. But for a few minutes after she'd heard that shot, her brain had shut down and all she could think about was Jack with a bullet hole in some vital place.

"No, wait," she said, when he tried to urge her in the direction of the camp. "Let me see your arm."

"Don't worry about it. It'll keep."

"So you say. But I don't want you losing an arm now, just when you're getting the hang of roping."

Hallie tried to sound as if she patched up wounded men every day of the week, and it didn't make any difference that it was Jack's turn. He saw right through her bluff; she sensed it the moment the words left her mouth.

He let her take a look at his arm without commenting, though, even going so far as to put up with her binding the bullet wound with her bandanna. Despite the blood, it was a clean wound, and Hallie inwardly breathed a sigh of relief she didn't have to dig any lead out of him. Jack's luck apparently went beyond the card table.

When she'd finished, she took the hand he offered and walked with him back to camp.

Tenfoot was there the moment they arrived. "What happened? Charlie was swearin' he heard a shot.

Seems like he was right,'' Tenfoot added, with a nod to Jack's arm.

"He was.'' Jack and Hallie quickly filled Tenfoot in on Hallie's attack and the shooting. By the time they'd finished, everyone in camp had gathered around them.

"You think it was that puncher who jumped Hal?'' Eb asked.

"The shot came from farther away,'' Jack said. "Besides, if it was him, he had plenty of time to finish the job. I never got a chance to take a shot at him. He turned and hightailed it out of there as soon as he saw me.''

Big Charlie snorted. "Figures, the yellow-bellied coward. Seems he was only brave enough to jump Hal from behind.''

"It might be a good idea if we took a look around,'' Tenfoot said. His mouth set in a grim line. "Stealin' calves is one thing, shootin' at folks is another.''

Jack nodded in agreement. "We've still got a few hours of daylight. If nothing else, maybe we can find our missing friend.''

"Are you crazy?''

Hallie blurted out the words at the same time Ethan said, "I want to go with you.''

Jack knelt down and took his son's shoulders. It hadn't been so very long that Ethan had lost his mother. Even though their relationship was still fragile, Jack guessed Ethan was probably afraid of losing the only parent he had left to claim.

"I need you to stay here and help Ben look after

Miss Hallie and Miss Serenity. I know I can trust you to help keep them safe.''

"You're hurt," Ethan said, with a glance at Jack's arm. Blood had seeped through the bandanna, and Ethan quickly looked away. "You shouldn't be ridin', should you?''

"It's only a scratch. I'll be fine. Now…" He lifted Ethan's chin so the boy looked him in the face. "Can I count on you?''

Ethan licked his lips, his expression doubtful. But he nodded and stood a little taller when Jack smiled and squeezed his shoulder.

Ben walked up to him, cuffing Ethan lightly on the arm. "Come on, partner. Serenity needs a hand closing up the chuckwagon, and she's afraid there's some scorpions hidin' inside.''

The rest of the men went to round up their horses, leaving Jack and Hallie standing alone. She faced him, trying without much success to tamp down her anger.

It was bad enough that every man in camp suddenly seemed to accept Jack as the boss. But now he was determined to go looking for whoever had shot him, asking for more trouble.

And to top it off, he had the gall to stand there with that irritating half smile on his mouth, as if he knew everything she was thinking.

"Well, go ahead and get yourself shot full of holes, then," she snapped. "But you're not leaving me behind as if I were some pretty little thing in petticoats who can't take care of herself. I can outride and outshoot the whole bunch of you.''

"I don't doubt it. But haven't you had enough for one day?"

"Haven't you?"

"Hallie…"

Jack moved forward as if he intended to touch her. Hallie stepped back out of his reach. "Don't imagine you can sweet-talk me into thinking your way this time, Dakota."

"I wouldn't dream of it, darlin'." His gaze shifted to her mouth, and for a moment, Hallie thought he intended to kiss her right there, in front of God and the entire camp.

Then he looked straight into her eyes, his expression changing suddenly to serious. "I know you're capable of handling anything. But I don't like the idea of you out there making a new target for whoever wants to shoot in our direction."

"Oh, and I love the idea of it being you. Or anyone else," she added hastily when he lifted a questioning brow.

"Ethan needs someone to look after him."

Despite her resolve, Hallie felt herself softening in the face of his concern for her and especially his son. "Ben and Serenity are here."

"I want you."

The way he said it, Hallie wondered, for an instant, if he was still talking about her staying with Ethan, or about the way he made her feel when he looked at her as if he were blind to every other woman on earth. It wasn't real; it couldn't be. But sometimes…sometimes she surely wanted to believe it was.

She didn't want to fight him. But she also didn't want to be left behind and give the idea that she'd surrendered her hard-earned position as the boss at Eden's Canyon any opportunity to take root and flourish.

Before she could say any of that, Jack ended their brief skirmish.

"Okay, I know when to throw in the cards," he said, an equal share of amusement and exasperation in his voice. "You win, Hal."

Trying not to grin, Hallie said, "I hope you're not going to be a sore loser."

This time he did kiss her, a quick brush of his lips against her cheek. "Depends on what I get for a consolation prize," he murmured, before swinging up into the saddle. "Are you coming?"

Hallie didn't answer, but hurried to get her horse. As she tossed the reins over Grano's neck, Ethan came up beside her.

He fidgeted with a strand of the mare's mane for a moment. "Is the man who shot him still out there?"

He couldn't quite hide the worry on his face, though Hallie could see him trying. "I'm sure he's long gone by now," she said, deliberately making her voice matter-of-fact to put Ethan at ease. "Your pa will be fine. He's got lots of people with him."

When Ethan looked doubtful, Hallie put her arm around his shoulders. She glanced around them, then leaned close and said just loudly enough for him to hear, "Don't tell anyone, but I plan to herd these cowboys back to camp just as soon as I can, your pa included. I don't know about you, but I've had enough of living on the range for a while. I want to sleep in my own bed tonight.''

''You promise? We're all going back? Today?''

''Promise. We'll be home in time for bed. If I have to tie them all to their horses and run them home to do it.'' She smiled and got an answering grin from Ethan.

Ethan's smile dimmed a little. ''What about the rest of the branding? Don't we have to finish?''

''These cows aren't going anywhere, and we're close to finished anyway. Don't worry about that. Now, I think Ben could use your help finding those scorpions. If he misses even one, Serenity will scream so loud she'll start another stampede.''

She got Ethan involved in helping Ben and Serenity pack their gear, before getting on her horse to follow Jack and the rest of the men. As they rode out to the area Jack figured the shot had come from, Hallie sent up a prayer they'd seen the last of trouble for the day.

Jack leaned against the porch rail and let the cool night breeze sweep over him. By rights, he supposed he should be asleep on his feet by now. But he couldn't shake the sense of unease he'd had ever since he'd caught that cowboy attacking Hallie.

They hadn't found the puncher, nor any useful clues to who had shot at him and Hallie. After more than two hours of looking they had given up, agreeing to return to the ranch.

No one talked much about it at supper, and after a quick meal, everyone had gone off in different directions to settle in for the evening. Jack tucked an exhausted Ethan into bed, sitting next to him until the boy fell asleep, before coming outside to clear his head.

The door opened behind him and Jack turned to see Hallie poised there, her hand still on the knob.

"I didn't know you were here," she said. She glanced back toward the house. "I should probably go and see if Serenity needs any more help in the kitchen."

"Don't go." Jack moved to sit on the porch swing and patted the seat next to him, beckoning her to join him. "I promise, no sweet talk."

Hallie shook her head, but she smiled and came to sit at the other end of the swing. "You should have let the doctor look at your arm."

"Are we back to that again? Nothing's broken, you said so yourself. And you've got it wrapped so tightly, it wouldn't dare start bleeding again. Besides," he added, winking at her, "I've gotten worse than this arguing with someone over how many aces should be in a deck."

"I don't doubt that. It's amazing you're still walking the earth, Dakota."

Silence fell between them, broken only by the whisper of the night wind. Hallie stared at the toes of her boots and wondered what happened now.

Jack had probably done things like this with dozens of women who knew how to make small talk and flatter a man with their attention as easily as they breathed. She'd rarely in her life had a conversation with any man that didn't have to do with cattle or horses or the prices of supplies.

Hallie plucked at a nonexistent thread on her shirt-sleeve, and Jack smiled to himself. She looked as uncomfortable as he felt.

He disliked the feeling because he couldn't figure it out, and that irritated him. He'd never had this trouble around a woman before. It had always been simple. A look, a smile, a little talking, a bit of teasing and they both knew what they wanted. It was straightforward and easy.

It was never like that with Hallie.

Yet it didn't stop him from wanting to touch her, to hold her. He just didn't know how to do that without complicating his life so much he'd never get it straight again.

He should stop any notions of being more than partners with her. But even as he thought the words, Jack stretched an arm out and rubbed his fingers against her shoulder.

Hallie slowly looked over at him.

"Are you glad to be home?" Jack asked, more to hear her voice than her answer.

"Yes…although I like riding the range. This time, though—" she smiled ruefully "—it was a little more exciting than I bargained for."

"Much more." Jack turned serious. He'd thought a lot about this afternoon, and the image of her being attacked by the cowboy still stuck with him. He saw her looking at him curiously, and made himself smile. "And I thought gambling was a dangerous profession."

"More than mine. This is the first time I've ever been shot at, but you've obviously had that experience a time or two."

Jack waited, and when she didn't add anything, he slid a little closer to her. He slipped his hand under her braid and began to massage the nape of her neck. "So it's not the first time you've been attacked by a rogue cowboy?" he asked, half serious, half teasing.

Hallie shrugged, not looking at him. "It's the first time, like that. Sometimes, before, some of the hands have tried to…take liberties. It didn't mean anything. It's not as if it was because I…because, they wanted…well, you know." She floundered, recovered and flashed him a defiant look. "I always got away from them."

"I've no doubt of that. But…" Jack's hand moved to caress the curve where her shoulder and neck met. "I confess, sweetheart, I couldn't blame a man for wanting to take liberties with you."

It was hard to have a conversation with him touching her like that. In fact, it was hard to think at all. Hallie quickly got to her feet and went to stand by the rail.

She heard the swing creak and then Jack come up beside her.

"Running away from me?"

The challenge in his voice was enough to make her reluctantly turn and look at him.

"What happened to the woman who said she'd sacrifice her reputation for me?" he asked softly. "The one who kissed me like she wanted more?"

"That's not me. That shouldn't have happened."

"But it did. And I can't forget it. I don't think you can, either."

"You're wrong," she whispered.

"Prove it." Jack stepped closer so there was only a whisper of heat separating them. "Walk away."

"I…" *I should. I have to.* "I can't. Jack—"

Hallie didn't know what she meant to say to him, but in the next moment she was in his arms, and whatever she would have said was lost forever.

Jack didn't bother to hide his need for her. It had been building too long, and he intended to use it to burn away any thoughts she'd ever had of being less of a woman.

He kissed her deeply while he held her fully against him, telling her without words how much he wanted her. Only her.

Hallie kissed him back without the slightest hesitation. She didn't waste time pretending this wasn't what she'd wanted from the moment she'd come outside and found Jack alone.

Maybe this wasn't the way most decent women behaved with a man. But then, she'd never been like most women, and Jack made her feel things she'd never even imagined she could feel.

His mouth and hands became more demanding, and Hallie, infected by the building urgency in him, reveled in every kiss and caress until they finally broke apart, both breathless.

Jack pulled off the tie fastening her braid, unraveling her hair and combing his fingers through it until it fell like a waterfall down her back. He nuzzled her throat, breathing in the scent of sunshine and wind, the essence of Hallie, as he tried to rein in the desire threatening to overwhelm him.

She was pushing him to the edge, and at the same time, Jack didn't know how far to take her. He wanted her so badly it hurt, and her abandoned response should have had him scooping her up and carrying her to his bed.

Instead, he felt like it was his first time. He found himself fumbling his way without knowing exactly what to do to make it right for her. Why the hell did it have to be so complicated?

Without releasing her mouth, Jack guided her until he had backed her against the wall of the house. He held her against him with his fingers tangled in her hair while he worked free the buttons of her shirt and pushed it off her shoulders.

Looking at her, Jack traced his fingertips along the edge of her chemise. Hallie trembled at the whisper touch on her bare skin, and he smiled. "How could you ever believe you're not beautiful?" he murmured. "If you could only see yourself now…"

He bent and kissed her at the same time he slid his hand down to cup her breast. Sharply she sucked in her breath, then leaned into his caress, silently encouraging him.

The thin barrier of cotton suddenly frustrated Hallie. She wanted to feel his touch with nothing between them.

Jack, though, seemed content to tease her with slow, tantalizing caresses, pressing warm, nibbling kisses against her skin before returning to make love to her mouth with his lips.

He was deliberately driving her mad, and she wanted to do the same to him, although she didn't have the first idea how. Propelled by curiosity as much as desire, she tugged open his shirt buttons and spread her hands against his chest.

Her unpracticed caress was nearly his undoing. "You're playing with fire, darlin'," Jack rasped hotly against her ear. "If you keep doing that, I won't be able to stop."

"I don't want you to," Hallie said. She spoke from her heart, but she couldn't quite look at him.

"Hallie…" Jack hesitated, her bluntness unnerving him. "You don't know what you're saying."

She did look at him then, and the fire in her eyes was more than just passion. "I know my own mind. I want to be with you. I'm not—no one has ever…I've never felt like this with anyone. Only you."

Her honest confession hit Jack like a bucket of cold water. Her way of simply speaking her mind about her heart's desire, as innocently as she did about everything else, left him dumbstruck. And she had the right to expect the same from him.

But he couldn't figure out himself what he was feeling for Hallie Ryan, let alone express it to her.

"Neither of us is thinking straight right now," he said, groping for something to say. He wanted her, as much now as ever. Loving Hallie, though, wouldn't end with one or two nights of passion. "I don't want you to have regrets. You need—"

"You're scared."

Jack stared at her.

Hallie moved out of his arms, yanking up her shirt-sleeves. She faced him squarely. "It's not about what I need or me being sure. It's you. The idea that something you feel about a woman, especially a woman like me, might make you obligated has you running scared."

She waited, fully expecting him to give her some sweet-sounding fast talk to explain why he was pushing her away.

Instead, Jack shook his head and gave a short laugh. "Okay, I admit it. You scare the hell out of me, lady." He reached out a hand and touched her cheek. "That doesn't stop me from wanting to finish what we've started."

"I have no idea what we've started and I don't think you do, either. And to tell you the truth, it scares me, too." Hallie hurriedly rebuttoned her shirt, doing her best to ignore how close he still stood to her. "But if you ever figure it out, let me know."

Before Jack could do anything to stop her, she practically ran into the house.

Jack was right behind her. He followed her to her bedroom door, shoving a boot inside before she could slam it in his face. "It's not going to end like this."

"Please..." Hallie's temper suddenly left her. Tears pricked at her eyes, but she fought them back. She wouldn't cry, refused to cry in front of him. "Not now, not tonight."

Taking one look at her face, Jack cursed under his breath, stepped into her room and gathered her into his arms. She stood stiffly at first, but he held her there, softly stroking her hair and back, holding her close against his heart.

Hallie finally sighed and leaned against him, the fight drained out of her.

They stayed together like that for long minutes until an overwhelming tiredness overtook Hallie and she swayed a little on her feet. Jack scooped her up and carried her to her bed. Laying her down, he tugged off her boots and pulled the quilt up around her shoulders before smoothing the hair away from her forehead and gently kissing her there.

"Sweet dreams, darlin'," he murmured. He took one last look at her before closing the door quietly behind him, silently wishing her untroubled sleep, knowing his would be far from it.

Chapter Thirteen

Jack awoke the next morning, stirred by an old familiar restlessness. His sleep had been fitful at best, frustrated by dreams of Hallie in his arms, in his bed. Last night seemed some sort of tantalizing torture.

Hallie Ryan had a way of turning his outsides in and his insides out so that all that was familiar to him in his dealings with women—his easy words and gentle wooing—became impossible. With her, all that seemed ridiculous.

She made him feel as if she could see straight through him. She seemed to know exactly how he'd always avoided commitment to one woman and the boredom of an everyday life.

But one look from Hallie made him question who he'd always been and who he wanted to become.

He shoved himself out of bed, his feet hitting the cold brick floor. At his dresser, he splashed handfuls of water over his day-old beard, then swished his shaving brush in a jar of soap to make it lather. Adjusting the mirror above the dresser, he stroked the blade against his roughened cheek.

As he scraped the stubble from his jaw, the restlessness inside him grew stronger. For some reason, the idea of another day of fixing fences or digging irrigation ditches didn't sit well.

So far, working this ranch with Hallie had given him new challenges, so had held his interest.

But it had also added elements he hadn't counted on, disturbing feelings and frustrations, and questions he'd never asked himself before.

Jack swiped a hand towel over his jaw before pulling on a pair of black denim pants and an off-white cotton shirt and his boots. He needed to get away from here, to distract himself with something other than work. And he had to do it today or his insides would explode.

Hallie might be able to work nonstop day after day, but the routine, not the work, would kill him with boredom. Today, he intended to take himself and Ethan away from Eden's Canyon. And he'd bring Hallie with them even if he had to tie her to the wagon to do it.

Considering the notion as he headed toward the kitchen for breakfast, he decided it might come to that, because he doubted Hallie would come along willingly.

"Mornin'," Tenfoot and the others murmured in welcome as he strode in and took his usual seat near the head of the table.

"Morning," he answered, glancing at Hallie. She stood at the stove, flipping griddle cakes.

"Hello," she said, keeping her back to him.

"You look mighty duded up for ditch diggin'," Big Charlie said.

Jack laughed easily. "That's because I'm not digging any ditches today."

That got Hallie's attention. Curiosity winning over stubbornness, she turned, spatula in hand. "What?"

"Ethan and I are going to town to do some shopping."

The room fell silent, forks stopping in midair, all eyes on Jack.

Ethan broke the silence. "Town? Really? Yippee! No work today!"

"That's right, unless you call shopping for shoes and clothes for you work."

"Oh." Ethan's enthusiastic squeal switched to a grumble. "I thought we were gonna do somethin' fun."

"Well, it'll be something different, anyway." Jack turned to Hallie, who looked more confused than annoyed. "I was hoping you'd come along with us. I've never bought clothes for a boy before and I thought you might give me some idea of what to buy."

Hallie crossed her arms over her chest. "I can't just pick up and waltz off to town for the day."

Still silent, the men at the table turned their eyes from Hallie back to Jack, breakfast temporarily forgotten in favor of the morning's unexpected entertainment.

"Why not?"

Hallie's eyes flared to bright green. "Because I can't. There's work to be done. The ditches are overgrown, the garden needs to be replanted—"

Jack shrugged. "It'll all keep for one day."

Eb cleared his throat. "You did work mighty hard out on the range, Hal. A day in town might do you good."

"Oh, go on," Ben urged. "Serenity will be glad to get out of this kitchen into the sunshine and give us a hand with the tilling." He turned to the girl and flashed a big grin. "Won't you?"

Serenity smiled back, obviously pleased. "That sounds mighty fine to me, Ben."

The others joined in with their agreement, leaving Hallie feeling outnumbered.

"Can I have a hard candy from the general store?" Ethan asked.

Jack reached over and tousled his son's hair. "Sure you can."

"Now, just one minute, all of you." Hallie spoke up loud and clear. "It's almost time for spring planting and we haven't even sorted the seeds. And those ditches have to be burned and cleared out or they'll clog." She looked directly at Jack. "You and Ethan can go while away the day in town if you want, but someone's got to keep things running here."

"The way you're goin' on, you'd think we'd got nothin' under our hats but hair," Tenfoot said, grinning widely when Hallie frowned at him. "We know what needs doin', Hal. We been at it long enough."

"Don't need to be a genius to dig a ditch," Charlie added with a laugh as he stabbed a forkful of griddle cake.

Jack tried on his best smile. "I'd sure appreciate your help with Ethan," he coaxed. He could see her wavering, and pressed his slight advantage. "And I'd be pleased to take you and Ethan to lunch for your trouble."

Ethan shoved his chair back from the table and carried his plate to the sink. "Please, Miss Hallie? You can't work all the time, can you?"

Hallie stared down into Ethan's eyes, so like his father's. Then she made one sweeping tally of the faces in the room and confirmed that she didn't have one ally. Untying her apron, she tossed it aside and wiped her hands.

"Well, it seems I'm going to town." She turned to Jack and Ethan. "You two get the wagon and I'll get my hat."

She hurried out of the kitchen, irritated at how easily Jack could convince everyone to fall in with his whims, and at the same time, pleased that he and Ethan wanted her to share in indulging those whims.

If only she didn't feel as if he was slowly stealing her authority at Eden's Canyon. If only she didn't feel as if he was slowly stealing her heart.

Last night... Hallie burned inside with embarrassment and a need she didn't want to name every time she thought about it.

Last night she'd nearly given in to Jack's tempting caresses and gentle words. Oh, how she'd wanted him. All of him. He'd seemed so sincere, boyish almost in his advances, so unlike the smooth-talking ladies' man she'd expected.

Was it all an act? Had he sized her up and figured out exactly how to break down her resistance? Had he seduced so many women that he could change, quicker than hell could scorch a feather, into whatever they wanted him to be?

She'd probably drive herself crazy trying to find out.

Grabbing her hat from the bedpost, Hallie sneaked a glance in her mirror and immediately wished she hadn't. Wild strands of hair sprang out around her face and all down her braid. Her cheeks and nose still glowed bright pink from being under the sun all the days of the roundup. And her hands! She didn't dare look at the stains and charred black grime under her nails from branding.

Well, she couldn't magically change herself into someone with a pretty dress and neatly curled hair. Jack would have to be seen with her as she was or he could leave her at home.

Hallie tugged on the hat Jack so often called ugly and, with a defiant nod to her mirror image, and a lift of her chin, marched out to meet him.

The bell jingled on the door of Bellweather's General Store as Hallie, Jack and Ethan stepped inside.

Joe Bellweather looked up from where he stood arranging a stack of canned goods, peeping over the spectacles on his nose. "Mornin' Hal, Mr. Dakota."

Hallie and Jack returned the greeting as Ethan scampered off to inspect the candy jars.

"What can I do for you?"

"I need two sacks of flour, a sack of sugar and a tin of lard for Eb's brother's family," Hallie said. "And Mr. Dakota's boy here needs some new clothes." She gestured toward Ethan.

The store owner looked down to where Ethan stood at the counter. "Better get the missus to help you there." Joe glanced back over his shoulder and shouted toward a room behind the front desk.

"Rosa, come on out here. Hal Ryan's here with the Harper boy from the saloon. The kid needs some new duds."

Hallie winced. Jack scowled and glanced at Ethan. Luckily, his preoccupation with the candy jars seemed to have kept him from paying any attention to Joe.

But Jack was pretty sure at that moment he knew the feeling that had driven Ethan to knock young Brett Peller on his rear.

Rosa bustled in from the back room, wiping her hands on her apron. "Well, Hallie, we haven't seen so much of you in months," she said. She looked at Jack; then back at Hallie, and smiled brightly. "First the church social, and now you're here in town. I'd have thought after roundup, you'd be so busy we wouldn't see you again until almost time for the drive."

"Miss Hallie generously offered to help me find some clothes for my son," Jack said, laying slight emphasis on his last two words as he glanced at Joe. "The few he's got are worn to threads and he's outgrowing what's left of them by the day. And he needs some new boots, too."

Hallie began rifling through a stack of denims, avoiding Rosa's avid curiosity and Joe's open speculation as he watched her and Jack. She motioned to Ethan. "Come on over here and let me hold these up on you for size."

Eyeing the boy from head to toe, Rosa cocked her head and considered. "We have one pair that might do, but you'll have to roll them up for a few months until you stretch up a little."

"He needs Sunday clothes, too," Jack said.

"How about socks and drawers?" Rosa asked.

Jack shrugged, looking to Hallie for help.

Hallie nodded. "Those, too. Serenity has mended what he's got until there's nothing left but the darning."

After an appealing look at Jack got him nowhere, Ethan reluctantly let the women fuss over sizes and lengths of shirtsleeves and britches. All the while Jack watched his son glance around the store, following as the boy's curious eyes swept past the bolts of calico and polka dot fabrics lining the shelves on the back wall, to colorful tins and gray sacks of food, returning again to the rainbow of candies in jars on the front counter.

Then Ethan's attention fell on a single pair of shiny black boots displayed in the front window.

As Hallie held up shirts against Ethan's shoulders, measuring for size, the boy scarcely noticed, his gaze riveted on the finely crafted boots.

Jack smiled to himself and strode over to the display. He lifted one boot and looked it over. When the workmanship passed his inspection, he turned to Ethan and held the boot high.

Ethan's eyes lit up. His teeth caught his lower lip, but he didn't say a word. It was as though Ethan wouldn't dare let himself dream Jack might be thinking of buying the boots for him.

"Where did these come from?" Jack asked Joe.

"Those? Mighty fine, aren't they? The new cobbler up the street made them. I told him I'd put a pair in my window to help folks get familiar with his shop."

"Do you like these, Ethan?" Jack carried one boot over to Ethan, who ran his fingers across it.

The boy nodded slowly. "Sure do. They look like yours."

Everything Jack had in mind to say suddenly stuck in his throat. Whatever he'd expected from Ethan, it hadn't been that.

Jack looked at Hallie, and she could tell he needed rescuing and that he counted on her to do it.

She stopped folding the pants she'd chosen for Ethan and smiled at Jack. She could feel Rosa watching them, but right then it didn't matter.

"Do you want a pair of boots like your pa has?" Hallie asked Ethan.

Ethan's eyes widened even more. He glanced from Jack to Hallie and back again, seeming as much at a loss for words as his father.

Jack laid a hand on his son's shoulder. "It's all right. If these are the boots you want, we'll go up the street and see about having a pair made in your size."

"You ought to have them made two sizes up," Rosa suggested. "He'll be growing like a weed and those boots won't come cheap, let me tell you. He can always wear an extra pair of socks for a spell."

Jack looked at his son's worn shoes. "I expect he's long overdue for a new pair, and they might as well be good ones so they'll last. Ethan's going to be doing a lot of riding and helping out on the ranch now that he's got his own pony.'' He smiled indulgently at his son. ''Isn't that right?''

''I got my own saddle now, too,'' Ethan finally managed to blurt out. ''Ben gave it to me. It used to be his.''

Rosa lifted a brow. ''My, my, you all are becoming quite a nice little family, aren't you? Who would have thought?''

No one, Hallie told herself, until Rosa spread it all over Paradise that Hallie Ryan and Jack Dakota were more than just business partners. Hallie couldn't make up her mind whether to be upset or pleased that anyone would believe that.

''We're finished here, aren't we?'' she asked.

The slight rise in her voice told Jack she was unhappy about something. Probably the knowing gleam in Rosa's eyes when she took in the both of them.

''I'll send Eb in to pick up those supplies for his brother's family,'' Hallie said to Joe.

Jack wondered at Hallie's purchase. She'd bought nothing for herself since he'd known her, yet here she was, taking care of another family apart from her own.

He was still thinking it over when he sent Ethan to choose a handful of candies, while he waited for Rosa to tally up their purchases.

Rosa clucked her tongue when Jack paid the bill for Ethan's clothes. ''You're spoiling the boy, you know.''

''Oh, I don't think a shirt on his back and boots on

his feet are too much. Besides, Ethan could use a little spoiling."

Outside the store, Jack started laughing as he took Hallie's elbow. "She'll have us married before sunset."

"And you think that's funny?"

"Come on, Miss Ryan, don't you think we'd make good partners?"

Liking the feel of his hand on her skin through her shirt, Hallie chose to ignore the whispers and stares of the townsfolk as the threesome strolled along the boardwalk.

"Nice idea, but I'm used to working alone and being in charge," she said, half teasing.

"That suits me fine. I like a woman with spirit," Jack teased back. "Careful now, you're smiling. Folks might think you're enjoying being with me."

As usual, Jack's infectious charm got the better of her. "Too late. It feels like it's written all over my face."

Jack turned to her and paused. Gently, he took her chin in his palm. "It is. And it looks beautiful there."

Hallie blushed. They'd stopped right smack on the main street, where everyone could see him touch her. Even Ethan was staring at them curiously.

"Jack, people are staring."

He glanced over her shoulder to the dress shop window behind them. "If you were wearing that green dress in the window, they'd never stop staring."

"Oh, don't talk nonsense," she said, following his

eyes. "What would I do with that? I don't have money to waste on something I'd never use."

"That's because you take care of half the county. How long have you been providing for Eb's relatives?"

"As long as they've needed a little help. They'll get back on their feet. But until then, I'll do what I can."

"I don't doubt it."

"Eb is family." She glanced ahead of them to where Ethan, tired of their talk, was swinging around and around a post, a peppermint stick dangling from his mouth. "You're learning how much that means."

Jack smiled as he watched Ethan. "I think I am."

Turning back to Hallie, he gave her elbow a gentle squeeze. "Let me buy you that dress."

"You'd do better to save your money for the ranch. You don't know how fast you'll be spending that big jackpot of yours."

"Jackpot?" For a moment Jack looked puzzled, then he laughed. "Have you been worrying my well is going to run dry? I'm afraid I misled you there, darlin'. I've got enough saved up to keep us going for quite a while."

"I never did believe that story of yours, about buying Eden's Canyon on one night's winnings," Hallie said. "But then, it's harder to believe you ever saved a dime."

Jack shrugged. "I didn't want to end up living under a cactus in my old age. And good thing I've been putting it aside, considering what it's going to cost me to keep Ethan in boots and britches.'' He looked back at the green dress again. "So there's more than enough for that. And I promise you, you'll have reason to wear it. Besides, I'm scared to death the next time you do wear a dress it'll be that orange nightmare.''

His expression of mock horror made Hallie laugh despite herself. "Was it that bad?"

"Worse."

"I don't doubt it. Still…" She looked at the dress again. "I don't think—"

"That's right. Don't think. It's better that way."

After telling Ethan to stay close, Jack ushered Hallie into the dress shop.

With more than a little urging from him and the shop girl, she found herself behind a curtain, out of her clothes and into the dress.

"I feel like red paint on a church door," Hallie muttered as she pulled at the sleeves and wriggled against the unfamiliar snugness of the bodice.

"Let's see," Jack coaxed.

Wishing herself anywhere else, Hallie inched out from behind the curtain.

Jack couldn't help but stare. He'd imagined she'd look enticing in a dress that actually fit, but nothing had prepared him for the effect it would have on him.

The soft, clear green cotton hugged her curves and accentuated every feminine angle. The long skirt slid easily over her slender hips, falling in graceful folds to the tips of her boots.

Jack smiled.

"What? Is it so bad? Oh, go ahead and laugh then and get it over with!" Hallie turned to duck back behind the curtain, but in a flash Jack had her by the shoulders.

"You look even more beautiful than I imagined," he said softly. At the same time, he flipped off her ugly hat and smoothed the wild tangle of curls back off her brow. "I only smiled because I see the cobbler will have two new pairs of shoes to make. Those boots might be perfect for the range, but they do very little for this dress."

Hallie looked down to her mud-encrusted, worn boots. "Oh. I guess you're right."

Jack turned to the shopkeeper. "We'll take the dress and any undergarments she needs to go with it." He looked back at Hallie. "I don't know about you, but I'm starved. Why don't you get dressed and gather up your packages, and I'll go find Ethan for lunch?"

"Jack, I really can't," Hallie said, indicating the dress with a sweep of her hand. "This is all too—"

He touched a finger to her lips. "It's not. Say yes. Just this once."

Hallie couldn't say no. "Yes," she told him. "But why do I have the feeling it won't be just this once?"

After a stop at the cobbler's, Jack, Hallie and Ethan made their way to the Santa Anna Hotel for lunch. Hallie had set foot in the elegant hotel only one other time in her life. And that was only after hearing rumors of a big poker game to be held there one night, to ask whether or not anyone had seen Ben amid the players.

The hotel was small, but clean and whitewashed inside and full of sunlight. Jack asked for a table near a window and it took only a smile and a few words from him for Hallie to find herself seated and being catered to as if she was an important guest, rather than just plain Hallie Ryan.

Leaning toward him, Hallie whispered to Jack, "Did you pay them to be nice to us?"

Jack laughed. "Don't you have any faith in my famous charm, darlin'?" Not giving her time to answer, he winked at Ethan, then reached to take Hallie's hand. "You and Ethan deserve the best, so that's what you're getting."

Again, he'd utterly baffled her. There he sat, looking completely sincere, nothing but generosity and kindness in his actions. Nothing but warmth in the brush of his fingers atop her hand. His charm came honestly and naturally, making it near impossible to refuse him anything.

Hallie sighed. "I swear, I don't know what to do with you, Dakota."

"I might have a few suggestions, ma'am." A man's gruff voice came from behind her.

Hallie swung around to look.

Jack immediately tensed, his jaw tightening. His hand slid to his holster instinctively. "Barlow. What the hell are you doing here?"

"Now what kind of a greeting is that for an old

gambling buddy?'' Redeye Bill Barlow asked. ''I was just enjoyin' a friendly little game in the back room.''

''You're supposed to be in jail,'' Jack said.

''And you're supposed to be dead, or at least with a lot less of my money in your pocket. I'd like the first one a sight better.''

''You tried to kill my brother!'' Hallie exclaimed, ignoring Jack's warning glance. ''You should still be locked up.''

Jack wanted nothing better than to end it with Redeye then and there. But not with Hallie and Ethan at his side. Although if Barlow so much as breathed in either Hallie's or Ethan's direction, he'd kill him, and damn the consequences.

''Try is about all Bill does,'' Jack said, leaning back in his chair.

Redeye blew cigar smoke toward Jack's face and let out a hoarse laugh. ''Now, where's those pretty manners of yours, Dakota?''

''You must have bought your way out of a cell again. Why don't you do us both a favor and spend your way right out of town?''

''Oh, I dunno.'' Redeye leaned back on his heels and looked around. ''I got a likin' for this town. At least it's got one fine hotel, and one fine saloon. What else does a man need?'' He cast a condescending eye toward Ethan, then back to Jack. ''You sure found everything you wanted over at the Snake. And a whole bushel more, eh, partner?''

With that Jack shoved himself to his feet. ''Outside. Now.''

''Whoa, there.'' Cigar dangling from his bottom lip, Redeye held up his palms. ''I don't want trouble with you. Only wanted to say hello, seein' as we're old friends and all. Don't worry, partner,'' he added, patting the gun on his hip, ''we'll settle our differences sooner or later.''

With a tip of his hat to Hallie, Redeye walked out of the hotel restaurant, leaving Jack fighting a nearly overwhelming urge to follow him and end their feud in broad daylight on the main street of Paradise.

Chapter Fourteen

The day was fading and the late-afternoon sun was losing some of its brilliant heat when they headed back to the wagon. Jack, with Hallie's hand tucked in the crook of one arm and his other hand on Ethan's shoulder, was doing his best to talk the two of them out of the somewhat subdued mood they'd fallen under since lunch.

Not wanting the encounter with Barlow to completely ruin their day, he'd shoved the unpleasant episode aside and sidestepped Hallie's questions. There'd be time enough to tell her about his and Barlow's past later—if he worried her with it at all.

He started to make some lighthearted suggestion that they get away from the cattle more often when he noticed his son glancing in the direction of the Silver Snake.

Jack saw that Ethan, by looking slantways, was trying to pretend he had no interest in the saloon where he'd grown up. His attempt to seem oblivious didn't fool Jack. He glimpsed the longing on Ethan's face that the boy couldn't hide. The only thing that surprised Jack now was that Ethan didn't ask outright if he could visit his old home.

Hallie saw it, too, and she caught Jack's eye. "There's no hurry to get back. We've got a couple of hours, at least, until supper."

"Is that a hint or an order, ma'am?"

Jack hadn't intended the slight edge in his voice, but Hallie shrugged it off. "Neither. I just mentioned it, that's all."

"Right." Jack looked back at Ethan. For several reasons, he would rather take his son almost anywhere other than the Silver Snake. One of them being he was hardly eager for a second run-in with Redeye. But Jack knew Ethan well enough by now to realize that once the boy got an idea in his head, he stuck to it like a burr on a horse's tail.

And something deeper warned him Ethan would never be satisfied with living at the ranch until he'd had a chance to settle with his past.

And maybe in that they weren't so different.

Stopping near the porch of the saloon, Jack turned to Ethan. "Would you like to go back, one more time?"

Ethan stared up at him as if he hadn't quite heard him right. "You'll let me go back?"

"This once, with Miss Hallie and me, if Miss Hallie agrees."

"If you want me to come, I'd like to," Hallie told Ethan.

Looking from Jack to the saloon, then back again, Ethan nodded, his eyes shining.

The delight on his son's face was enough to quiet

the worst of Jack's misgivings about offering to take Ethan to the saloon. "All right then, let's go."

A loud burst of laughter and the scrape and shuffle of chairs greeted them as Jack ushered Hallie and Ethan ahead of him into the Silver Snake.

The rugged adobe saloon hadn't changed since the last time Hallie had come here to drag a drunken Ben away from trouble. It wasn't fancy, but she knew the miners and cowboys and gamblers who frequented it didn't come to admire velvet curtains and polished wood.

They came to drink, or test their luck, either at cards or with one of the half-dozen women who earned their way satisfying a man's pleasure.

Three of the girls stood near one of the tables now, watching a card game between a grizzled cowboy and an old man with a gold tooth and a face like a well-broken saddle. They glanced up when the saloon doors swung open, dismissed Hallie with one look, but broke into smiles when they recognized her escort.

"Why, Jack Dakota!" A blonde in red satin walked up to him, stroking her fingers over his arm. "We weren't expectin' you back so soon."

"But you sure are welcome, honey," another practically gushed. She tossed her black curls as she eyed Hallie's cowboy garb with a scornful smile. "Even if you have gone and turned all respectable now."

"Well, now, darlin'," Jack drawled, flashing a lazy smile, "*respectable*'s such a vague word. It doesn't mean I've forgotten the pleasure of your company."

The woman giggled and preened, and Hallie barely

kept from grinding her teeth. If she'd ever needed a reminder of the life Jack had led before acquiring Eden's Canyon, this would have been more than enough. Last night he'd been practically in her bed, and today he'd slipped back into that slick talk as easily as he walked and breathed.

She opened her mouth to remind him that they'd come for Ethan's benefit, not so he could sweet-talk every woman he laid eyes on, but just then a slender girl in a low-cut blue dress that matched her eyes came up to them. To Hallie's surprise, the girl smiled only briefly at Jack before turning to Ethan.

"I'm glad to see you," she said. "I've been hopin' you'd come back. I got a few of your mama's things I been keepin' for you."

"Thanks, Kitty. We'll take them with us," Jack answered for his son. "Ethan wanted to see Mattie's old room again, too. I know it's yours now, but we won't stay long."

"Aw, it don't matter," Kitty said with a wave of her hand. "There's hardly been a soul in all day, least none with any money to part with. Come on up."

After a quick word with the other girls, Kitty led them upstairs and into a room at the end of the hall-way. Snatching a discarded petticoat off the floor, she went to a shabby wooden dresser and plucked up a small wooden cigar box.

"Not much here," she said, handing the box to Ethan. "But since it was your mama's, I thought you might want it. Stay as long as you want," she added, before slipping out the door and closing it quietly behind her.

Jack looked around the room as Ethan went to sit on the narrow iron-frame bed with his treasures. It hadn't changed much, even after all these years. Mattie had loved bright yellow and it showed everywhere, like splashes of sunshine between the disarray of Kitty's petticoats and stockings and discarded shawls.

Jack caught Hallie watching him as if trying to read his thoughts. Moving behind her, he scooped an armful of quilt and a slightly dented straw hat off the only chair in the room, pulled it closer to the bed and offered it to her. She sat down after a moment's hesitation, and Jack went to sit by his son.

Ethan perched on the edge of the bed, chewing on his lower lip as he eyed the box.

"Let's see what you've got there," Jack said, touching the lid.

He watched as Ethan carefully lifted the lid, almost as if he feared the box held something momentous—or nothing at all.

The faint smell of lilies lingered inside the box, stirring more memories for Jack. All these weeks, he'd fought to keep Ethan away from the saloon, telling himself the boy didn't need reminders of his past. Now he wondered if he himself needed to be protected from remembering, not Mattie, but the life he'd promised to turn his back on for good.

A lace handkerchief, yellowed at the edges, lay on top. Ethan gently picked it up and studied it a moment before putting it aside. "That was Ma's favorite. And this, too." He held up a silver coin, hung from the end of a watch chain. "She used to let me play with it. She said it was her treasure from the best night she ever had.''

Ethan proudly showed the coin to Hallie. She turned it over in her palm, rubbing the worn surface with her fingertip. ''That's a mighty fine treasure, Ethan. I'm sure your ma would be pleased to know you have it now.''

She handed it back to him and Ethan held it up for Jack to see.

Whatever Hallie expected him to do, she wasn't prepared for the odd way he looked as he stared at the coin in his son's hand. For a moment, he seemed to leave them for a place only he could see.

''Jack…what is it?''

''Nothing,'' he said, shifting suddenly as if shaking off a memory. ''I'm just surprised to see this, that's all.''

''Do you recognize it?'' Hallie asked.

Jack half smiled. ''It was mine.''

Both Hallie and Ethan looked at him, and after a moment's silence, Jack touched a finger to the box. ''I see your ma kept that fancy ribbon she liked so much.'' As Ethan drew out the frayed bit of shiny yellow satin, edged with lace, Jack added musingly, ''I bought that ribbon for your ma the first day we met because I wanted to see her smile. There was another girl here with a green one like it, and your ma had her eye on it from the start.''

''She liked pretty things,'' Ethan said.

''She was a pretty woman. I remember the bright yellow dress she wore that day, and how she tied that ribbon in her curls and wouldn't take it out for three days in a row.''

Toying with the end of the ribbon, Ethan didn't say anything. Then, lifting his head to look at Jack, he asked, "If you thought she was pretty, why didn't you stay with her?''

Hallie felt she might have walked out then and neither of them would have noticed. She hurt for them both—for Ethan, who didn't understand his mother or the choices she'd made, and for Jack, who only now had a chance to be a father.

And strangely, she ached inside, in a place that belonged only to her, because Jack would never think about her with that soft look in his eyes and remember her as pretty and laughing.

She told herself fiercely that she didn't want him to think of her that way, that she wanted to be more than just a pretty woman with a smile men longed to see. Pushing away her foolish yearnings, she looked back at Jack and could almost hear him considering the best answer to Ethan's hard question.

"Your ma and I were just friends," he said at last. "We didn't have enough time together to love each other. But I would have stayed and taken care of you both, if I had known about you. I hope that one day you'll believe that. I never would have left you behind.''

Even as he said the words, Jack wondered if they were true. Eight years ago, would he have accepted the responsibility of Mattie and a baby? He wanted to believe he would have, because of his own childhood. He hoped that even then he would have wanted more for his son.

And he hoped that Ethan would believe him now.

Ethan seemed to consider his words, looking hard at Jack. "You came back for me," he said at last.

"Yes. And I'm staying."

"Yeah? Well, I guess…" Ethan glanced around the room. "I guess I am, too. It's strange here now. I thought… Everything's different. It ain't like it used to be when Ma was here."

"No," Jack said quietly. "And it's not going to be again. We belong at the ranch now. This is the past. Maybe it's time to let it go."

"Are you going to let us stay there?" Ethan abruptly asked Hallie.

His sudden question took her aback. "Of course," she said. "It's your home now."

"Are you staying there, too?"

He asked the question without any apparent interest. But Hallie could see from the way he looked at her that her answer meant something to him.

Coming to sit next to him on the bed, Hallie put her hand on his shoulder. "It's where I belong, too. It's home. I'm not leaving."

Jack put his arm around Ethan, including Hallie in the embrace. "None of us is leaving. Besides," he said lightly, "we're just starting to get good at this ranching business. And Storm is going to need someone to train him to a saddle."

"And I'm going to need the both of you to help me finish digging out those ditches," Hallie added.

Jack and Ethan both let out a groan, and then the three of them started laughing.

"Come on," Jack said finally, getting to his feet and pulling Ethan and Hallie with him. "If we don't go now, Charlie and Eb are going to have our share of supper. Let's go home."

As they left the room, closing the door on Ethan's memories, Hallie thought that, for the first time, Jack calling the ranch home meant something to all three of them.

Hallie's lighthearted mood lasted as far as the swinging louvered doors of the Silver Snake.

Just as Jack pushed the doors open to usher them outside, a man built like a snake on stilts shoved the doors inward, nearly colliding with Hallie.

The man started to apologize, stopping midsentence when he spotted Jack behind her. "Jack Dakota, just the man I was lookin' for. I should've known I'd find you here. You saved me the trouble of askin' for you."

Hallie swiveled to look at Jack. He smiled at the newcomer, extending a hand, but she could tell the smile was pure cover for the irritation she saw in his eyes. It was obvious that, whoever the man was, Jack didn't relish running into him with her and Ethan around.

"What are you doing here, Mike?" he asked. "Last time I heard, you were making a living off the San Francisco hotels."

The man didn't seem to notice Jack's abruptness. "And the last time I saw you, you were picking the pockets of some lucky miners while trying to sweet-talk Miss Lucy Linn out of her petticoats.'' He eyed Hallie as if he couldn't quite believe Jack was with her. ''Where are those nice manners of yours, Jack? You haven't introduced me.''

As Jack made the introductions, Hallie decided she disliked Mike Mallory on sight. He smiled too much, talked too fast and never looked you straight in the eye.

''I thought you might be interested in knowin' Creed Walker is in town,'' Mallory said, dismissing Hallie and Ethan with a nod.

''Why would I be?'' Jack kept his tone deliberately neutral, but something quickened inside him at the name. Glancing at Hallie, he saw she'd noticed, and wished she hadn't.

Mallory snorted. ''Is this where I'm supposed to pretend you haven't been trying to get the best of Walker for the better part of ten years now?''

''I'd say it's been the other way around.''

''You could say it, but how about you prove it? Walker and me got a game up for tonight. We heard you were back here, and figured with you and your old friend Redeye, it'd be just like the old days.''

Jack tensed. ''Bill is going to be there?''

Mallory shrugged. ''If we can find him. He always hated losin' to you, so we figured he'd jump at the chance to best you for once. So, if you're not worried you'll be emptying your pockets for us in the first hour, then join us.''

Memories of his past games with Walker, and the illicit temptation of testing his luck for high stakes, goaded him, but even so, Jack might have resisted then and there if not for one other enticement—Redeye Bill Barlow.

He hadn't felt easy about Redeye since the day he'd set foot in Paradise. Their confrontation over Ben had been one too many for Redeye, that was obvious from the threats Redeye had tossed his way when they'd met at the hotel.

That meeting had given Jack a bad feeling. If there was a chance Redeye might wind up playing tonight, it could give him an opportunity to find out just how far his longtime enemy would go to settle a score—without putting Hallie and Ethan at risk.

Before good sense could kick in and Jack could think of any reason to say no, Ethan tugged at his sleeve. "You're gonna do it, ain't you?"

Jack exchanged a glance with Hallie. She stared at him without expression, but her eyes sparked. "Ethan, I—"

"You're better than they are," Ethan said. He looked contemptuously at Mallory. "No matter what anybody says. I'd sure like to see you beat 'em all," he added wistfully.

"And I'd like to have you with me," Jack said. "But you'd be better off breaking in those new britches at the ranch than learning from me how to win at cards."

Ethan didn't bother to hide his disappointment, but Hallie felt relieved Jack hadn't agreed to let him stay. It was bad enough knowing Jack would be at the saloon tonight. At least he had sense enough to keep his son at home.

She'd hoped, when he hesitated in jumping at Mallory's challenge, that he'd actually turn down the offer, especially when Mallory mentioned Redeye. Hadn't that low-down varmint caused them both enough trouble for one lifetime?

Just by looking at him, though, Hallie could tell Jack couldn't resist. Honestly, how could she have thought otherwise?

"I'll be back, as soon as I get them to the ranch," Jack told Mallory. "Keep a chair for me."

"Sure thing," Mallory said, "though it ain't like the old days, is it? Looks like your little woman here's got you walkin' the fence."

"Only on fine days," Jack replied easily.

Hallie, though, could see the barb had gotten under his skin, and her stomach clenched. As she went outside with him and Ethan, the fledgling hope she'd nursed during the day, that maybe he was at least tempted to settle down for good, died.

All during the drive back to the ranch, she only half listened to Ethan questioning Jack about the card game and who'd be there, and demanding Jack tell him all about it the next day.

As soon as Jack pulled the wagon to a halt, Ethan jumped down and raced to the barn to find Ben, wanting to show him his fancy coin. Hallie ignored the hand Jack offered her and climbed down on her own, grabbing their packages and starting toward the house without a word to him.

He stepped quickly in front of her, stopping her in her tracks. "I'd rather hear you say it, than pretend I'm not here."

"Fine." She crossed her arms over her chest and faced him squarely. "Good luck and we'll see you in the morning, if you're able to drag yourself out of bed."

"It's only a game."

"That's all it ever is with you, isn't it?"

"No, and I don't understand why you're so riled up about this one."

"No. You probably don't."

She made to push past him. Jack stepped in front of her again, blocking her way.

"I'm not making it that easy for you, darlin'." He stopped her attempt to sidestep him by taking hold of her shoulders. "It's only a couple of hours in town. I'm not leaving you."

"I'd be better off if you did," she retorted. "You've been nothing but trouble from the first time I laid eyes on you."

"Hallie—"

"Oh, go on, or you'll lose your chair! You need to be doing what you want to do. And if that means you'd rather be gambling than ranching, then that's all the better for me—"

Hallie abruptly stopped, embarrassed to find herself close to tears. It all came back to her in a flood of worry, fear and anger. She'd said almost those same exact words to her pa and to Ben, while they smiled and told her it was just a game, leaving her to fret about the ranch and all the people on it.

Now Jack was doing the same thing.

She couldn't depend on him. But she didn't have any choice.

She'd never had a choice when it came to Eden's Canyon.

The fight suddenly went out of her. Jack could see it in the slump of her shoulders and sheen of tears in her eyes. He hated seeing her that way. It stirred up guilty feelings in him he would have just as soon done without.

He considered explaining to her about Redeye, but he didn't want to upset her any more by bringing up the name again. She probably wouldn't believe Redeye was his main motive for playing tonight, anyway.

And truth be told, Redeye wasn't the only reason he'd agreed to the game. Jack didn't truly want to rein in the restless urge to return, if only for a few hours, to the life he felt completely at ease with, to taste that excitement again.

It didn't mean he would do anything to jeopardize the ranch or Hallie, or Ethan's future, although he doubted he could ever convince Hallie of that.

"I told Ethan I'm staying and I mean it," he said at last. "This is only one night. It doesn't mean anything to what we have here."

"It means everything. You just don't see that."

Jack's hands tightened on her. "I'm not your father, Hallie, and I'm not Ben."

She shook her head, but Ethan running up to them, Ben beside him, stopped her from saying anything more.

Ethan talked excitedly about the new mustangs Ben and Eb had brought in that day, and told Ben all about Jack's game. Ben's eyes lit up at the mention of it

until one look from Jack killed any ideas he'd started
to have about talking his way to the table.

Leaving Hallie to talk to Ben about the horses, Jack
walked Ethan to the house and helped him find a
place for his treasures on the dressertop in his room.
After repeating his promise to tell Ethan everything
about the game in the morning, he squeezed his son's
shoulder and started to tell him good-night.

Impulsively, Ethan threw his arms around him and
hugged tightly. "I'm glad you came back for me,"
he blurted out. Then just as quickly he let Jack go,
ducked his head and was out the door with a mumbled
explanation about needing to check on Storm.

Jack stood where Ethan left him, stunned. A rush
of satisfaction hit him that was so sweet he stayed
there for several minutes, savoring it.

He carried it with him a few minutes later when he
went to find Hallie, walking in on her and Serenity
setting out plates and pans in the kitchen.

Hallie raised a brow at the grin he wore, not sure
what to make of it or him.

She didn't want to waste time thinking about him.
But he made that impossible just by being Jack. Now
she tried instead to convince herself she had no call
to imagine he could ever care about the ranch or her
enough to trade his past for a life here.

It wasn't as if she cared about him, either, she told
herself, other than as her partner in business. She
didn't need him for any other reason.

Did she?

It wasn't as if she had any feelings for him.

Was it?

A woman would have to be crazy to give up even a little bit of her heart to a man like Jack Dakota.

Wouldn't she?

Hallie refused to listen to the taunting little whisper in her mind any longer. Averting her eyes, she asked, "You're leaving?"

"I'll be back, and in time to be up with the sun so I can help you with those mustangs tomorrow. You have my promise," he said. "Now wish me luck, darlin'."

Striding up to her, Jack made Serenity giggle and blush by catching Hallie by the shoulders, swinging her around and kissing her briefly but thoroughly on the lips.

"I can't lose now," he murmured against her ear. Then, with a wink and a smile, he was gone.

Chapter Fifteen

It was past midnight by the time Jack rode up the dirt drive to Eden's Canyon, his pockets jingling with coins, his head light with whiskey. He whistled a happy, if slightly off-key, tune, one he fancied Ace might enjoy on the ride home.

But his lighthearted mood faded when he saw the lamps still aglow at the ranch house.

Was Hallie waiting up to confront him? Or had something happened? Redeye had never showed up at the game. God forbid he'd paid Hallie and Ethan a visit, instead. Why the thought even crossed Jack's mind didn't really make any sense, except that he knew how much Redeye hated him and that the bastard was probably capable of anything, if he thought it would give him some kind of victory over Jack.

Jack gave Ace a swift kick and galloped up to the house. Relief washed over him when he saw Hallie standing on the front porch, with Tenfoot, Eb and Charlie around her. In the next instant, relief tightened into unease when he saw the looks on their faces.

Sliding off Ace, he tied his reins to the rail and

strode up the front porch steps. The gathering fell silent and he noticed that mud caked everyone's boots, clothes and faces. "What happened?"

Hallie glared at him, almost too angry to speak. "You would have known if you'd been here instead of at a poker table," she said through clenched teeth.

"Now, Hal, gettin' yourself all painted up for war ain't gonna help," Tenfoot said.

"A man's gotta have his vices," Big Charlie added.

Eb leaned over from his spot in the cane rocker to where Hallie stood stiffly. He laid a hand on her arm and spoke in a low voice. "Give the fella some rope, Hal. He ain't had a lot of time to get used to this kinda livin'."

Jack's patience snapped. "Is someone going to tell me what the hell is going on?"

Tenfoot paced across the porch. Realizing Hallie wasn't about to give Jack a decent answer, he decided to take the reins. "This afternoon, we found one of the irrigation ditches filled up in several spots."

"And?" Jack asked impatiently, not quite grasping the significance.

"And," Eb continued, "in this heat, we'll have cattle droppin' like flies without water."

"But I thought the ditches were full," Jack said. "I know we have to dig them out to improve the water flow, but I didn't realize they were that bad or I never would have gone to town today."

Hallie crossed her arms over her chest and faced him squarely. "That's just it. They were working fine. Someone deliberately stuffed the main ditch full of grass, shrubs, clumps of earth, branches, sticks—anything he could get his hands on to stop the water flow.''

''How's the herd?''

''Several of 'em are weak, and we may lose a few,'' Charlie said. ''Luckily, we caught it early enough so most of 'em weren't that bad off. But if Eb hadn't checked that particular main today…'' He held up his hands, his meaning clear.

Moving restlessly to the railing, Hallie gripped it so hard her fingers ached. ''Who knows? We all know!'' She whirled on the group. ''My herd—'' The remembrance that it wasn't hers anymore hit her hard, and she dug her nails into her palms to keep from shouting. She nodded sharply toward Jack. ''*His* herd would be dead.''

Jack wrestled with an equal mixture of guilt and frustration.

He shouldn't have gone back to town. Waiting around for Redeye to show up had been a waste of time. Sure, the game had been fun, had scratched an itch. But that didn't justify his not being here when he was needed. When he could have helped.

At the same time, he wondered when Hallie would get past this notion of hers that he spent all his waking time trying to find ways to undermine her authority. He might own the deed to Eden's Canyon, but everyone in the territory knew who was in charge.

''How are the ditches now?'' he asked, though the layers of mud on everyone's clothes gave him part of his answer.

''We dug a lot of it out this evenin' when Eb found

it," Tenfoot answered. He rubbed at his jaw as he sat down heavily on the swing. "But night closed in on us and we had to quit."

"Some water's gettin' through, but not near enough," Charlie added. "We'll need to get back at it come daybreak."

"Fine. I'll be there."

Hallie thought she might explode if she didn't let go of some of the fierce emotions rolling inside her. Now he wanted to take on the responsibility, now that the worst of the work was done. He'd probably been wasting money, one arm around a blonde in red satin, while they'd been fighting to save the herd.

"Don't bother," she snapped. "We can take care of this."

Jack turned on her fast, and she didn't need to see his expression to know she'd pushed him too far. "If I lose cattle, I lose profits. And if I lose profits, we all lose."

It was the first time he'd deliberately laid claim to the ranch without including her as his partner, and he might as well have slapped her.

Part of her knew he was reacting to her anger, but it still hurt. Suddenly, drained from hours of endless digging and shoveling out ditches, she felt too tired to fight him.

After all, he'd won it all the day he'd paid off her debts. And she had willingly agreed to stay on and keep the ranch going.

Right now, it seemed like the worst mistake she'd ever made.

She knew one thing, though. He might have won

poker games from Denver to Tombstone. He might have won the interest of countless females in a dozen counties. He might even have won the right to call Eden's Canyon his own.

But one thing he'd never win. Her heart.

"All right," she said, heading for the door. "I think enough's been said for one night. We all know where we stand."

Mumbles of agreement sounded all around, and the men said their good-nights and began to trudge back to the bunkhouse.

Jack realized he'd chosen the wrong time to assert his authority as owner of Eden's Canyon. He'd let her needling get to him, and for a few moments, his control had slipped. Being able to make him lose his composure goaded him more than anything else, because only Hallie could do it to him.

Following her inside, he took her elbow and stopped her from stalking off to her room. "Wait. Please."

"Let go of me."

"Look, Hal…" She tugged at his hold and he released her. Letting out a long breath, he shoved his hand through his hair, trying to come up with something to say that would take the edge off her anger. "I should have been here. But I did have reasons for staying in town other than just wanting to play poker."

Hallie faced him, searching his eyes. It seemed she wanted to tell him something, but then her expression hardened and she turned aside. "Save your explanations for someone who wants to hear them."

* * *

Despite his restless sleep, Jack made certain he was up before sunrise. He started the coffee, grabbed a leftover biscuit and headed out to saddle up Ace. Following the main irrigation ditch, and the trail of weakened and parched cattle, led him to where the channel was still clogged with debris.

Sliding off of Ace, he examined the grassy area at the edge of the first blocked passage. Several boot prints leading back and forth from the brush to the ditch made it clear that perhaps half a dozen men must have helped create the blockage that had wreaked so much havoc so quickly.

As Jack sat on his haunches near the prints, noting different sizes and shapes, Hallie and the others rode up. The ranch hands stopped a few feet upstream from him.

Hallie rode up next to Jack and stared down at him kneeling in the grass. "Doing penance this morning?" She almost regretted the jab as soon as it was out.

Jack rolled his eyes. At this rate, he'd never live last night down. He stood and looked up to where she sat in the saddle. "No, I don't have anything to repent. Though you're starting to make me wish I did."

Hallie smiled a little and handed her reins to him. She threw a leg over Grano and slid to the ground inches from Jack. He smelled of soap and leather. And when he smiled back, she felt a sweetness spread through her, easing the tense anger she'd held on to for too long.

"Okay, truce," she said, inching back a little to

keep from falling completely under his spell. "I was frustrated and worried, and digging in the mud for hours doesn't put one in the best of moods. Too much has happened around here lately. I just can't shake the feeling that someone is out to ruin me."

"Or me," Jack said quietly, unable to resist brushing a wild curl from the side of her face.

Hallie backed up a step. "Don't even try to sweet-talk me, or touch me like that. I'm still plenty riled at you."

"I can see that. And maybe someone else is, too."

"You?" She let out a little laugh. "Mr. Charming? I don't think so. It's me. And I've got a good idea who wants to see me fail."

"Peller."

"The one and only."

Tenfoot rounded the backside of her horse then and jammed a shovel in her hand. "You'd make better use of your time with this than with your crazy ideas about Whit Peller."

"Hallie, what proof do you have?" Jack tried to smooth Tenfoot's blunt attempt to throw water on her fire.

"Why, Dakota, that's a good point. And since you're here today, you can take my place," she said, thrusting the shovel into *his* hand. Taking her reins from his other hand, she swung back into the saddle. "I'm going to go on over and get myself some proof right now."

Jack and Tenfoot exchanged an exasperated glance. As Hallie whirled her mount around, the cowboy slapped Jack on the back. "Nice goin', partner. Now she's gonna fix everything up just fine."

"Hal! Come back! That's not the way to—"

But determined as a hawk after a prairie dog, she kicked Grano into a gallop across the grassland, heading in the direction of the Peller spread.

Jack jammed the shovel into the ground. Shaking his head and cursing under his breath, he sank his boots into the ditch and started shoveling.

Tenfoot stared after her. "Ain't you goin', too?"

"If I go now, she'll only think I'm trying to undermine her position as ranch boss, more than she already does."

"That's what's gonna happen, anyhow. Whether anyone likes it or not, it's your ranch now. Might as well settle it between you two before she gets herself into real trouble."

Utter frustration forcing his hand, Jack jammed the shovel into the side of the ditch and untied Ace's reins from a nearby tree. He swung his leg over the stallion and looked back over his shoulder at Tenfoot.

"It's not even about the ranch anymore."

Jack caught up with Hallie just as she reined in her horse a few yards from Peller's front door. Jack slid off Ace before the stallion came to a skidding stop, and sprinted around her to block her headlong rush toward the house.

"Don't," she said, holding up a hand as if to ward him off. "I have to do this."

"Not now. You're too mad to think straight. All you're going to do is buy yourself more trouble."

"All I'm going to do is finish this. It's gone on long enough." Hallie tried to think of the words that would make him understand. "Don't you see? I'm responsible. If I let him do this, there won't be any Eden's Canyon. I can't let that happen. I won't."

"And what if you're wrong? What if it's not Peller?"

For a moment, a sliver of doubt made a crack in Hallie's belief in Peller as the man trying to ruin her—to ruin them. She immediately pushed it away. "I'm not wrong. It has to be him."

Before she could slip around Jack, the door of the house opened and Whit Peller stepped out, coming off the porch toward them. Behind him, Rachel hovered in the doorway, her hands pressed tightly together as she watched them.

"Well now, we weren't expectin' visitors," Peller said. He smiled, but a tenseness around his eyes and jaw betrayed his outward show of friendliness. "You look like a lady with a problem, Miss Hallie."

"I am," Hallie said, before Jack could soften the blow. "In the past few days, someone's blocked up our main drainage ditch. We've lost nearly a dozen head so far."

Peller frowned. "You're sure it was deliberate?"

"I'm sure. It's not the first time we've had trouble in the past few weeks. We lost six calves, and there was a stampede I can't explain. Then, while we were out on roundup, someone shot at us."

"Rustlers?"

"I don't think so," Hallie said. "I think someone wants us to give up Eden's Canyon."

"And you think it's me." Now Peller was clearly annoyed. He swung his eyes to Jack. "You with her on this?"

Jack wanted to back Hallie, to show Peller she wasn't alone in her suspicions about everything that had gone wrong lately. He hadn't missed her talking as if she and Jack had an equal stake in the ranch. It made him feel, for the first time, as if she truly thought of him as a partner, not just an obstacle she'd gotten stuck with.

On the other hand, he also wanted to keep Peller from getting mad enough to kick them off his land. They'd never get any answers then.

"We're just trying to find out the truth," Jack said at last.

"It don't sound that way to me. If you're accusin' me, Miss Hallie, then get on your horse and ride into town and bring the sheriff back with you."

"Sheriff?" Rachel hurried off the porch to her husband's side. She reached out a hand to Hallie in appeal. "Why, you can't think Whit had anything to do with this."

"Now, Rachel—" Whit began.

Jack held up a hand. "No one's calling in the sheriff." Hallie made a movement beside him, and Jack knew she itched to do just that. "But everyone knows you were pressing Hallie to sell the ranch, even before her father died."

Peller's mouth pulled into a hard line and he appeared on the verge of telling them to go to hell. Rachel put her hand on his forearm. "Whit…"

"It's okay, honey," he said, forcing a smile for her.

He turned back to Hallie. "You want the truth? The truth is I knew about your pa's gambling debts. Hell, everyone in Paradise knew. I figured your pa would be willing to sell to clear them. He turned me down every time. When he passed on…" Peller shrugged. "I thought you might be glad to be rid of the responsibility."

"I'll never give up Eden's Canyon without a fight."

"I figured that out real fast, Miss Hallie," Peller said with just a touch of a smile. "You know, I could have bought your place from the bank. But I didn't think it was right to run you off your land so quick after your pa died. Most of the other ranchers around here felt the same. That's why a stranger ended up with it."

Peller stared pointedly at Jack.

Jack didn't flinch. "I didn't know. I needed a place and it was for sale."

They all looked at Hallie and she felt a slow heat burn up her neck into her face. She began to wish she'd listened to Jack and waited until her temper cooled to confront Peller. Now she started to have the sickening feeling she'd just made a first-class fool out of herself.

Except for one thing Peller had said that didn't quite ring true. "I can hardly believe anyone in Paradise holds me in such high regard that they'd pass on buying Eden's Canyon."

Peller shrugged. "Everyone knows it was you keepin' that ranch together, long before your pa died.

Your pa and that brother of yours were always much better gamblers than they were ranchers.''

"She's taught me more than a thing or two about running a spread," Jack said, grinning at Hallie. "I wouldn't have lasted a week without Miss Hallie."

Whit laughed outright. "To tell you the truth, we figured you wouldn't last a week anyhow. You were so green when you came to town, we decided you wouldn't know a cow unless it was dished up in stew."

Hallie didn't know which embarrassed her more, their praise of her or her complete turnaround from thinking Peller guilty enough to be hanged, to innocent.

She straightened her spine and looked her neighbor straight in the eye. "I'm sorry I suspected you. I was wrong."

"No harm done," Peller said. "Do you have any ideas about who it could be?"

Hallie started to confess she hadn't the first idea, when Jack spoke up. "A few," he said, surprising her. She tried to figure out if he meant it, but his expression didn't tell her anything.

"Well, I don't know about all of you," Rachel said, "but I've had enough of standing about in this sun. Why don't we all go inside and have a glass of lemonade?"

"That sounds like the best idea I've heard all day, ma'am," Jack said.

He touched a hand to Hallie's waist while they went inside, and stayed close to her as Whit showed them into the elegant front parlor.

Hallie tried to keep from fidgeting after she'd perched on the edge of the dainty little couch and sat waiting for Rachel to fetch the drinks. Jack stood next to her, his hand resting casually on the cushion behind her, not touching her, yet near enough to make it obvious he offered his support to her.

Now that they'd gotten past her mistaken accusations, Peller relaxed and talked easily to Jack about the problems of owning such a large spread.

Hallie caught Jack glancing at her from the corner of his eye more than once. After a few minutes, he drew her into the conversation, and she found herself in a spirited debate with Peller over which breed of longhorns made for better beef.

She expected her awkwardness to come back when Rachel returned with their drinks and she found herself seated next to her hostess. Instead, with Jack there, approval clear in his eyes, she felt more sure of herself, even confident.

She could even see a bit of humor in the scene. What a pretty pair they must make—Rachel in her dainty flowered dress and her smooth chignon, sitting next to Hallie Ryan, the hoyden of Paradise.

Rachel didn't seem to take any notice, though, and chatted to Hallie about small daily household things Hallie was familiar with.

"This is a nice room," Hallie said impulsively, looking again around the parlor. It was too fussy for her liking, but there was a restful warmth about it, and it was obvious every item there had been chosen with loving care.

Rachel smiled, following her gaze. "Thanks to

Whit. I wasn't too pleased about moving here from Ohio. But Whit did all he could to make it nice for me. Now I can't imagine living anywhere else.''

"Good thing, too," Whit said, winking at Rachel. "I'm gettin' too old to be lookin' around for another wife.''

"You mean you couldn't find one willing to put up with your ways," Rachel countered.

They smiled at each other, obviously sharing some private joke. Watching them, Hallie felt something tug inside her.

She found herself meeting Jack's gaze, knowing he was watching her. They looked at each other and it was as if he somehow understood the inexplicable longing seeing the loving relationship between the Pellers had stirred in her.

For a moment, it felt as if she and Jack were alone in the room. Then Whit's question about her corrals broke the odd sensation, and the four of them talked a little longer before Jack and Hallie got up to leave.

Both Rachel and Whit made them promise to come back with Ethan and Ben one evening for supper, waving them off as they started back to Eden's Canyon.

"You were right," Hallie said to Jack, when they'd ridden a fair distance from the Peller house.

He glanced at her, his face hidden in the shadow cast by his Stetson. "I was?"

"I shouldn't have gone off like that, ready to string him up."

Jack started to make some teasing reply. He stopped himself, seeing how hard it was for her to admit she was wrong, especially to him. "You did what you thought was right for the ranch. And as it turned out, we made some new friends."

Hallie nodded, keeping her eyes fixed ahead as they neared the boundary of Eden's Canyon.

Jack left her alone with her thoughts. He figured she'd had enough for one day, and only hoped whatever she was thinking was less disturbing than the notions in his head.

He'd bet his last dollar, though, she already knew that although Peller was innocent, someone out there was waiting for his next chance to ambush them.

Chapter Sixteen

Hallie scratched a few more entries on the ledger page, then rubbed at her forehead, stifling a yawn. She hated working with figures. But the task had at least one redeeming factor: it distracted her from thinking about anything—or anyone—else. Almost.

After her confrontation with Peller, she'd had plenty of time to consider the obvious. If Peller wasn't responsible for the trouble they'd had, then someone else was. The answer was a long way from obvious, and Hallie had run her brain in circles thinking about it. She needed to learn the truth, but she didn't know where to look for it.

Despite that, she was about to push all those worrisome thoughts aside until tomorrow when footsteps sounded behind her, and before she could turn, a hand reached out and plucked her pen out of her fingers and tossed it aside.

"I don't allow anyone on my ranch to work this late," Jack said in her ear.

"Well, you can rest easy. I was just about to turn in." Dousing the oil lamp on the desk, Hallie slid sideways out of her chair and started toward the other lamp burning in the parlor.

Jack beat her to it. With one swift motion, he flicked off the lamp. Only the moonlight brightened the darkness. "Now you're finished." He reached out and took her hand. "Come on."

The night shadows made it impossible to see his expression clearly, but Hallie heard the laughter and anticipation in his voice.

She sighed. She wasn't in the mood tonight for his games. She'd given up being angry with him over deciding to gamble the night away. However, it was a sore point that still lay between them, waiting to be settled, and she didn't want to try to settle it tonight.

"I have a surprise for you," Jack said as he gently tugged her toward the front door. Her feelings had been made clear in that one expressive sigh, and he knew they needed to talk. But not now.

"I suppose you'll stick to me like a burr and annoy me until I go with you," she grumbled, allowing him to lead her outside to where he had tied Ace to the front porch railing.

She eyed Jack suspiciously as he freed Ace's reins and offered her a hand into the saddle, swinging up behind her. "Where are we going?"

"You'll see," was all he would say while they rode away from the house.

"Jack..." she began warningly.

"Just enjoy the ride, Miss Hallie," he murmured, leaning in close so she felt his breath on her cheek.

"Do I have a choice?"

"Sure. But it's better if we both simply relax."

Hallie couldn't think of anything suitable to say to that so she gave up trying to figure out what he had in mind and took his advice, letting Ace's smooth pace and the press of Jack's body against her back lull her into a kind of peacefulness.

They rode toward the foothills, until they reached a small outcropping of rock. Pulling Ace to a stop, Jack offered Hallie a hand down, tethering the stallion before taking her hand and leading her up to where the rocks flattened out to form a small plateau.

Hallie waited near the edge, gazing out at the night-time vista of land and stars, while Jack fidgeted a moment with something behind her. Suddenly, a pale golden glow sprang up around them, and Hallie turned to see him spreading out a blanket beside the lamp he'd lit.

"What's the matter," she teased, "didn't you get enough of sleeping on the ground during the roundup?"

Jack smiled back at her. "Sleeping, yes. This is just dessert."

"Dessert?"

He laughed at her confused expression. "Dessert," he said, holding up his saddlebag. "You skipped it at suppertime, and as far as I'm concerned, that means you missed the best part. I'm remedying that now.

"Besides..." he beckoned her to sit by him on the blanket "...you work and worry too hard. You need to forget your troubles once in a while."

"One of us has to work and worry," she bantered back. But there was no edge in her words, and she came to sit across from him, watching as he took a bottle, two tin cups and a small box from the saddle-bag.

"Here," he said, pulling off the lid and offering her the box. "Try one of these. They're chocolate. You'll like them, I promise."

Looking at the small piece he gave her, Hallie asked, "Where did you get it? I don't recall anything like this at Bellweather's."

"That's my secret," Jack said with a wink. When she looked unconvinced, he added, "You don't think I play for money all the time, do you? Go ahead, try it."

Hallie tentatively nibbled at the confection, then a slow smile spread over her face. "Oh, this is wonderful. I've never—" She popped the whole nugget into her mouth, closing her eyes to savor it.

Jack followed the tip of her tongue as she licked the taste from her lips. Looking away quickly, he poured her a cupful of wine and handed it to her. "Now this is wonderful. Besides, it's the best way to eat chocolate. I promise you, I've learned from experience."

"Does this have something to do with Miss Lucy Linn and her petticoats?" Hallie asked, looking at him over the rim of her cup with innocent eyes that didn't fool him for a minute.

"Not exactly." Jack shifted closer to her so his shoulder brushed hers. He put his own cup aside, freeing his hand to lightly stroke down her cheek. "Since you asked, though, there is one more ingredient we need to make this perfection."

Sliding his fingers into her hair, Jack touched his

mouth to hers, softly at first, tasting the sinful mix of chocolate and wine. Hallie rewarded his efforts by putting her arms around his neck and kissing him back, once more turning his game into something deeper and more disturbing.

Something more exciting.

"So what do you think of my dessert recipe?" he asked, when they finally pulled a little apart, breathless.

Hallie appeared to consider his question carefully. "Mmm, maybe a little more chocolate," she said, then burst out laughing when he shook his head and feigned exasperation.

"Next time I'll leave the chocolate and wine behind so there won't be anything to distract you from the real treat."

Hallie responded when he kissed her again, leaning in closer to him and liking the feel of him under her hands and against her mouth. But after a few minutes, he eased back, searching her eyes.

"What is it?"

"What…? Nothing," she said. She put her hand to his face to draw him back to her, but Jack resisted.

"It's something." He leaned back, studying her, then suddenly snapped his fingers. "Damn, I knew I should have checked to make sure I had all of you before we left. I've gone and left half your attention back at the house."

"I suppose you think you're funny."

"Maybe a little. Tell me," he said, taking her hand. His thumb drew slow circles against her palm. "What is it?"

Hallie sighed. "It's everything that's happened. After today, I don't know what to think. I was so sure it was Peller."

"Well, it's certainly someone who doesn't think kindly of us."

"I've been thinking about that, and maybe I was wrong before. You must know dozens of people who fit that description," Hallie said.

Jack's hand stilled on hers. His face didn't show it, but Hallie felt the tension spring up in him. "Probably," he answered without looking at her. "But I don't know too many who'd get any satisfaction from causing me bits and pieces of trouble. If they wanted to settle a score, they'd just shoot me and be done with it."

Even though he said it flippantly, a cold shiver chased over Hallie. "Someone already tried that."

"They didn't try too hard," Jack said, giving her hand a squeeze. That incident bothered her more than the rest, although he didn't want to consider the reason why too closely. All he wanted to do now was reassure her, to take some of the worry away and coax her into sharing a little of that responsibility she carried around like a lead weight on her slender shoulders.

"Well, you're inviting them to finish the job when you run off to play cards every time one of your disreputable friends comes to town," she retorted.

"Ah, I knew we'd get around to that." Jack took both her hands in his and tugged her around to face him. "Which bothers you more, my leaving or the gambling? Are you afraid I'll turn out like your father, leaving you alone with nothing but debts and trouble?''

"It's not like that," she protested, but her words lacked conviction.

"Hallie…" Jack let go of one of her hands to cup her chin. "We're in this together, for as long as it lasts. You have my word. I don't want to take your place at Eden's Canyon. I want us to make it work together."

The caress of his fingers on her face tempted Hallie to forget all the talk and go back to kissing him. It was so much simpler when they didn't have to think about all the whys and why nots. Unfortunately, the questions wouldn't quit pestering them.

"It may not last much longer, if we don't find out who's got a grudge against you," she said.

Jack let her go, shaking his head in exasperation. "There's no one in Paradise who—"

He abruptly broke off. Hallie looked up at him, questioning. "What?"

"Nothing," Jack said. For a moment, an image of Redeye Bill Barlow had flashed into his thoughts. Barlow certainly carried a grudge, but all the trouble they'd had seemed like too much time away from the gaming tables for him. "I was just thinking about my disreputable friends," he finished, catching Hallie looking at him expectantly. "Speaking of disreputable, what about someone from your past?"

"My past?" Hallie laughed at the very idea. "What could possibly be in my past that would bring all this on?"

"Your father was a gambler and Ben's done his

share. Maybe it's someone with a grudge against them.''

"That's ridiculous!"

"Is it?"

"Of course! Ben is just a kid and my father…my father would never have… Neither of them would have gotten themselves into that kind of trouble,'' she ended as she pushed herself to her feet.

She walked a few paces from Jack, feeling suddenly edgy and unsettled. She wanted to be mad at him for even suggesting such a thing about her family. The truth was, she hated to admit he might be right.

Behind her, Jack stood and came up beside her. "It's just something to think about."

"We'd be better off thinking about somebody from your past," she said stubbornly. "I'd say that was a better bet."

"What we should be doing—" Jack took her by the shoulders "—is working together to resolve this, not fighting each other."

"I know," Hallie said, so quietly it was almost a whisper. She tried a smile. "I'm not quite used to this sharing part yet, I guess. I don't want to fight with you. You're right. We do better on the same side."

Jack answered her with his crooked grin. "Yeah, we do. And we both need to work on the sharing, although we haven't done too badly." He pulled her to him and held her against his heart, gently stroking her back. "We just need a little more practice."

Hallie put her arms around him in turn. For tonight it was enough simply to be in his arms. It felt so good.

Yet at the same time they had so much between them, unresolved, that she couldn't help but wonder if it would always keep them apart.

The next evening, Hallie was finally nearly finished with the books when Serenity burst in without a warning or a knock.

"You *have* to go to the dance!" she said without any preliminaries.

"Serenity—"

The girl stood next to her, twisting her hands against her pale blue skirts. "Mr. Dakota said you weren't going. Charlie is taking Miss Elizabeth, and Tenfoot went to town. Eb's not going, and I can't go alone with Mr. Dakota. It wouldn't look right."

Hallie rubbed at the ache between her eyes. "Isn't Ben taking you?"

"He was supposed to, but he's not back from town."

"I'm not surprised, but if he promised you he may show yet." Hallie shook her head and pushed her ledger book aside.

"But if he doesn't, I can't go tonight," Serenity said. "And I need to be there."

"Why do you *need* to go to the dance?"

Serenity pulled her shawl tighter around her shoulders. "Oh, Miss Hallie, I care a lot for Ben, and he's the only one I want to be with. But if he doesn't turn out to be a man I can depend on, then I need to find someone else. Besides…" She studied her hands to avoid looking at Hallie. "Drew Peller asked me to go with him. I said no because of Ben, but Drew will be there and…''

"You're so young, Serenity," Hallie told her. "You have plenty of time to think of all that."

"I'm eighteen already. Where I come from girls are usually married by thirteen or fourteen, and have several children by the time they're twenty."

"But you're not a part of that life anymore. And here you'll be your husband's only wife for as long as you both live, so why the hurry to get settled?"

"Well, no offense, Miss Hallie," Serenity said, fidgeting with the tassels on her shawl. "You've been real nice to me and all."

After a long, uncomfortable pause, Hallie pushed herself away from her desk. "Go on. You can speak your mind."

Finally, Serenity looked directly at Hallie. "You see, I've been watching you."

"Me?"

The girl nodded. "You work so hard, all alone, running things around here, doing a man's work and more. Not that the others don't help, but look who's up doing the books now when everyone else is already at the dance. Everything from sunup to sundown around here begins and ends with you."

Hallie had started to stand up, but sank back into her chair.

"I don't want to be alone like that." Serenity pressed on. "I want a man around to take care of the big things, the things I'm afraid of or that are just plain too hard to do. And if I don't find someone to be that kind of a man for me while I'm pretty and young, then—'' she glanced around the room lined with books and papers, all involved with the weighty matter of running the ranch ''—then I might never find anyone.''

Hallie couldn't say anything for a moment. Serenity's words churned up emotions in her she didn't want or need.

Was that how she appeared to the others? As some sort of tireless ox, born and bred for work alone? Not liking the image, but finding no way to get rid of it, she sighed.

''Why not just go with Jack and Ethan? I'm sure they'd be willing to take you, and you're too young for anyone to think anything of it.''

Serenity looked doubtful. ''Haven't they left already?''

''I don't think so. Jack tried earlier to press me to go, and when I kept refusing he told me he wouldn't leave until I changed my mind.''

''I'll go and see if they've gone,'' Serenity said. She hesitated at the door. ''Won't you change your mind, please? He might not go if you won't.''

Hallie smiled. ''I'm sure that once you explain your situation, he'll be pleased to come to your rescue, with or without me.''

With a shy smile and a delicate shrug of her shoulders, Serenity turned and hurried out of Hallie's office.

Hallie busied herself with clearing away her papers and pen, deliberately avoiding thinking about the image Serenity had painted of her.

If that was what the others thought of her, then it

was all well and good. She'd never shied away from responsibility. She took pride in her ability to run the ranch. All that nonsense about needing a man at her side didn't apply to her.

Did it?

When Jack, Serenity and Ethan appeared in the doorway a few minutes later, she didn't notice them until Ethan spoke up. "Evenin', Miss Hallie."

She started, caught staring blindly at the wall.

Jack, standing behind Ethan, smiled as if he guessed what she'd been doing. He looked impossibly handsome, his whiskey-and-sunshine hair falling in an easy wave over his brow, his white shirt stretched across his broad chest and accented by a coffee-colored leather vest.

Ethan, too, had already begun to take on his father's style. Sandy hair brushed neatly off his brow, wearing his new black boots and his slender leather bolo tie, he looked polished and sharp, ready and equal to any challenge the evening might present.

And Serenity looked lovely—every bit the flower ready to bloom beneath the right mix of sun and rain, love and attention.

Hallie caught a glimpse of herself in the bookshelf glass and almost laughed at the contrast. Her skin too rosy and tanned from the sun and wind, her hair springing out of a loose braid, her shirt and pants baggy, dirty and disheveled, she would never be the belle of the ball.

"We're hoping you've changed your mind," Jack said, both challenge and anticipation in his face.

"You'll come with us, won't you?" Serenity echoed.

Ethan nodded. "We want you to come, Miss Hallie."

Somewhere inside, Hallie felt a pang of longing. Part of her, a part she'd never dared indulge until Jack Dakota had come along, ached to go with them, felt the need to do something enjoyable and lighthearted.

But, she hastened to remind herself, last night's surprise dessert with Jack had been pleasant. That was enough. Being alone with him, relaxing, was all the social mixing she wanted.

She couldn't—wouldn't—encourage any part of her that wanted more. So many times she'd given in to Jack's tempting offers to play, and forgotten her responsibilities. She had to remember her work came first. She didn't need anything else.

Of course she didn't.

"Like I told you, I don't go to dances." She backed away from her desk and stood, waving them off. "But you all go on or you'll miss the music and dancing."

The light in Jack's eyes faded. Hallie expected him to try to tease or challenge her into going along. Instead, for the first time, he seemed to accept her words with an air of resignation.

He laid his hands on Ethan's shoulders, turning the boy away. "All right. If you insist on staying here alone, then there's nothing more we can do. Good night."

With a wistful glance over her shoulder to Hallie, Serenity followed Jack and Ethan to the front door.

The instant the front door shut, an onslaught of regrets blindsided Hallie. She felt left out, alone, disappointed.

"What nonsense," she muttered to the empty room.

Moving out of the study, she drifted into the parlor, stopping by the piano to plunk out a few notes. She'd never regretted missing a social event. And in fact, she preferred an evening of quiet and solitude where she could catch up on things uninterrupted.

Besides, she didn't even know how to dance.

She was better off avoiding social gatherings. She'd only wind up saying the wrong thing or feeling foolish.

Deciding to find something to keep her busy, she went in the direction of the kitchen, thinking she'd check the pantry supplies. But her mind refused to focus.

Instead, when she stared at the cans and sacks, she saw Jack's smiling, handsome face. He'd have every woman at the dance swooning over him before the night was over. And he'd be dancing his way through a crowd of women looking for husbands.

And what a catch he was! With his charming manners, good looks and a successful ranch, what woman wouldn't jump at the chance to try to seduce him into marriage?

Images of Jack dancing with this woman and that one, each set on capturing him for herself, annoyed Hallie. Of course, he'd probably lead them all on, too, with that lopsided smile and his easy ways. He'd win their hearts without any intention of claiming them.

Slamming the pantry door shut, she walked back to the parlor, restlessly pacing the room and finally settling on the piano stool. The clock on the mantel ticked on relentlessly. She ran her fingers over the piano keys and thought of Jack sitting here, playing her a sweet ballad.

What was he doing now? Who was he dancing with? Why should she care?

She shouldn't.

But she did.

The question was, what was she going to do about it?

Stay here and make herself loco imagining things? She'd never given in to such silliness before.

Or she could do something about it. She could stop feeling sorry for herself, stop shutting herself off from everyone and everything but Eden's Canyon, dig that green dress out of her cedar chest and go see for herself what he was up to.

Jack had proved time and again that he liked her, Hallie Ryan, and wanted her with him. Now she had to prove it to herself.

Chapter Seventeen

Jack twirled a young lady, whose name he'd already forgotten, on his arm in a lively reel. He'd had no lack of partners since he'd arrived at the community hall, but somehow the whole affair wasn't the pleasant distraction he'd planned.

The three-piece ensemble with fiddle, piano and harmonica were playing out their hearts and souls to the grateful crowd, who stood clapping, tapping their toes and whooping out calls to the girls.

He ought to be having a great time. Ethan seemed to be, after all. Jack had been watching his son as, shyly at first, he went from one little girl to the next and asked them to dance. The smile on his boyish face and the bit of cockiness and swagger in his walk grew with every success.

Only once had he shied away. And that was when Jessica James had asked him to dance. Jack watched the two bantering, his son shaking his head, Jessica pulling him by his hand. In the end the girl had won, practically dragging Ethan to the center of the floor.

Since that dance, though, Ethan hadn't looked for another partner.

Even Big Charlie seemed to be enjoying himself, dancing and talking with Elizabeth. The two stood to the side now, watching Ethan and Jessica, pointing and whispering like watchful parents.

The sight turned Jack's thoughts immediately to Hallie. He wanted her here to see Ethan, smiling, happy, at ease, the way a child should be.

He knew she'd be sharing the moment with him, feeling the same satisfaction he felt. They had somehow become that close.

How could he convince her that people could and would accept her if she only gave them a chance?

He and Ethan had been greeted tonight with genuine warmth and kindness, quite opposite to the cool reception Ethan in particular had faced in the past. Together with him and Ethan, Hallie would be just as welcome.

At last the dance came to a stop and Jack absently thanked his partner. As he backed away from the whirl of couples, he realized he'd practically ignored the girl throughout the dance because his real partner, in mind and spirit anyway, had been Hallie.

Hallie?

It took Jack a full minute to convince himself it was Hallie there, not some vision he'd conjured up by thinking about her every moment since he'd left the ranch.

She'd not only come, but she'd worn the dress he'd bought her. He'd been right about one thing: she looked beautiful in the soft green, with her hair loosely tied back. He just never expected she would look so…different.

As though the sheer force of his willing her there had drawn her to him, he indulged in the sight of her, a vision in the dress that hugged her every curve and lit up her eyes.

She was a beauty, beyond his imaginings, and he felt a surge of pride, and an even stronger rush of desire.

He wanted her now more than ever. Yet something foolish and boyish turned his feet to lead. Words failed him. Every move, every gesture, every turn of a phrase that came so effortlessly with any other woman, abandoned him. All he wanted to do was to walk over to her and ask her to dance.

Yet, at this moment, all he *could* do was stand there gaping like a love-struck boy.

Rosa accidentally nudged his arm on her way to the punch bowl, and Jack scarcely acknowledged her apology, his eyes fixed on Hallie as he gathered his confidence and strode through the crowd toward her.

Having gotten as far as the door, Hallie poised there, trying to hold on to her slippery courage. She was relieved to see Jack notice her there, until she saw the expression on his face. He appeared almost stunned, and she couldn't tell if it was because she'd shown up in a dress or shown up at all.

"You're here," he said, coming up to her.

Hallie couldn't resist a smile. "Obviously. Although from the expression on your face you'd think you'd never seen me before."

Jack lifted her hand and raised it to his lips, brushing a lingering kiss against her knuckles. "You look beautiful."

"You look silly. You're staring," she said, aware that nearly everyone close to them was staring, too. It didn't matter so much, though, with Jack gazing at her like that, as if he wanted to do much more than simply hold her hand.

"Hallie! You came after all!"

Serenity's voice intruded, and Jack reluctantly let go of Hallie's hand. He suddenly didn't want to be here. He wanted to whisk Hallie back out the door, away from everyone.

"Where's Ben?" Hallie was asking Serenity. "I thought you came to find him."

Serenity glanced over her shoulder. "Oh, I don't know. He wasn't happy about my dancing with Drew." A small smile curved her mouth. "It was only one dance."

"One too many, apparently," Jack said with an answering grin. "You're a wicked woman, Miss Serenity."

He laughed at Serenity's blush, but Hallie wondered if he'd still be laughing if she herself decided to dance with one of the men eyeing her now.

She immediately dismissed the notion. It felt strange to have them staring at her, although she suspected that was due more to the novelty of seeing Hallie Ryan in a dress than because she was so lovely.

Casting a sideways look at Jack, she caught him watching her. He smiled and she hastily looked away. Then, unable to resist, she glanced back to find him still looking at her with that smile that made her breath catch.

A cowboy from the Peller ranch claimed Serenity for a dance, and Jack was about to tempt Hallie outside for a few minutes when Ethan saw them together and rushed over to say hello to Hallie.

"You sure look pretty," the boy said. "Like a real girl."

"Ethan—" Jack began, but Hallie only laughed.

"Thank you, Ethan," she said, "that's a fine compliment."

"I see I'm going to have to teach you a few things about charming the ladies, Son," Jack said, smiling and shaking his head.

"Why do I need to learn *that?*" Ethan scrunched up his nose. "That's no use on the ranch."

"Oh, no," Jack said, slapping his forehead in mock despair. "She's turned him into a rancher. I see there's no hope of my son ever being disreputable now."

Hallie nudged Ethan. "I think he's trying to be funny again."

Ethan grinned and the three of them laughed together, talking for a few minutes until Jessica came up in a whirl of pink calico and petticoats to tug Ethan over to the lemonade.

The fiddlers struck up another tune, this one more slow and dreamy, and Jack took advantage of the moment to pull Hallie into his arms and whirl her around on the square of floor being used for dancing.

"Jack," she protested, "I don't know how to do this."

"Just follow me and don't think too much about it. You'll get the idea."

Hallie got the idea that Jack's notion of dancing—holding her close, caressing her hand, focusing all his attention on her—wasn't exactly the conventional way, from the interested and knowing looks they kept getting.

"If you don't stop, no one is ever going to believe we're just partners," she whispered. "They're all going to think—well, you know."

"Mmm...wouldn't that be too bad?"

"Jack!"

"Are you still mad at me?"

"Mad?" Hallie couldn't remember why she was supposed to be, and didn't care. Right now, she didn't want to think about anything else but the way Jack made her feel. "No," she said softly, looking up into his eyes. "I'm not mad."

Jack smiled and tightened his hold on her a fraction. "You know, one of the things I'll always love about you is that I never know where I stand. You're a challenge, Hallie Ryan, and something tells me you always will be."

Spinning around with her on the dance floor, Jack sensed a difference about her, as if something between them had subtly changed. Unexpectedly, she'd chosen to meet him halfway tonight, to put aside work and responsibility, and risk her pride in a situation where she so often felt out of place.

"Why did you change your mind?" he asked, moving away just enough so he could look in her eyes.

"I didn't want you to take your plan to become respectable too far by letting one of these women talk you into marriage," Hallie answered honestly. A little embarrassed at the meaning he might give to that, she added, "Where would I be then?"

"Women? Are there other women here?"

"You've probably danced with most of them."

"Why, Hallie Ryan, if I didn't know you better, I'd say you were jealous." When she blushed, he smiled, that endearing, lopsided smile that always made her heart turn over. "You shouldn't say things like that unless you mean them."

Jack swept her closer and around in a whirl, until they were both lost in the dance and each other.

All too soon for him the music ended and they were almost immediately surrounded by people greeting Hallie, talking, avid to know just what the relationship was between Hallie and her gambler.

Whit distracted Jack from Hallie by asking him a question about their irrigation ditch. By the time he'd answered and talked with Whit a few minutes, Hallie was on the other side of the room, chatting to Rachel and Rosa.

Seeing Jack's focus on Hallie, Rosa nudged her. "He certainly has his eye on you."

Hallie didn't need to ask who had inspired Rosa's knowing smile. She glanced over Rachel's shoulder and easily found Jack. He smiled at her and she returned his smile until she realized both Rosa and Rachel were eyeing her with avid interest.

"He's not—we're not…we're just friends," Hallie finished in a rush. Neither of the women looked convinced, and Hallie couldn't blame them. She didn't sound convincing to herself.

Rachel arched a brow. "Of course."

"Of course we don't believe you," Rosa said with a good-natured laugh.

Starting to refute them, Hallie stopped. All these weeks, she'd been telling herself over and over that she and Jack were just partners, barely even friends.

But Jack was the reason she had come tonight. Maybe it was time to be honest with herself and admit why.

Before Hallie could go any further with that thought, John Bellweather came up to her and asked for a dance. To give Rosa and Rachel something else to think about besides Jack and her, Hallie accepted and let John whisk her off to the dance floor.

Jack watched them, his gut clenching. Did she have to look so happy about being with someone else?

"Miss Hallie sure has blossomed," Whit commented, following Jack's intent stare. "I don't recall noticin' before, but she's a real pretty little gal."

"Yeah, isn't she?" Spotting Ethan in a group with Jessica, her mother and Charlie, Jack excused himself to go and talk to his son. "I'm taking Hallie home a little early," he told Ethan. "Are you about ready to leave?"

To Jack's surprise, Ethan balked. "Could we stay just a little longer? Jessica and I were talkin'."

"I'd be glad to bring him home with me," Charlie said, turning from where he'd been talking with Elizabeth. "I'm taking Elizabeth and Jessica home, so I won't be keepin' him too late. Ben can bring the wagon home. I'm sure Miss Hallie will give you a ride back in the buckboard,'' Charlie added with a grin.

Jack hesitated, then relented at the pleading look on Ethan's face. He went down on one knee to say his goodbyes to his son. ''Miss Hallie and I'll be waiting for you at the ranch.''

Ethan nodded solemnly. ''I understand.''

''You do?'' Jack asked, not sure what Ethan meant.

''Sure, you want to be alone with Miss Hallie 'cause that's what you do when you're courtin'.''

''Courting?'' Jack jerked back. ''Where did you get that idea?''

''I don't know. I just figured you liked her, and you bought her things, so you must be courtin' her,'' Ethan said. ''Anyway, that's what Mr. Charlie said. See you later.''

With a wave of his hand, Ethan went off to join Jessica, leaving Jack standing there, slightly stunned.

He'd never thought about *courting* Hallie. Fighting with her, working with her, talking, laughing, teasing her, yes. Kissing her, oh, yes, too many times, enough to keep him awake nights.

But courting her?

His gaze settled on her again, watching as the cowboy swung her around. It was the one thing he'd never done. Maybe he ought to give it a try.

The music wound to a close as Jack strode up to Hallie and took her elbow. ''I need to talk to you,'' he said, dismissing John with a glance.

Hallie stared at him a moment, opened her mouth and closed it again.

Instead of refusing Jack, she thanked John for the dance, then let Jack lead her through the crowd and outside before she spoke up. "You know, you've been badgering me for weeks to leave the ranch more often, and then, when I take your advice, you drag me out so fast the whole town will be talking—"

Before she could finish, Jack pulled her into his arms and kissed her so thoroughly she gasped for breath.

"Let them talk," he rasped against her ear. Scooping her into his arms, he carried her to the wagon and put her in the seat.

Hallie supposed she should at the very least be annoyed at his high-handed tactics. Instead she felt a warm rush of pleasure that left her almost giddy.

"You're making a habit of whisking me away whenever it suits you," she said when he set the horses in motion with a sharp snap of the reins. "Should I bother asking where we're going this time?"

"Home. Ethan tells me I have some courting to do."

Courting? Hallie stared, not sure she'd heard him right. Did he mean that? Jack Dakota, courting her? What was she supposed to say, let alone do?

During the ride home, she said and did nothing. And Jack kept the silence between them until they'd reached the ranch, unhitched the horses and were standing on the front porch, facing each other.

"Well...we're here," Hallie said, aware of how silly she sounded, but unable to stand the quiet anymore.

Jack shifted uncomfortably, feeling like a fool. Hell, he'd never done this before. He'd flirted, teased and seduced, but he'd never wooed a woman. He did have a feeling, though, that dragging her out of the hall and tossing her in the wagon wasn't a good start.

"I'm sorry," he said, lifting his hands. "I shouldn't have...I only wanted to—" He broke off when Hallie started to grin. "You know, you're not making this any easier."

"Oh, this from the man who pushed his way into my life and did his best to annoy me every chance he got." Hallie folded her arms and tried to look stern. "You aren't going to get any sympathy from me, Dakota."

"*Sympathy* wasn't exactly what I had in mind, Hal," Jack drawled.

"That's right, you were going to do some courting. All right." Sitting down on the swing, Hallie arranged her skirts around her and primly folded her hands in her lap, then looked up at him expectantly. "Go ahead."

Jack smiled. This was his Hallie, giving him back measure for measure, challenging him at every turn. "You know," he said, coming to sit beside her, "I haven't had much experience at this. You'll have to tell me what you like."

He took her hand, gently rubbing her fingers with his. As he did, he watched her face soften. He kept his caress deliberately light, although he wanted to do more, much more. She deserved gentleness, though— all that sweet talk and those tender kisses she'd never known because the men in Paradise had been too blind to see beyond her pants and ugly hat.

Jack just hoped he could do it right, for her.

His odd hesitant mood confused Hallie. One minute the man was practically roping and tying her and putting his brand on her, and the next he acted as if he'd never been with a woman before.

She didn't know the first thing about the proper way a man and woman decided they cared for each other and then acted on it. She did know she was tired of waiting to find out.

All these weeks, she had tried to ignore and deny the way she felt about Jack. Now it was time to be honest with herself.

She did care for him, admire him, more than she should, more than she admitted. And, right or wrong, she wanted him to kiss her, to hold her and touch her, and make her feel again the way only Jack could make her feel: that she wasn't just plain Hallie Ryan in her britches and hat, but a woman he cared for, a woman he desired.

"Since neither of us knows what we're doing, maybe we should just skip this part," she said, and leaned forward and pressed her mouth to his before he could say anything.

For one heart-stopping instant, Jack didn't respond, and Hallie feared she'd been too bold in showing her feelings.

In the next instant he slid his hand into her hair, his arm around her waist, and pulled her up hard against him, parting her lips with his and kissing her deeply.

Hallie put her arms around his neck and pressed closer. She had never allowed any man such liberties, never wanted them, yet with every kiss, every touch, she invited Jack to show her everything she'd only imagined him doing.

The fire flared so quickly and hotly between them that Jack couldn't think. She didn't give him the chance.

Blood pounded in his head and he felt as if the solid ground under him suddenly shifted and left him scrambling for a footing.

Too quickly, he was losing control. He didn't know how to stop it. He'd never lost it before, with any woman.

But then he'd never loved any woman before.

The thought immediately cleared his head like a dousing in cold water. Love?

Is that what it was?

He drew back and Hallie stayed still in his arms. He couldn't see her face clearly in the darkness, despite the moonlight. He remembered, though, the night he'd touched her here. The night she'd told him to tell her when he'd figured out what they'd started.

"Maybe I have figured it out."

His words made no sense to Hallie, not here, not now. She hesitantly touched his cheek. "What is it?" she asked, almost afraid to hear his answer. "What's wrong?"

"Nothing," Jack said, gathering her close again. "Nothing in the world."

He kissed her with a coupling of tenderness and passion that started a slow, hot trembling inside her.

Hallie only vaguely knew when Jack lifted her off her feet and carried her into the house. Only his closeness, his mouth making love to hers mattered anymore.

Until he set her on her feet again and she realized they were in his room. All at once, a rush of uncertainty hit her.

"Hallie..." Jack slid his hands over her back, so their bodies fit together and she could feel the need for her she'd roused in him. "It's all right, sweetheart," he whispered, kissing her temple, her cheek. "I'll only give you what you ask for. Tell me what you want."

Too shy to tell him, too honest to pretend, Hallie reached up and kissed him.

It was all the answer Jack needed.

Their tongues mated, echoing the rhythm of the dance to come, while he worked free the buttons of her dress, finally pushing it off her shoulders to the floor.

Hallie sucked in a breath when his hands covered her breasts, stroking her through the thin chemise. An aching pleasure blossomed deep within her and, clutching his shoulders, she let her head fall back, wanting to prolong every second of it.

Gently moving her backward, Jack guided her down on his bed. He sat beside her and trailed his hand lightly down her arm, over her waist and hip, smiling when she trembled.

Taking his time, making them both restless with anticipation, he drew off her stockings, just grazing her bared skin with his fingertips.

Then, just as slowly, he pulled the first three ribbons of her chemise free, enough to give him a tantalizing glimpse of the curves beneath.

He sat back and looked at her, bewitched by the promise and temptation of Hallie. "You're beautiful," he murmured. "You don't need satin skirts and ribbons. You're so much more than that."

Tears welled in her eyes. "Only with you."

"No, you're a special woman, Hallie Ryan. I want you to believe that. But this…" He pulled free the remaining ribbons of her chemise and spread it open. Almost reverently, he skimmed two fingers down the hollow between her breasts. "This I want to be only for me. For always."

She didn't believe his words, so Jack showed her the truth with every kiss, every caress.

He licked fire along her skin as he started kissing her throat, her shoulder, then lower, nibbling, tasting, intensifying the longing in her so it matched his.

Hallie's fingers clenched on his shoulders, digging in hard when his mouth closed over one hardened nipple.

"Jack," she gasped, then arched to him as he suckled one taut peak and then the other, using tongue and teeth to prolong the pleasure until it was so tight and hot inside her, Hallie thought she might resort to begging him to give her some release from it.

He did, but in a way she never expected. Moving his hand over her hip and thigh, he slipped his fingers through the opening in her pantalets and stroked her there, lightly at first, and then deeper, quicker.

She clung to him, moving, shuddering, and finally

an incredible feeling burst over her, sweet and wild, and sent her flying and falling.

Jack held her, trembling against him, until she pulled back to look at him in wonder. "I never knew," she said simply.

He laughed and kissed her, lingering over her lips. "Oh, I promise you, darlin', it gets much better," he murmured.

Levering away from her, he pulled off his vest and tossed it aside, and began unbuttoning his shirt. When it joined his vest on the floor, he looked back at Hallie, only to find her staring at him, wide-eyed.

"Sweetheart?"

Hallie's heart thudded crazily in her ears. It was ridiculous to feel afraid now, but this was more than Jack touching her. This was Jack in her bed, ready to do much more.

Smiling a little, Jack bent and gently kissed her forehead. "I only want to love you. But if it's not what you want, then this is as far as it goes. Hallie…" He cupped her cheek, making her look into his eyes. "I only want what you want."

"What I want scares me," she whispered. "I've never…"

"I know. But I've never, either. Not when I've loved someone."

Astonishment shot through Hallie, driving every coherent thought from her brain. Before she could make herself believe she'd actually heard those words from him, Jack covered her mouth with his and began those tormenting caresses that made thought impossible.

In between the fire and the pleasure, he stripped off the rest of their clothing and took her in his arms with nothing between them but heat.

Jack seized the chance to do the things he'd been imagining since the first day he'd kissed her. Now, he took his time, memorizing the texture of her skin, the shape of her body, the scent of wind and sunshine that belonged to Hallie alone.

Hallie moved restlessly against him, the flood of pleasure almost an unbearable ache. The intimate press of his body, hard and insistent, reminded her there was no going back now, in body or in heart.

She loved Jack and she was about to prove it to herself and to him.

Jack moved over her, nudging her legs apart with his. This close to her, he forced himself to hold back, mindful of her innocence.

Yet Hallie being Hallie, she arched and opened herself to him, offering him everything, and in the middle of a long, dizzying kiss, he pushed inside her.

Hallie stiffened and bit at her lower lip. Jack stayed still, soothing her with kisses and his touch, whispering praise in her ear, until she softened again and he began to teach her the rhythm of loving each other.

Holding him tightly, Hallie moved with him, straining, faster and hotter, toward the feeling he'd shown her, until it crashed over her. As it slowly faded to echoes, she found herself shaking, wanting to laugh and cry all at once.

She lay with her head against Jack's chest, listening to the rasp of his breath and the uneven thud of his heart, wondering if he felt the same.

Making love to Hallie left Jack shaken. Never, in all his experience, had it been that intimate before, a true joining of body and heart. She'd touched him, deeply and irrevocably, and it was far too late to deny it.

Shifting up on one elbow so he could look into her face, he gently touched her cheek. Just seeing her beside him, warm and tousled from their lovemaking, flooded him with emotion.

"I love you, Hallie Ryan," he whispered, then bent and covered the lips that parted in surprise with his before she could respond.

He didn't want to talk now. He only wanted to show her again, and forever, that nothing he'd said had ever been more true.

Chapter Eighteen

A gust of wind caught the tail of the shirt Hallie had just pulled from the laundry basket, nearly tugging it from her fingertips. She held tight to the sleeve, shaking it out before pinning it to the line. The smooth feel of the fine white cotton told her it was Jack's shirt. The shirt he'd worn to the dance last night.

The shirt he'd shed to make love to her.

After pinning it carefully to the line, she pulled the soft fabric close to her nose and breathed in, hoping to catch a remnant of his scent. But soap and water had washed away all traces of him. If only it were as easy to wash him out of her thoughts.

But after last night, he would forever be in her, a part of her, no matter what happened from this moment on.

Last night... Last night had been everything she'd longed for and nothing she could have imagined. It was as if all her life she'd been waiting, saving every joy, every wonder, every tender feeling and her most secret desires, only to experience them all in Jack's arms.

Then he'd said he loved her.

Hallie closed her eyes, his shirt pressed to her cheek. She'd wanted to hear those words from him, but how much, she hadn't realized. She also hadn't realized how much they frightened her. Could she believe him? Could she ever believe in them?

Confused, her emotions scattered from ecstasy to distress, she'd slipped out of his bed this morning at dawn, before she could give in to the fierce desire to stay there in his arms.

She'd skipped breakfast, unable to face him in front of the others. If they saw her face, they would know her feelings. They would recognize the change between her and Jack, and she wasn't ready for anyone else to know. Instead, she'd started straight in on the laundry, hoping the work would make her forget.

It hadn't. And she knew it never would again.

"My, but you've got it something awful for him, don't you?"

Serenity's voice startled Hallie out of her dreams. She let go of Jack's shirt and hurriedly picked up the next item in her basket—a pair of pants—and started pinning them to the line.

"Oh, I—I was only checking to make sure it's clean," Hallie said, wincing at her pitiful lie.

Putting down the basket of freshly washed linens she was toting, Serenity laughed. "Don't try to fool me. I know you were thinking about Mr. Dakota. Oh, it's okay," she said when Hallie looked distinctly uncomfortable, "I do the same thing with Ben's shirts. I love the scent of him. It makes me feel close to him just holding his shirt against my face."

"Well, I don't think we want this to go any further than the laundry line," Hallie said. She bent to pull a pillowcase from Serenity's basket, anxious to change the subject to anything but Jack and her own foolish yearnings. "How are you and Ben, anyway? He seemed a little put out at the dance last night."

Serenity shook out a towel and took a clothespin from between her teeth. "Who can say? One day he's doting on me and treating me like a princess. Then I don't see him for days because he's either gambling or in bed sleeping off a night in town."

"It's hard for a gambling man to change his ways." *Isn't it?*

"I suppose that might be true. But I can't help believing that if he has something more tempting than a fistful of spades to come home to, he'll choose home."

Hallie drew another of Jack's shirts from the basket. A sweet feeling swelled up in her. Such a simple domestic chore, but it warmed her heart to do it for *him*. Until the near panic set in again.

She couldn't do this. She couldn't love a gambler.

"It's hard for any woman to compete with the excitement of the game," she said aloud, more to convince herself than Serenity.

"I know. But I still think sooner or later even a gambler needs more than a pocketful of coins, a bottle of whiskey and a stranger with a painted face to be happy."

Hallie hung the shirt with hands that weren't quite steady. She hesitated, then turned to Serenity, trying to check the raw emotion in her voice. The look on the girl's face told her she failed miserably.

"It sounds so simple, but I want to believe that, too."

Serenity reached across the basket separating them and took Hallie's hand in hers. "Then do it."

"Do what?"

"Believe in him."

Jack stabbed a pitchfork into a bale of hay and thrust it down from the barn loft to where Ben and Ethan handled the wheelbarrow below. He was glad for the work this morning. Thoughts of Hallie had been all-consuming since he'd awakened alone, and only hard physical labor seemed to give him any reprieve.

Their loving had been as close to paradise as he ever dreamed he'd get in this life. He'd thought she'd felt the same. Then he'd discovered she'd left him, and now he had no idea how she felt, what she wanted from him—if she wanted anything from him at all.

"We missed you at breakfast," Ben called up. "Have a late night?"

Jack didn't miss the teasing jab. "No later than most of yours."

"My sister sure raised some eyebrows last night, didn't she? Who'd have guessed she'd clean up so nice?"

"She was the prettiest one there!" Ethan declared with a sincerity that made Jack smile.

An image of Hallie glowing with womanly sensuality, cheeks flushed with desire, lips tempting his kiss, nearly sent him accidentally tripping off the edge of the loft.

"Yes," he murmured, catching himself, "Hallie is beautiful."

"So, what happens now?" Ben looked up, shielding his eyes with the back of his hand against the onslaught of hay.

"What do you mean?"

"Well, it's obvious enough to anyone with eyes that you and Hal are in love."

Taken aback, Jack stopped his work. "Is that what people are saying?"

"'Course it is. Right, Ethan?"

Ethan nodded enthusiastically. "Yep. You two were staring at each other all mushy-eyed the whole night. And she even wore a dress. Miss Hallie *never* does that, so she must love you."

Unsettled at everyone knowing what he'd just figured out for himself, Jack fiddled with a piece of straw, turning it between his fingers.

"So?" Ben pressed the issue.

"So what?" Jack asked, his tone growing terse with impatience, more at himself and his uncertainty over where he stood with Hallie than at Ben's probing.

Ethan stepped around the wheelbarrow. Setting his hands on his waist, he looked up at Jack. "Why don't you just go on and marry her, Pa?"

Jack didn't know which stunned him more—Ethan calling him Pa, as if he'd been doing it all along, or his son's direct question.

Both released a surge of happiness in him that suddenly made everything seem simple.

Why didn't he just go ahead and marry her? He loved her. And after last night he believed she loved him, too.

They were good partners and friends, better lovers. Together, they and Ethan could truly be a family.

Ben laughed at the silly grin on Jack's face. "You might as well. It'd solve everything. Well, almost everything."

Still caught up in his golden vision of the future, Jack almost missed what Ben had said. "What do you mean?" he asked, when the words finally sank in.

Ben glanced at Ethan first. "Sure you want me to say now?"

"Ethan's old enough to know where things stand." Jack handed the pitchfork down to Ben before he backed down the loft ladder to face the two boys.

Squaring his shoulders, Ethan said, "Yeah, I ain't no baby."

"Okay then," Ben said with a shrug. "I heard talk at the dance from a couple of men who run with Barlow. They didn't know I was standin' in hearin' range."

"Go on."

"They said Barlow would have an easier time gettin' the best of you now that you'd gone all soft over Hal."

The muscles in Jack's neck and jaw tightened. Unconsciously, his gun hand flexed against his hip. "What else did they say?" he muttered, barely concealing his growing rage.

Ben glanced once again at Ethan. When Jack didn't say anything, he added, ''Barlow figures if he ruins Hal and the ranch, he'll destroy you, too. I'm guessin' you've crossed Redeye once too often?''

''Ben, all your wasted nights at the Silver Snake might just have paid off,'' Jack said, not bothering to satisfy Ben's curiosity. ''You two finish up here. I have something I need to do.''

''What're you gonna do?'' Ethan asked, his eyes wide with a combination of wonder and fear.

''Don't worry, Son.'' Jack laid a reassuring hand on Ethan's head. ''You showed me it's time I took the biggest gamble of my life. I'm going to ask Miss Hallie to marry me.''

Striding across the backyard, Jack stopped at the clothesline and swept a bedsheet out of Hallie's hands, tossing it back in the basket. He turned to Serenity. ''You don't mind finishing up without Miss Hallie, do you?''

Serenity smiled sweetly and pulled the basket away from Hallie. ''Not at all.''

Jack took Hallie's hand firmly in his and urged her along beside him.

''What's wrong?'' she asked, bewildered by his sudden appearance and the determined, almost serious look in his eyes.

''Nothing's wrong. Let's just say it's time we made something a lot more right.''

Jack led her to the front porch and sat her beside him on the swing. ''Not ideal by far, but it'll have to do.''

Hallie let him take her hands in his. Fear started in her, overriding all the other mixed-up feelings she had about Jack being close again. "Something is wrong. Tell me."

"This isn't the way I might have planned it," Jack began, holding her hands tightly.

He looked at her solemnly, and she had a fleeting impression he was almost apprehensive. It was so unlike Jack it made her even more uneasy.

"It doesn't matter, though, as long as you know how I feel," he said.

Hallie frowned, trying to make sense of his intentions. "I don't understand."

"Don't you? Hallie, I love you. I want you to be mine. Not just because of last night and not for a few days or weeks. Forever."

Hallie stared at him, speechless.

Last night, he'd told her he loved her. But there in the darkness, she'd found it easy to convince herself he'd only been caught up in the emotion of their loving. If he'd felt anything like she had, she could easily see how he could lose his head and say the words he thought she wanted to hear.

Now, she could see him clearly. And she saw nothing but honesty and tenderness for her in his eyes when he said those words again.

Jack lifted her hands and gently, almost with reverence, kissed the backs of them. "Maybe this seems sudden. But it shouldn't, to either of us. It's been between us for a long time now."

When she still continued to gaze at him with that astonished expression, Jack smiled a little. "I'm not doing this very well.'' Sliding off the swing onto one knee in front of her, he tried to find the words to convince her he was sincere. ''You're what I've needed all my life. You and only you make me complete. Hallie, I'm asking you to marry me.''

Hallie's heart jumped. Marry Jack? Jack Dakota wanted to make her his wife?

A hundred old doubts, fears, rushed through her mind, clouding her feelings, confusing her. ''Jack, I— I don't know what to say.''

''How about yes?''

When she didn't answer, he moved to sit beside her again. ''I guess I should have waited for a moonlit stroll or a candlelit dinner, but once I realized this was right, I didn't want to wait to know whether you'll have me or not.''

''Jack—''

The sound of a horse galloping toward them turned them both to the front yard.

''It's Tenfoot,'' Hallie murmured distractedly. She glanced back at Jack, reluctant to leave things so unresolved.

But Jack was already starting down the porch stairs. ''The way he's riding, it looks like trouble.''

Hallie followed him, and they met the cowboy halfway to the house.

''West pasture's caught fire,'' Tenfoot called out as he pulled his horse to a halt in a cloud of dust. ''Eb and Charlie are already out fightin' it. I just sent Ben and Ethan out with a wagonload of shovels and buckets. I'm goin' back. We need every hand out there now.''

As Tenfoot wheeled his horse around and kicked him into a run, Hallie looked to Jack and saw a cold anger settle over his face.

"Barlow," he muttered.

"Bill Barlow? What's he got to do with this?"

"Everything. This is his doing. And once we're done here, I'm going to find him."

Jack spun around and headed for the corral before Hallie could ask him anything. By the time they'd saddled their horses and were galloping full out to the west pasture, the threat of fire drove every question she had to the back of her mind.

The pungent odor of burning grass assaulted their senses as they reached the pasture. Ahead, flames leaped and danced across the tall, dry grasses, threatening to destroy grazing land.

Leaving the horses a safe distance away, Jack and Hallie ran to the edge of the fire, where the others were already working furiously to contain the blaze.

"We need to dig a circle around it to keep it from spreading," Hallie shouted through the waves of heat, over the crackling flames. "Is the main ditch open?"

Ben nodded as he jammed his shovel into the earth. "Ethan's following the water back, to tell us when it's coming."

Jack ran over to the wagon and grabbed two more shovels. "Then all we can do in the meantime is dig," he said, handing one to Hallie.

Plunging in at strategic points, they all dug furiously, clearing a swath of earth around the fire so nothing would be left there to feed the flames.

Though they struggled for what seemed hours, the

fire was clearly gaining ground, with no hint of irrigation waters in sight. Battling the blaze, Hallie didn't hear Whit Peller, his two oldest sons and several of his men ride up behind her until Whit called her name.

"We came to help," Peller yelled out. "Rachel saw smoke from the kitchen window. I brought the boys over to help put it out before it ruins us both."

Hallie could only smile and wave in thanks. When she saw the group of over a half-dozen men already dismounting and Jack meeting them, pointing out the work that still needed to be done, relief washed over her, sweet and strong.

"Whit said the water's almost here," Jack said, when he'd finished. He came up beside her and put his arm around her shoulders, squeezing lightly. "They rode through it on the way over."

"Thank the Lord." Hallie squeezed her eyes shut for a moment, tears threatening. "For a while there I was afraid we'd lost."

Jack bent and kissed her brow. "I know. But your ranch is safe. And I'm going to make certain it stays that way."

"What you said earlier, about Barlow—"

"Don't worry," Jack said, pulling her into his arms for a hug. "I never want you to worry about Eden's Canyon again." Not giving her a chance to try to stop him, he let her go and started striding away in the direction of his horse.

"Jack!" Hallie threw down her shovel and ran through the ashes after him. "Where are you going?"

By the time she caught up to him, he had already

mounted Ace. His eyes were hard as flint he looked down at her. "I'm going to finish this with Barlow once and for all." Momentarily his gaze softened. "And when I come back, Miss Ryan, I'll want my answer."

With a tip of his hat, he pulled the reins against Ace's neck and turned him toward Paradise.

Hallie watched until he vanished from her sight before walking slowly back toward the others.

Ben, Ethan at his side, met her near the edge of what now was a muddy, ashen mess.

"Jack went to town," she said, feeling strangely empty.

Ben hesitated a minute. "Because of Barlow. We know."

"What do you know?"

"Just that Redeye's been tryin' to ruin Jack. The day Jack shot him, he'd been braggin' how he was finally goin' to take it all from Jack," Ben told her. "But it was the other way around, and seems that's what's always happened between them. Barlow blames Jack for his sour luck. He figured if he ruined Eden's Canyon, it would pay Jack back for all those times Redeye went home with empty pockets."

A sick feeling lodged in Hallie's stomach. "And now you're saying that instead of calling in the law, Jack's gone on his own to settle with Barlow?" She thought of him facing down Redeye on Paradise's main street. "He wouldn't... No. He's going to settle it at the card table. Isn't he." It wasn't a question.

Ben nodded reluctantly. "He didn't say. But that'd be my guess."

* * *

"Third room on the left, but he ain't gonna be happy to see you. He's with Eva," Lila Lee told Jack.

Jack didn't bother to answer her. He quickly found the room and, without warning, shoved open the door on the unsuspecting couple tangled together under the sheets.

"What the hell—" Redeye sat bolt upright, his hand fumbling at the holster slung over the bedpost. He leaned back when he recognized Jack, his smile goading. "Where's your manners, Dakota?"

"Meet me downstairs in five minutes or I'll show you just how unmannerly I can be."

By the time Jack got back downstairs, a small crowd had gathered, watching him expectantly. Jack pushed through them and, picking a table in the center of the saloon, found a deck of cards and slapped them down.

A few minutes later Redeye joined him, his fat fingers still fighting the fasteners on his suspenders.

"I need a bottle," Redeye called to Lila.

A growing crowd of curious onlookers moved in close as Jack and Redeye took their seats opposite one another.

Eyes dark and unreadable, Jack expertly shuffled the deck, never taking his gaze off Barlow. "Here's how it is. I want you out of my life for good. If I win, neither you nor any of your scum will ever come within ten miles of Eden's Canyon or so much as look at Hallie, my boy or anyone else on the ranch."

"And what's in it for me? 'Cause it sure ain't the pleasure of your company."

Lila brought the whiskey then and two glasses.

Jack poured himself a shot and held up his glass in a mock toast. "This is the last time I want to see your face across the table from me. So it's winner take all."

Redeye lifted one heavy brow suspiciously. "You tellin' me you're gamblin' your ranch?"

"I said winner take all. All that's mine or all that's yours. You in?"

"Hear that, boys?" Redeye asked over his shoulder. "You're my witnesses." Several snickers and nods from half a dozen gritty cowboys answered him.

Lifting his own glass, Redeye smirked at Jack. "I'm in. Deal, Dakota."

Exhausted from hours of turning over wet, blackened earth to make certain every cinder was doused, Hallie plunged her shovel in one more time, ignoring the ache in her arms. Everything from her shoulders to her toes hurt.

But all her pains didn't compare to the anguish in her heart. Despite the grueling labor, not a moment passed that she wasn't thinking of Jack.

Now, of all times, how could he leave to play cards? He may have been sincere in wanting to stop Barlow, but it was obvious the only way Jack knew how to deal with trouble was by playing games.

Knowing how she felt about his gambling, he couldn't have been serious in his proposal. She wanted to believe he could change, give up that wild, reckless living.

He couldn't change, though. Gambling was in his blood, poisoning everything good that came his way.

Just as it had her father.

Just as it could her brother.

She glanced over to where Ben now sat on a fallen log with Serenity, who had ridden out with water and food for everyone. Ben was young. Maybe Serenity's faith would save her brother, if anything could.

Ethan hovered nearby, poking at odd pieces of charred wood, burned down to strange, fascinating shapes. Since Jack had left for town, the boy had been distant and quiet, absorbed in playing with refuse from the fire.

Hallie wondered what she could say to him to comfort and reassure him that his father would be all right. If only she believed it herself, it would be a lot easier.

She set her shovel aside and slogged through the mud to the boy's side. "You did a lot of work here today. You helped save the pasture, you know that?"

Idly, Ethan kicked at a pile of charred sticks. "I wish Pa was here."

Hallie's heart went out to him. She put her arm around him and hugged him. "Your pa had something very important he had to do. He'll be back."

"If you say so," Ethan muttered. He looked around, saw Charlie and Eb hacking at a large fallen tree and, his interest momentarily piqued, ran off to watch.

Hallie sighed and had started to follow him when the sound of a song on the wind drew her attention toward an approaching rider. As he closed in, the rider swept his Stetson from his head and waved it.

Despite everything, Hallie had to smile to herself. Jack. The man who always made an entrance.

Thank heavens he wasn't hurt or worse…! Something inside her loosened a little and she could breathe easier again.

She sighed, seeing his familiar lopsided smile. No doubt he'd beaten Barlow again, but she didn't see how that was going to solve their problems. If anything, Redeye would be more determined to ruin him.

Riding right up to where she stood knee deep in black mud, her face spattered with soot, her hands smeared with ash, Jack pulled Ace to a halt and slid down.

Not giving Hallie a moment to protest, and uncaring of the mud and mess from the fire, he lifted her in his arms and spun her around once before kissing her soundly.

"Jack, are you crazy?" Hallie gasped when he finally set her on her feet, keeping her in the circle of his arms.

"Crazy about you." He grinned at her, soot smudging his face and his hat pushed back at an odd angle. "I've come for my answer."

Hallie shoved away a little but he held on to her. "Jack, you're impossible! I'm so angry, so frustrated with you, you make my head spin!"

"And I hope I always do, darlin'."

She couldn't stay mad in the face of his infectious joy. But she couldn't make herself believe in a dream, either.

"Jack, you don't need to marry me," she said, forcing out every word. "The ranch is yours already. And you know I'll teach you all you need to know to run it."

"You still don't get it, do you? It's not about the ranch. It never has been. I love you, Hallie. And you're wrong about Eden's Canyon. It's not mine."

It took a moment for his meaning to sink in, but when it did, all Hallie's fears came crashing back.

"Barlow... Tell me you didn't—oh, Jack, tell me you didn't gamble away Eden's Canyon."

"Not exactly."

Breaking out of his arms, Hallie faced him with her hands fisted at her side and her eyes blazing. "Jack Dakota, you have some fast explaining to do."

"Whoa, there." Jack held up his hands. "The ranch is safe. I never risked it in the game. Barlow only thought I did. Obviously you did, too."

Hallie silently blessed the soot on her face for hiding her shame at not trusting him. "I—I'm sorry, I shouldn't have thought such a thing. I should have trusted you. But..." Drawing in a shaky breath, she let it out slowly. "I was afraid...."

"Hallie Ryan, afraid? The woman who's faced down stampedes and rogue cowboys?"

"They're nothing compared to you," she said with a touch of spirit.

"That's my Hallie." He touched her cheek. "Trust me, sweetheart. I won't let you down."

And he hadn't. He had stood by her, encouraged her, challenged her, loved her for herself. Even now, when she was covered in mud and ashes, he looked at her as if she were the most beautiful woman in the world to him.

"But I don't understand. Why did Barlow think you were gambling the ranch?"

"I told him we'd play one final game, winner take all, to end it between us." Jack's smile returned, this time gleeful. "What I didn't tell him is I signed the deed over to you before I went to the Silver Snake."

"You…Jack, I don't know what to say."

"You're the rightful owner. I don't want Eden's Canyon. All I want is you." Reaching for her, Jack thought she'd never looked so beautiful to him as she did now. "Look into my eyes and tell me you can't see that."

"Oh, Jack." A tear slid down her cheek. Hallie didn't bother to brush it away, nor to hide the emotion in her eyes. "I do see it. And I love you, too."

"Then you have to believe the only reason I gambled with Barlow was to protect you and Ethan. The only rules Barlow respects are the rules of the game."

"He caused us all the trouble, didn't he?"

"And the only way to stop him was to do it at the table."

"So he won today?"

Jack looked at her with mock indignation. "This is me we're talking about."

"Modest as ever, too," Hallie said, unable to stop her smile. "But if you took everything from him, he'll only hate you more. We'll never be rid of him."

"I haven't taken anything. Yet. And I won't, unless he or any of his friends ever come near my family."

"Your family?" Her heart nearly bursting with love, Hallie echoed his words.

"That's what we're going to be, aren't we?"

"Pa!"

Ethan came running up to them, throwing his arms

around his father's neck as Jack swung him into a hug. "Miss Hallie was right. You did come back."

"Miss Hallie is usually right about things like that. But she is a little slow in answering an important question."

"What important question?" Ethan demanded.

"I asked Miss Hallie to be my wife." Keeping an arm around a grinning Ethan, he reached out to Hallie and drew her into their circle. "So, are you going to give me the answer I want to hear?"

"Oh, yes." Hallie lifted her hands and took his face between her sooty palms, holding his eyes with hers. "I'll gamble my heart on you for the rest of my life, Jack Dakota."

"Darlin'," he murmured, his lips brushing hers, "that's no gamble at all."

*   *   *   *   *

SAVOR THE BREATHTAKING ROMANCES AND THRILLING ADVENTURES OF THE OLD WEST WITH HARLEQUIN HISTORICALS

On sale March 2003

TEMPTING A TEXAN by Carolyn Davidson

A wealthy Texas businessman is ambitious, demanding and in no rush to get to the altar. But when a beautiful woman arrives with a child she claims is his niece, he must decide between wealth and love....

THE ANGEL OF DEVIL'S CAMP by Lynna Banning

When a Southern belle goes to Oregon to start a new life, the last thing she expects is to have her heart captured by a stubborn Yankee!

On sale April 2003

McKINNON'S BRIDE by Sharon Harlow

While traveling with her children, a young widow falls in love with the kind rancher who opens his home and his heart to her family....

ADAM'S PROMISE by Julianne MacLean

A ruggedly handsome Canadian finds unexpected love when his fiancée arrives and he discovers she's not the woman he thought he was marrying!

Harlequin Historicals®
Historical Romantic Adventure!

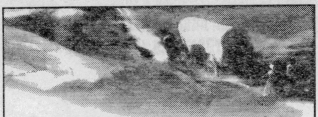

Don't miss the breathtaking conclusion of
New York Times bestselling author

HEATHER GRAHAM'S

popular Civil War trilogy
featuring the indomitable Slater brothers....

If you *savored* DARK STRANGER
and *reveled* in RIDES A HERO,
you'll *treasure* the final installment
of this intoxicating series!

In January 2003 look for

APACHE SUMMER

*Born and raised in frontier Texas, beautiful Tess Stuart needed
a hired gun to avenge her uncle's murder. But the only one willing to
help was the infuriating, smolderingly sexy Lieutenant Jamie Slater—
the man whose passion set her soul on fire.*

You won't want to miss the opportunity to revisit these classic tales
about the three dashing brothers who discover the importance of
family ties, loyalty...and love!

DARK STRANGER	RIDES A HERO	APACHE SUMMER
On sale August 2002	On sale November 2002	On sale January 2003

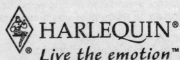

HARLEQUIN®
Live the emotion™

Visit us at www.eHarlequin.com

Steeple Hill Books is proud to present
a beautiful and contemporary new look
for Love Inspired!

HEARTWARMING INSPIRATIONAL ROMANCE

Love Inspired®

As always, Love Inspired delivers
endearing romances full of hope, faith and love.

Beginning January 2003
look for these titles
and three more each month
at your favorite retail outlet.

Steeple
Hill®

eHARLEQUIN.com

Calling all aspiring writers!
Learn to craft the perfect romance novel
with our useful tips and tools:

- Take advantage of our **Romance Novel Critique Service** for detailed advice from romance professionals.

- Use our **message boards** to connect with writers, published authors and editors.

- Enter our **Writing Round Robin**— you could be published online!

- Learn many writing hints in our **Top 10 Writing lists!**

- **Guidelines** for Harlequin or Silhouette novels—what our editors *really* look for.

Learn more about romance writing from the experts— visit www.eHarlequin.com today!

From Regency Ballrooms to Medieval Castles, fall in love with these stirring tales from Harlequin Historicals

On sale March 2003

THE SILVER LORD by Miranda Jarrett

Don't miss the first of **The Lordly Claremonts** trilogy!
Despite being on the opposite side of the law,
a spinster with a secret smuggling habit can't resist
a handsome navy captain!

BRIDE OF THE TOWER by Sharon Schulze
(England, 1217)

Will a fallen knight become bewitched with the
mysterious noblewoman who nurses him back to health?

On sale April 2003

LADY ALLERTON'S WAGER by Nicola Cornick

A woman masquerading as a cyprian challenges a
dashing earl to a wager—with the stake being an island
he owns against her favors!

HIGHLAND SWORD by Ruth Langan

Be sure to read this first installment in the
Mystical Highlands series about three sisters
and the handsome Highlanders they bewitch!

  Harlequin Historicals®
Historical Romantic Adventure!

HHMED29R

COMING NEXT MONTH FROM

HARLEQUIN HISTORICALS®

- **THE SCOT**
  by **Lyn Stone**, author of MARRYING MISCHIEF
  After overhearing two men plotting to kill an earl and his daughter, James Garrow, Baron of Galioch, goes to warn the earl. Instead, he meets the earl's daughter, freethinking, unruly Susanna Eastonby. Despite the sparks flying between them, James and Susanna enter into a marriage of convenience. Will this hardheaded couple realize they're perfect for each other—before it's too late?
  HH #643 ISBN# 29243-0 $5.25 U.S./$6.25 CAN.

- **THE MIDWIFE'S SECRET**
  by **Kate Bridges**, author of LUKE'S RUNAWAY BRIDE
  Amanda Ryan is escaping her painful past and trying to start a new life as a midwife when she meets Tom Murdock. As Tom teaches Amanda to overcome the past, they start a budding relationship. But will Amanda's secrets stand in the path of true love?
  HH #644 ISBN# 29244-9 $5.25 U.S./$6.25 CAN.

- **FALCON'S DESIRE**
  by **Denise Lynn**, Harlequin Historical debut
  Wrongly accused of murder, Count Rhys Faucon is given one month to prove his innocence. In order to stop him, the victim's vengeance-seeking fiancée, Lady Lyonesse, holds him captive in her keep and unwittingly discovers a love beyond her wildest dreams!
  HH #645 ISBN# 29245-7 $5.25 U.S./$6.25 CAN.

- **THE LAW AND KATE MALONE**
  by **Charlene Sands**, author of CHASE WHEELER'S WOMAN
  Determined to grant her mother's last wish, Kate Malone returns to her hometown to rebuild the Silver Saddle Saloon and reclaim her family legacy. But the only man she's ever loved, Sheriff Cole Bradshaw, is determined to stop the saloon from being built and determined to steal Kate's heart....
  HH #646 ISBN# 29246-5 $5.25 U.S./$6.25 CAN.

KEEP AN EYE OUT FOR ALL FOUR OF THESE TERRIFIC NEW TITLES